# SWEDISH CULTS

# ANDERS FAGER

TRANSLATED BY IAN LEMKE AND HENNING KOCH

VALANCOURT BOOKS
Richmond, Virginia
MMXXII

*Swedish Cults* by Anders Fager
Originally published in Swedish as *Svenska kulter* in 2009
First Valancourt Books edition 2022

All stories translated by Ian Lemke except 'The Furies from Borås',
'Fragment I', and 'Grandma's Journey' translated by Henning Koch,
revised by James D. Jenkins and Anders Fager.

Published by Valancourt Books, Richmond, Virginia
http://www.valancourtbooks.com

The cost of this translation was defrayed by a subsidy from the Swedish
Arts Council, gratefully acknowledged.

ISBN 978-1-954321-56-4 (hardcover)
ISBN 978-1-954321-57-1 (trade paperback)
Also available as an electronic book.

Set in Bembo Book MT Pro
Cover by Vince Haig

# CONTENTS

For Anna-Lee. Without you I would be nothing.

# THE FURIES FROM BORÅS

DEEP IN THE WOODS STANDS Underryd Dance Hall. Between the towns of Värnamo, Borås, and Jönköping. In a black-as-night corner of north Småland. There has always been dancing in Underryd. Since God knows when and long before that. First on stony heaths and then at the actual crossroads, where the roads from the three towns meet. To the sound of shawm and fiddle, then the accordion. The dance pavilion built in the 1920s evolved into a park right in the middle of the forest. In the eighties, the festivities were moved into a barn, a large one, which someone had the idea of painting purple. It grew into a dance palace with five bars, three dance floors, and a pizzeria. They built a parking lot worthy of a major supermarket, and the best acts were booked. Thorleifs for mom and dad. Jerry Williams for the rockers. Freestyle, Pontus & Amerikanerna, and Petter for the kids. Underryd rocks. Everyone in the village works at the Dance Hall.

They dance five days a week in Underryd. There's disco on Wednesdays, oldies on Thursdays, a dance band on Fridays, disco again on Saturdays, and a senior citizens' dance on Sunday afternoons. At seven o'clock on dance nights, the purple Dance Hall buses make stops in Värnamo, Borås, and Jönköping. The ride to the big parking lot outside the purple barn is free. On the bus they drink, put on makeup, make out. No matter which crowd is being driven. Those who get too rowdy are left on the side of the road. At half past two the last buses go back.

★

Most of the girls take the 8:15 bus from Borås. They sit together and talk about school, boys, and music. They get texts from girlfriends who are also on their way. They fix their hair. Check out boys. Did you invite anyone? He was pretty cute, but he was with his friends. That one's cute. 'He's doing auto mechanics at Almås Vocational School,' says Sofie. 'Dumb as a rock, but pretty to look at. He'll end up working at a garage and going to all of Elfsborg's home games. Oh, what an idyllic life.'

'Why does everybody have to make fun of me just because I live in Töllsjö?' Laughter and pushing. Alexandra has to get the hell out of the sticks.

'It's not like you're meeting any geniuses in Borås.'

'It's not like there are any geniuses in Borås.'

'It's not like you care.'

'It's all about timing,' Elin explains. 'Right now I'm going to hit on cute guys, okay? When I'm ready to have kids I'll go cruising at the Chalmers University library.' Laughter and more taunts. 'Or I'll make sure I get knocked up by some hottie at the gym and then marry Olle the Nerd, the one who hangs out in the library. Someone with thick glasses and a thirty-grand-a-month starting salary.' More laughter and high fives. Elin Andersson from Lundby is really cool.

Text message from Kari Cederlind on the Gothenburg bus. 'Nice piece of meat climbing all over me. Could be something.' Lenni Larsson texts from Värnamo: 'Nothing but drunk kids here. And me.' More laughter. The buzz of more voices in the bus. The noise level has doubled since they left the bus stop. The girls laugh louder and get a bit more vulgar. The boys just shout. Their phones don't stop ringing. They beep, chime, burp, and fart. Who has the coolest ring-tone? Anna's phone howls like a wolf. Elin's plays Shakira.

They're greeted by the smell of vomit as they swarm off the bus. Dusk is falling. The parking lot is full of hormones, H&M, and hooch. The girls gather at the entrance. Kiss each other's cheeks and comment on clothes. They're into cheap mail order, Pink, and too-short skirts. Or more of an emo vibe. Long nails are hot in either case. And jewelry with snakes. Roxette is booming out from inside the barn. Guys walking past stare at them. Kari points out Meat standing alone nearby, smoking. Good-looking, dark, a little over twenty. Nikes on his feet and headphones around his neck. White sleeveless T-shirt and Levi's.

'Is he an immigrant?'

'No, from Hisingen.'

'Do people really live there?'

'Doubt it.'

'Why is he by himself?' Anna is suspicious. Guys on their own in bars can be trouble. Sex maniacs. Psychos leaving their house for the first time in fifteen years.

'He's meeting his team here.'

'Team?'

'Handball team.'

'Is he famous?'

'Maybe in Hisingen. He plays like once a week with his friends.'

Anna looks at Meat and smiles enthusiastically. 'Is the fucker on steroids?'

'How the fuck should I know?' says Kari and waves at him. He smiles back.

Anna sighs. 'He'll do for now. Let's go in.'


The dance is on in Underryd. As it has been for eons. Boys and girls strutting. Jumping and prancing and showing off. Boozing and staggering around. Just like their parents once did. Sometimes you even see someone who can dance. For real.

The girls hang out at the bar by the small dance floor. One floor up. Separated a bit from the worst of the trash. They sit, stand, and dance, evenly scattered across the space. They ooooown that bar. Anna sits drinking wine on the fanciest sofa. On a throne, like a mafia daughter. Bob haircut, white blouse, and chalk-stripe vest. No one bothers Anna Lundman from Parkstaden. Wherever Anna is, you can smoke inside Underryd Barn. Because Anna does. Nonstop. She looks out over the dance floor. Elin and Lenni are dancing with each other. Sexy. Kari and Meat are sitting at the bar. Meat is talking about handball. Sofie sips a parasol drink and checks the place out. Ash-blond Alexandra and a few of the younger girls are sitting at the table behind Anna's. Alexandra tells stories and the girls listen. They're all ears. Especially little Nalim and Emma from Nitta, who haven't been here before. 'This is what the girls do,' says Alexandra. Listen and learn. Where to sit, where to stand. Alexandra lays down the law. We ooooown the place.

'This is all you need. You're gonna own it.'

'What do we tell our parents?'

'Nothing.'

'So this is where to go?'

'It's the best place to come. A couple of times a year is good.'

Alexandra explains the dangers. Kari is standing next to Meat now. Feel-his-breath close. Soon they'll start making out. It's only a matter of time until he falls into the trap. Elin and Lenni are making out on the dance floor. They're treating Meat and the other boys to a teenage lesbo show. Scare the shit out of them with tongue-kisses and hands under tops. The bartender looks away with a blush. The DJ plays Shakira. Colombian hip-rolling music. People stare and breathe heavily.

Anna takes a gulp of wine and gazes at the world through the bottom of her glass. It almost looks more normal like that. Like if a funhouse mirror made everything look the right way. She closes her eyes, lets everything spin around. She thinks about the daughters of daughters of daughters of the snakes. About eons of light. About forests of slowly swaying arms. Tentacles as thick as tree trunks. About death. Her dreams these days are a total acid trip.

Sofie sits down with her.

'Meat seems okay.'

'No friends?'

'He said hi to a few people but they're keeping away. He went and chatted with that guy over there a while ago.' She points at an immigrant guy with dark, curly hair sitting by himself at a table, texting.

'Cute,' Anna mumbles.

'Yeah. But our friend Meat wants to be left alone with his hookup.'

'Anything else?'

'He shoots up heroin and has AIDS and leukemia and hepatitis,' Sofie snickers.

Anna ignores her. Sofie grimaces. Damned mafioso manners. But she knows. The girls want healthy meat. No drugs, no steroids, and no harelips.

Anna nods. It's all looking good. The girls give her sidelong glances. All the others are staring at Elin and Lenni.

'Well then,' Anna says. 'Come, you Thousand Young.'

They whisper together. Sofie hugs her hard. Like, best friends, you know. The queens of Underryd. Sofie walks past Meat and nods. Kari nibbles Meat's lower lip. Mid-sentence, as he's talking about free throws. He freezes and all the girls sneak a peek. Holding their breath. Then he starts up with a lot of tongue. The girls exhale. Quick glances say: 'It's working.' 'Get ready.' Meat fiddles with his glass of beer. Sets it down behind him and grabs Kari's ass instead. They have a makeout marathon, leaning against the bar. Anna closes her eyes, sees primeval swamps behind her eyelids. Swamps and rain and kisses. The Pussycat Dolls' 'Don't Cha' blares through the speakers. Sofie scans the place. She's thinking about her history project. There's a lot going on in your head your final year. Industrialism in the Västergötland region and bogs and kisses.

Sofie circles the dance floor. A teenage girl, not too tall, with frizzy blond hair, black jeans, and a Nirvana T-shirt. Nobody you'd stare at. But Sofie sees everything. Like a hawk. Look over there: Elin and Lenni have gone to the bar and are standing a couple of steps behind Meat. Alexandra and the younger girls are also swarming around the bar. Alexandra offers them all candy. Special girlie candy. Small black lumps that taste like tar. Very exclusive stuff. One time Sofie treated some crackhead's Rottweiler to a nice sample. The evening paper wrote two pages about it, without mentioning that the goddamn dog tried to fuck its owner while eating his face.

Justin Timberlake whimpers. More people are dancing. From where Sofie's standing you can hardly see Meat for all the girls round him. They're circling him like a school of fish. Hiding him from his friends. Sofie has checked out three guys who probably know him. They're sitting a little way off, laughing over their beers.

'Some people have all the luck.'

'We won't be seeing him again tonight.'

They don't see Alexandra lacing Meat's beer. They don't see Kari rooting around inside Meat's clothes. Undoing his belt. Digging in his trousers. The air is thick in the middle of the swarm of girls. The girls pretend to look anywhere except at the couple by the bar. And yet they know. They look out of the corner of their eyes and whisper details. Hear the boy's breathing. Kari's ballsy. She's going to study law at the university in Lund after high school. She licks her palm. Spits on it. Then her hand disappears inside Meat's trousers. While she kisses him like a snake.

Anna nods at Sofie. Midnight soon. 'Get them moving.' Sofie checks that the big girls are in position. She nods at Alexandra and Elin. Checks that Saga is with it. Saga is sitting at a table next to Meat's friends, big and heavy and alone. Saga stares down people trying to take photos. She looks mean. Take a photo and I'll crush your fucking phone against your forehead.

Alexandra hands out more candy. Alexandra is good at chemistry. She'll finish high school with top grades in everything. Become a doctor or something. Sofie swallows one of the bitter little lumps. There's a stinging in her throat. Her stomach grows warm. The crowd around Meat gets thicker. The flock moves away from the dance floor. Towards the emergency exit by the bar. People look away. Don't stare. Don't annoy them. Be glad it isn't you.

One of the youngest girls comes up to Sofie. Black skirt. Tights. Fifteen years old. Might be a freshman. Her tank top says 'Porn Star'. Malin? Ida? She looks excited and nervous at the same time.

'I don't know if this is important . . .'

'What?' The warmth in Sofie's stomach turns to a corrosive bubble.

'I think he took a pill. The guy, I mean.'

'When?' Panic rises in Sofie's throat. She's missed something. A guardian doesn't miss things. 'Tell me!'

'I think he got something from that guy over there.' Ida/Malin points at the cute immigrant boy, who's still sitting fiddling with his phone.

'Got what?!' Sofie cries. In a loud candy-voice.

'A tablet. Or something.'

The flock gradually makes its way out using the emergency exit. Slowly, so nobody will notice what's happening. As if they cared. As if anyone wanted to notice them.

Sofie shoves Ida/Malin against the bar. Shakes her. Hard.

'And you're telling me *now*?'

Ida/Malin looks terrified. Her eyes fill with tears. 'I didn't know if it was important.'

'Let me be the judge of that, you stupid bitch!'

Big Bad Saga stands beside them. 'What's going on?'

Sofie takes a deep breath. Swallows the vomit. 'We have a problem.'

The flock heads down a dark spiral staircase. They escort Kari and Meat. Have some more candy. The darkness is filled with footsteps, tittering girls, and music. The Ark from one direction and Robbie Williams from another. Meat holds Kari's hand. She laughs and pulls him along. He doesn't give much thought as to why the other girls are tagging along. He doesn't think very much at all. He just wants to get into the dark and fuck. Nothing else is of any interest. And the girl holding his hand knows the way into the dark, the wet, hot dark. The girl has told him she'll show him things he's never seen before. Things he'll never get to see again. Things the guys on the team will never experience in their pathetic lives. There's going to be fucking like no one's ever fucked before.

The cute immigrant guy wants to be called Juju. Fucking ridiculous. 'Juju has whatever you need.' A pair of blue, girlish eyes light up and want to talk about the price. Someplace where it's quieter. He doesn't ask what she's after, just shambles along behind Sofie into the handicap toilet. Sofie locks the door without turning on the light. Saga head-butts Juju in the dark. Sofie turns on the light and watches Saga shove his head down the toilet. She flushes twice before allowing Juju to breathe a bit. Sofie waits impatiently. Saga is mean, but she takes a while getting to the point. She kicks Juju in the kidneys and stomps hard on the hand that's fumbling towards the top of his boot. Crunch. No little knife for Juju.

'What did you give him?'

'Fucking whore!' spits Juju. Saga smiles. The idiot is giving her every excuse in the world. 'My friends are gonna murder you and that fat fucking whore friend of yours.'

Saga kicks Juju in the head. Awfully hard. 'Fat? Did you say fat, you asshole?'

'Calm down.' Sofie squats down beside Juju. Tries to focus. There's blood running into Juju's eyebrows. 'My friend gets a bit worked up. Just tell me and everything will be all right.'

Juju doesn't answer. Saga has him halfway down the toilet again by the time he tries to say something. Fuck it, Saga flushes anyway. Back in Borås, Saga goes to a special needs class. People say she 'acts out'. She cracked her mother's ex-boyfriend's skull. With a hot iron. Killer girl power. Don't mess with the gals from Tosseryd.

'Viagra!' Juju roars once he gets some air. 'Viagra!'

'Viagra?' says Sofie. That was unexpected.

Saga slams Juju's head into the toilet bowl so hard that the porcelain cracks. Water gushes onto the floor.

'Viagra?' Sofie repeats.

'What old guys take to get it up,' says Saga.

'But why does Kari's guy need it?'

'It's a fuck-fix,' slurs Juju.

Sofie gives him a kick for each syllable. 'Why does a fucking jock need *that*?' Kick, kick, kick. The rush of vomit comes again. And Juju can't answer. Sofie understands what'll happen now anyway. She pulls Saga out. Out of the bathroom and towards the fire escape.

The flock has already had time to get away. Saga and Sofie run down the stairs, stumble in the dark, into the night. They're light-headed and out of breath.

The summer night is warm. There's a smell of grass, Yellow Blend cigarettes, and six kinds of shampoo. Sofie stops and looks around. Saga runs into her. She's panting like an eighty-year-old. It's dark behind the barn, but Sofie can see the path leading to the forest. The path to Underryd bog. The moon illuminates broken blades of grass. A road of silver. Thousands of years old. The road from the dance pavilion to the grove by the bog. The bog where the tree branches look like slowly swaying octopus tentacles. The road taken by the flock every fourth full moon.

She sees them. The flock has already reached the place where the forest gets dense. The place where cigarettes are stubbed out and phones turned off. Just to be on the safe side. Sofie catches a glimpse of a girl's white top through the trees. Hears a laugh. The candy is buzzing like a wasps' nest in her head. It's like all the sounds are far away. But the candy also gives her night vision. It intensifies the light. The world turns black and corrosively white. Looking at the moon hurts her eyes. The slightest sparkle in the grass becomes a star.

They run along the path. Through a tunnel of black and white. Saga is right behind them. She'll never be a runner. She trips in the grass. It sounds like an elephant when she crashes into the bushes. Sofie keeps running. To the edge of the trees, where she slows down. This is no place for running. The forest doesn't appreciate it. The forest has no sense of humor. No patience with excuses. People disappear here. And the police in Gislaved don't waste very much time looking for them. There's no point. In 1996 a whole family disappeared. Why were they picking berries there? the farmers muttered. In Underryd? There are no berries there. There's nothing at all. Sofie heard that story in middle school. One of the 9th grade girls had been to the bog. Found clothes and a pair of child's shoes. Sofie wanted to know more. She was curious and bored and tired of hanging out at the riding stables or gawping at the rednecks on mopeds. The first time she followed the others to the forest she was fourteen years old.

A bird shrieks. Some kind of bird of prey, maybe an owl. Sofie takes deep breaths. It's pitch-black between the trees. Just the odd shard of moonlight makes its way down to her, lighting up leaves and branches and mist. It's always misty here in the forest. Something to do with geothermal heat. Sea smoke. Primeval forest and bog. Sofie is crap at Natural

Sciences. But when you walk in the front of the flock you see how the haze and moonlight make the cobwebs glitter. The webs hang like curtains of silver across the path. It's easy to see things through curtains and swathes of mist. Even things that don't exist.

Sofie hears the wails from afar. They come riding on the corrosive veils of mist. They echo between the trees as if that's what they've always done. Girls roaring as if they're at a football match. Roaring like horny monkeys. Roaring like a bunch of lunatics. Roaring as if calling down a god.

Out on the bog there's a fuckfest going on. Kari and Meat are rolling in the grass. They're yapping and clawing each other like two dogs. The girls stand half-naked around them in a breathless semicircle. They hold each other's hands hard. Stare at Kari arching her back. Her panties hanging on a juniper bush. Meat is pounding like a maniac. They pant and snort and scratch and tear. Alexandra's candy is kicking in hard now. Kari's eyes have turned black. She sees fire and trolls and trees with huge cocks. The trees promise to fulfill her wishes. She drools. Bloody disgusting. Babbling while she fucks like she's speaking in tongues. A machine that pounds and pounds and pounds. A machine with blood under its fingernails. The moon turns the blood black. And all skin becomes white and milky. The girls howl when they see the blood. They lean forward to get a better look. They wish for beautiful children and happy lives. Journeys far beyond Borås. That is what the Goat promises. The girls press themselves against Anna, who's standing at the center of everything. They pant, they fumble for each other and stare at the blood. Then the first sounds are heard from the bog. Whispering, crazy tittering, and then a branch snaps with a crack. A few of the girls don't know which to look at anymore, the fucking or the darkness. Some of them keep staring at the fucking so they don't have to see. There's sobbing and panting. Elin wrestles one of the high school girls to the ground and starts tearing at her tank top. Kari takes Meat's throat in a stranglehold. He grins like an idiot when she starts squeezing.

Anna untangles herself from the jumble of girls' limbs. She walks past the fuckheap, towards the darkness. The lunar haze spins around her. Sweat glitters on her naked legs. She raises her arms to welcome the thing approaching through the forest. They can all hear it now. The sound of the Messenger. The spawn of the Goat. The thing making the trees sway. Wrapped in moon-mist and partially hidden by branches it comes closer. It wades through pools and steps into quagmires. Trips over rotten stumps. Splashes like an elephant, a big fucking monster elephant, in fact. At the edge of the bog it snaps a pine at the roots. Twenty-five meters of tree come crashing down. Its crown hits the ground in front of Anna. A cloud of pine needles and water washes over Meat and the girls. For anyone with candy-eyes it looks like the bog is exploding in a cloud of diamonds. Anna does not back away. She raises her arms toward the madness behind the tree crown and howls. The girls howl with her and the Messenger answers.

The Black Goat has a thousand young. The howls echo between the trees. Hoarse girls' voices and the roar of the Messenger from beyond time and space and reason. The sounds carry all the way to the barn. The security guards tell people to come inside. In Underryd you stay indoors on nights like this. You could catch cold if you hang around outside. In the parking lot, people look away nervously. They exchange glances as if to say, 'It's time once again.' Turn up their car stereos. Knock back another drink. Hurry into the barn. The mist hanging over the parking lot is full of death. Death, which can only be stopped by lust. You there, get in the car. With me, in the back seat. People act like total pigs. Fighting, shouting. Cars rock to and fro in the mist. Children are conceived, young people are crying. In a ditch a seventeen-year-old girl lies covered in vomit, calling for her mother.

The roar makes Sofie stumble on the path through the undergrowth. She falls over a juniper and tears up her arms and face. Hits her head on a rock. She vomits wine and black magic mushrooms and cheap Chinese food. When she closes her eyes she sees spirals of eerie light circling Aldebaran. Wet and bleeding, she stands up. Gets back on the path. Guardians do not lie vomiting in ditches. The guardian in Underryd has a responsibility and tradition to watch over. Her mother was a guardian once. And her grandmother's sister. It has been like this for years. For bloody eons.

She reaches the glade by the bog and sees everything in flashbulb white. Trees and mist. White girls' bodies in a panting heap. Their paper bags full of practical things tossed at the end of the path. The small piles of clothes. Jackets and trousers they don't want to get dirty. And then: Kari on top of Meat. Anna, her arms upraised, turns towards the thing that is just emerging from the thickets by the pools. The girls cheering and screaming like mad. Kari wailing orgasmically. Meat's legs thrashing. Half-strangled he shoots the wad of his life. Then catches sight of the living mess of arms and branches and mouths. He roars without a voice. He flails with his arms and points. Can't you see how big it is? Says 'For fuck's sake, run!' with his eyes. Croaks like a raven.

Then Meat sees that the girls are not afraid. They look happy to see the thing rising above the bushes. He's the only one scared out of his wits. He starts to get it. Drugged and drunk and strangled and fucked he may be, but he isn't stupid. The girls don't look scared. They're howling with excitement. Not fear. They're totally in on this. Meat tries to shake Kari off him. He arches his body. Tries to hit her. Claws her hands. The girls grab his arms. Press him down. Laugh at his panic. Cover his mouth.

The Black Goat has a thousand young. The forest echoes with the yells of the girls and the Messenger. Sofie remembers her first time in the forest. Remembers the rush. Fourteen years old. High on magic mushrooms and red wine. Someone's hand inside her top. Standing so close to the people fucking that she could see everything. Just like in a hardcore porn film. And then that big, unfathomable thing standing there, rocking, at the edge of the trees. Like a ten-meter-tall piece of kelp on legs like bridge-piers. Lit up by the moon it looks like a dead tree. One that moves. It lashes out here and there with its tentacles and bellows. An arm as thick as a fire-hose makes its way towards Anna. Another whips the moss on the ground like an enormous dog's tail. A third tentacle gropes towards the moon. Sofie pissed herself the first time she saw it. Then she screamed nonstop for five minutes. It took a week before she could talk again. She couldn't remember what she had wished for.

But the sickest thing of all. The most fucked up. It's what happens next, once the Messenger has acknowledged them. Sofie is surprised every time. Even though she has been in Kari's place. She doesn't see who strikes the first blow. But suddenly there's blood everywhere. And girls clawing, girls tearing, and girls kicking. Girls who throw Kari aside so they can also have a ride. Kari tumbles over the moss, lies there with her ass bare. Meat keeps humping in his drugged death throes. His brain dies but his cock fights on.

Sofie stumbles towards the jumble of teenage girls. She remembers her Meat. Alexander from Rottne in the heart of Småland. Dumb as hell. Wanted to be a musician. Heavy metal. She still keeps his skull ring on a string around her neck. When she came home that morning her mother helped her shower. She washed her like she was a small child. Sofie remembers the smell of blood in her hair. And how her father started avoiding her. Never a harsh word from him again. Once you've been to the bog you can stay out late. The magic mushrooms make her trip over something. She rolls over the moss. The water is so close beneath the moss that her pants get wet. The water smells of blood and fucking and rotten plants.

The girls tear and tear at Meat. Cartilage and tendons crack. Elin and Lenni break one of his elbows. Snap it the wrong way. They bend and bend and bend. Twist it off like a goddamn chicken wing. Overhead, the Messenger looms. Checking out what Larsson, junior champion in gymnastics, and Andersson, soon to be a teacher, get up to in their spare time. The smell of blood gets it worked up. It trembles and bellows. Its arms lash the air above them. Then Alexandra holds up a bloody bundle over her head and screams shrilly. '*Iä! Iä!*' The girls cheer. '*Iä! Iä!*' Anna roars at the Messenger in a pre-Cambrian tongue. Blood-spattered hands wave strips of flesh. Sofie joins in with the shrieking. Forgetting her role. She wants to feast on the flesh. She tosses aside a couple of jabbering high school girls. Julia and Lova. Or Lova and Maja? Who gives a shit? Make way for the guardian. She sees a girl straddling Meat's hips while three others claw open his belly. Intestines everywhere. They split and stink of shit and vomit. Someone throws up. Someone comes, howling like a lunatic. Lenni gives a stupid grin, her mouth full of forearm muscle. Hunger tugs at Sofie. She bares her teeth and hisses. Lenni backs off a little. The whites of her eyes shine white in a mask of black blood. She defers to Sofie, who snatches the arm for herself. Sinks her teeth into a fleshy fold by the thumb. Briefly she catches sight of Meat's face among the jumble of girls. Meets his eyes. Sees his terror and pain. She thinks to herself, 'The stupid fuck is still alive' and swallows flesh.

'*Iä! Iä!* The Black Goat has a thousand young!' The girls fight over Meat. His flesh. The holy sacrifice to the Goat in the forest. The girls from Underryd. They are the girls from Småland. Sussilull and Sussilo feed each other raw, steaming flesh. The girls are like poppy flowers and lilies and peonies. Hardcore maenads the whole bunch of them. Wailing cannibal chicks feeding a monster of the abyss a smoking warm liver. Alexandra and Anna hold it up together towards the slither of arms. The Messenger shakes with excitement as he wallows closer. Mashing the peat and dry twigs. Blundering onto firmer ground. There's a rustling of thrashing tentacles and a stink of death and marsh gas.

A cluster of arms snatches up the liver. It disappears upwards in a spray of blood into the center of the Messenger. There's a glimpse of something that might be jaws. Chewing. Some of the girls toss it more meat. Little Nalim squats, her hands full of steaming gunk. She's crying. And laughing. Alexandra kisses Anna and they fall down in a heap. Wrestling and finger-fucking. Kari runs out into the bog. She's wearing nothing but a tank top and her skin shines white in the moonlight. She dances madly in front of the Messenger. Screaming, jumping up and down in a cloud of water drops. Then Sofie remembers her errand. There may be something wrong with the meat. That was it, yes.

'Wait,' she croaks, spitting cartilage and bits of flesh. 'Wait.'

She stumbles over to Anna. Anna is sitting astride Alexandra in the moss. There's blood and Alexandra's long hair everywhere. They feed each other strips of flesh. Bare breasts and stupid grins. The Messenger hangs over them. Big and stinking. It quivers. Makes monstrous jumps up and down on its elephant legs.

'Wait,' Sofie calls out. 'Wait, damn it!'

Alexandra and Anna look up at her. Some of the girls stop throwing meat. They have empty eyes, all of them. The Messenger sniffs her scent. Who disturbs my feast?

Sofie leans over Anna. Looks into her crazy-shimmering eyes. 'Listen! You have to listen.'

Anna collects herself. Nods.

'What?' screams Alexandra. Above them, an arm sweeps dangerously near. Sofie feels her terror breaking through. If the Messenger flips out they're all sooooo fucking dead. Soon she'll start running. To hell with everything and just go.

'Listen to what?'

'He was drugged.'

'WHAT?!'

'The asshole took Viagra.'

Alexandra mutters something and fumbles for Anna's breast. Anna pushes her away.

'What? What? What? How the hell could that happen? On your watch?' Sofie backs away. In the corner of her eye she sees one of the Messenger's eyes staring at them. It's as big as a basketball. It's ancient and altogether evil. And drugs and medicines make it go nuts. An empirical fact. It can cope with the livers of alcoholic dance band musicians. But paracetamol makes it unpredictable. And drugs make it crazy. It has killed two priestesses out of pure rage when it was poisoned before. In 1969 Marianne Utter was decapitated. The girls had tricked their Meat into taking LSD and three of them were seriously injured. Anna's oldest aunt was the other one torn to pieces, in 1978. All they found was her right hand. Anna still keeps it in a linen bag at home, on top of her dresser.

The girls sense something has happened. The gorging and heavy petting stops. Twenty misty pairs of teenage eyes stare in her direction. 'Go on,' Sofie wants to shout at them. 'Go on fucking around so it doesn't notice.' Twenty blood-black mouths jeer at her. Above her head, a tentacle stops in mid-movement.

Then Kari comes reeling as if out of nowhere. High on magic mushrooms and horror film sex. Her pussy bare and her hair on end. Sex hair and blood. The latest look for girls from Borås.

'Oh fuck!' she laughs. 'Fuck, fuck, fuck!' Every creature in the bog has its eyes on her. Sofie sees the movement before it has even begun. Mushroom-intensified perception. Not bad. A tentacle as thick as a tree trunk comes flying. Sofie rams Kari. A good rugby tackle. They fall into a puddle and the arm whooshes over them, hitting a clump of grass which explodes in a rain of water and pulverized vegetation.

'What the hell!' Kari shouts. 'Are you stupid or what?'

The next lash strikes ten centimeters from her head. The water gushes up like a fountain once again. Kari flat out screams. She's on her feet and halfway to the treeline in one single movement. All the girls back away. The Messenger staggers towards them. It shakes, quivers. Totters. And strikes. Sparks fly when a whip lash hits a rock. Sofie hears herself saying, 'Wow.' One of the girls screams. A scream of terror. This isn't fun anymore. They're exposed. Half-naked in the forest with a really nasty monster. A girl vomits up raw strips of flesh. Another one retches. Before long they're all running. They say this happened once before, in the late 1700s. The ritual failed and half the flock was killed. It took years and years to build it up again.

Sofie meets Anna's gaze. Controlled and sober by sheer force of will. She hears her voice as if inside her head. 'We have to fix this.' Sofie nods. Time slows down. The girls' screams fade away and the Messenger freezes mid-motion. Sofie mimes, 'Get the girls out of here.'

Anna nods. '*Iä! Iä!*' Sofie is as good as dead. Tomorrow she'll be sitting at the Black Goat's side.

The High Priestess rises slowly. Glances over her shoulder at the tangle of death hanging in the air overhead. The tangle of tentacles. Ten or so eyes. Total evil. This is heavy. She's covered in blood. Her panties are half pulled down and her white blouse shines in the moonlight. She has moss in her hair. She's as beautiful as a goddess – the sister of the Goat. The snare, the bitch, and that which grows in the dark. She's the witch that tames the Messenger from the black beyond. She's the cry in the forest that entices the girls to dance. She's Anna Lundman from Parkstaden in Borås. She's nineteen, going on ten thousand. She's the key to strange eons.

Anna walks towards the flock with upraised arms. Her blouse flaps like wings. Her face radiates, 'Come to me, children.' No panic, no fear. She's the reassuring schoolmistress, the mother, the calm the world revolves around. Follow me and you'll be safe. Now let's all stand up. Nice and easy. Let's walk away from this annoying monster. Miss Sofie will get rid of it.

The girls start getting up. Sofie holds her breath. Stares at the girls and stares at a telephone pole of a tentacle less than a meter from her forehead. A twitch and she's dead. Not much fun. And on top of everything she has an essay to hand in. She turns around with glacial slowness. The Messenger keeps its gazes on her. Or its gaze? What do you say about something with eyes everywhere? Sofie notices the way her thoughts keep running away. As soon as they get a chance they're off. Can so many eyes cast a glance? How does the world look to you if you can see in all directions? As if from the inside of a dome?

She bows to the Messenger. Lifts her hands. A legion of tentacles are raised slightly, by way of an answer. She has its attention. It recognizes her. The girl who comes bearing gifts. Do you hear? If there's anyone to be angry with, it's me. She sees Anna and the girls in the corner of her eye. They're inching back. Together they're saving the flock.

A girl, Sandra from Gislaved, stumbles over what's left of Meat. She falls over and crawls naked among the moss and pieces of flesh. The Messenger is startled. Its tentacles sway like seaweed. It loses interest in Sofie. Turns its eyes to Sandra and Anna and the girls. Picks up the scent of the flock again. Sofie feels the panic rising. Among the girls and inside herself. But she's the guardian. A custodae. One who has drunk the blood and waded in the darkness. One who preserves and protects. One who does not panic.

Sofie screams. With all her might. Roars to attract its attention. Howls at the night sky like a wolf. She calls for battle. Roars out, 'Take me, you ugly fucking slime monster. Do you hear me, you asshole?'

The Messenger turns to her again. It looks surprised. Or curious. It's been an eternity since someone shouted at it with defiance. It's been a long time since anyone challenged it. It lashes out at the little screaming thing with white hair. The bug ducks. It lashes out again. And again. The bug backs away, stumbles backwards over the tufts of grass.

Sofie sees all the eyes. Feels how anger causes its mess of arms to tremble and jerk one way, then another. The Messenger is pissed off. First, an offering laced with poison and now she stands there shouting at it. It climbs out of the moss and mud. Leaves the thicket. Comes swaying across the peat. Taller than ever it stretches towards the moon. As if wanting to show itself in all its foulness.

Sofie has an eternity to think. Then it attacks again. The first lash passes high above her. A careless sideswipe. The next one comes down slantwise from above. Shorter and straighter. She has time to jump out of the way. And again. She trips, falls over, rolls around in the moss and bounces up again. Her clothes are soaked. A blow that would have felled a tree hits the moss. And then another. Water and mud spurt up and Sofie jumps aside, then backwards. She can handle single strikes. As long as the Messenger only uses one arm at a time she can make it. And if she can just get in among the pines she can run. Easier said than done. She stumbles again. Something sharp stabs her in the thigh. Impales her. When she jumps up again it hurts all the way down to her calf. A tentacle crushes the spot where she just lay. Another one swipes her across the shoulder. A glancing blow. Another, thin as a finger, whips across her hand. A third over her thigh. The lashes burn, but she's still standing. She fumbles with her thigh and finds the sharp thing. A thick stick driven into her flesh. Losing her concentration for a moment, she takes a clout to her face that throws her like a rag across the tufts of grass.

A tooth snaps. She feels it on her tongue. Her head is thundering, and when she opens her eyes she sees the silhouette of the Messenger against the stars. She smells the stench of corpse and mud. Sees the eyes indifferently watching her crawl. They don't even hate. They just don't like the idea of her moving. Or breathing. Or even existing. It was given bad meat and now it wants to kill and smash. Sofie yanks the stick out of her flesh. The pain is unbelievable. She disappears into a hole of whiteness and when she comes back the Messenger has drawn closer. A thin tentacle scrapes against her calf. As if curious. Or horny. Another, thick as a thigh, is raised over her face. Ready to club her. Six eyes scrutinize her intently. More tentacles come slithering up her leg. One pulls at her shoe. Another forces itself between her thighs. Spreads them apart. It's so damned disgusting. The piece of shit is groping her. Tentacles on her stomach. On her breasts. She holds her breath. If she moves she'll get the club in her face. It's over. Sofie relaxes. Closes her eyes. She's dead. She'll be one of the young waiting in the dark forest. A sister who got left behind on the bog. A story to be told at home in the town. By all means go dance on the bog, but it's dangerous. Sofie Granlund, Bodil's daughter, got left behind out there.

She hears Anna's voice again. It comes in like a ghostly signal through the pain and terror. 'We're safe! Everyone made it. Thanks to you. You're holy, sister.' Sofie starts to cry. She'd like to tell Anna to go to hell but her voice has gone. Her strength is gone. All of it. All she can think about is the arm above her. She looks up again. The moon turns it blue-black and makes the slime shimmer. The gunk hangs down in threads, sticky as syrup. The skin beneath is rough. A glittering drop of slime drops in a long string of silver. It looks like a shooting star.

'Wait!' someone calls out. The Messenger freezes. The eyes register something behind Sofie. 'Take me instead, you fucking ...' The voice cuts off. Saga? '... fucked-up monster!' The tentacles draw away from Sofie. She takes a deep breath. It's forgotten her. You're stupid. And I'm too damn quick for you. Sofie rolls aside. Around, around. Away, away. Waits for the crushing blow. But nothing happens. She's soaked everywhere and her leg burns like fire. It's wonderful. She's alive.

She looks up. The girls have gone. The remains of Meat lie on the ground in a pile. And there: Big Saga striding over from the edge of the trees. With her hands in her pockets and shoulders thrown back. She lumbers along like always. Straight at the Messenger, who turns towards her. Tentacles and eyes and everything. And Saga doesn't stop.

'It was my fault. I'm the one you should take.' Saga's voice grows firm. Warlike. Mad. Sofie sees the blood in her hair. She must have fallen in the forest. It's run down and across her round face. She looks like one of those Japanese theater masks. The mask says: 'Sofie, take care of the girls. I'll handle this.' Sofie doesn't answer. What do you say to someone who's just decided to die in your place? You wave. 'Okay.' An okay-wave and a farewell-wave in one.

The Messenger stumbles towards Saga. Reeling across the quagmire like a drunk. Hissing and gurgling. Saga goes to her death. Saga, who wanted to be a guardian. Stupid Saga with her crappy grades and bloodied knuckles. Stupid Saga who no one dared bully even before she found her way to the flock. Saga the butcher, Sofie's shadow. Loyal as a dog. Kind as a dog. Crazy as a dog. Sofie waves again. The world's dumbest gesture. Ever.

The Messenger towers over Saga. She looks up at the mess of eyes and arms. She thinks she should say something. Anna would have said something cool, in some ancient tongue. '*Iä! Iä!*' Or something about that black goat. All that stuff Saga never really got. A lot of bullshit, really. This isn't a goat. It's a fucking slime monster. Standing two yards from her. Stinking like a garbage dump. So disgusting.

She sees the first blow coming in. Far to the right.

'Your little brother sucks old men's cocks!' she shouts. And attacks. She connects a few wheeling punches. It's like punching foam. Then the Messenger strikes back. From all directions. Saga is thrown into the air like a stone, through the branches of a tree. Half her bones are broken. She has time to think of Sofie one last time. Then the arms come together. She disappears in among them. Like a fish in an anemone, Sofie thinks. They'll never even find a finger.

And then it's over. Eons pass while the Messenger plows his way back into the bog. Everything goes silent. Sofie kneels in the mud. She sits with her back to the forest and looks out into the mist, where the Messenger can be made out, like a swaying tree. She sits there feeling the terror and the blood and the magic mushrooms releasing their hold on her. All that's left is a hunched-up girl freezing and staring at the swathes of mist.

Slowly they dare to come out. First Anna and Alexandra. They stand at the edge of the trees, Alexandra crouching and Anna erect. On their guard. Keeping an eye on the situation. Kind of.

Only when the Messenger has disappeared far into the mist do the girls emerge. Frozen and half-naked and dumbfounded. They tiptoe past Sofie like they're afraid of scaring her off. Pointing and whispering. Sneaking over to clothes and bags. Getting out their wet wipes, bottles of water, and clean underwear. They can't show up in Borås looking like Carrie, after all. They help each other in pairs. Blood is black in the moonlight. No one mentions Saga.

Anna and Alexandra go over to what used to be Meat. They root about in the mess. Pick out his wallet, phone, and jewelry.

'He has three missed calls from Lina.'

Alexandra gives a low laugh. 'Oh, must have been love.'

The valuables go in a bag. The bag will end up in the river. Far from the bog. The body will be grub for the badgers. The badgers in Underryd are diligent and fat as hell. There's the odd piece of bone and rags at the edge of the trees but that's it. Some of the clothes are old. Anna once found a bonnet that would have looked good on Strindberg's girlfriend. You could still see the bloodstains.

The girls rub and dry. The maenads disappear. Transform themselves into high school girls on a camping trip. With pine needles in their panties – and does anyone have a mirror? A couple of small flashlights flicker. A bottle of vodka makes the rounds. They take big swigs to calm their shaking.

Anna explains. 'Saga was with us all night. She went back with Sofie and the rest of you to Borås. Everyone said good-bye and goodnight at the bus station.' The girls nod. Few of them look up from their tank tops and paper napkins. 'Say you think she went with Sofie.' No one answers.

'Sofie?'

Sofie stands up. All the eyes of the flock on her back. Slowly she turns around. 'She came with me.'

'Good. How's the leg?'

'I can walk. I think.' She outstares everyone. Her cheek is swollen from the monster slap. 'No, I don't need any help.' She's the guardian. The girl who stares down monsters. She walks without help. Otherwise there are others who would like to be guardians.

'You need some clean clothes,' tries Alexandra.

'Fuck it.' The steely monster-stare. Alexandra backs off.

Together they walk back to the barn. Anna in front. Sofie last. The girls are silent. It makes Anna suspicious. Worried. Usually they start chatting and giggling as soon as the bog is out of sight. And singing. Elin and Lenni can do a hilarious white gospel act. 'I want to thank God,' in breathy voices, ' 'Cause I used to be in the arms of the devil.' But not tonight. The girls are waiting for her or Sofie to do something. Anna just doesn't know what. A couple of times they hear sobbing. The owls call after them. It's cold in the forest. Someone's racing an engine somewhere far away. One of the village idiots. The drunks in their Volvo 240s. The ones you never want to turn out like. The ones you want so badly to avoid that you end up going to the bog to feed monsters. It's cold in the forest by the bog. The monsters may even eat you. But at least you avoid the Volvo. The young of the Goat drive Porsches. And succeed in everything they want. Unless they're torn to pieces.

Halfway to the barn, Sofie says, 'I need a fucking cigarette.' You don't smoke in the forest. Smoke is not appreciated. Sofie doesn't give a damn. Try and make me put it out. 'Does anyone have a smoke?'

She gets seven packs shoved in her face. She says something silly about 'One at a time, said the milkmaid.' The girls laugh so loud that you must be able to hear it up at the bog. She takes a Prince. Lights it and takes a monster puff.

Her head spins from the nicotine. She tries to catch Anna's eyes. She's standing in the background. In her leader pose. Staring out into space. Bloody diva.

Kari comes up to her. Her face is still dirty.

'You saved my party. Thanks.'

Sofie nods. 'Thank Saga.'

'I do, all the time.'

Sofie nods again and looks away. We all thank you. Sleep now. With the young of the Goat. You're one of the thousand now. We'll never forget you. Bloody lunatic.

The girls go down to the party spot in Underryd. Where the roads from three villages meet. They laugh and make a lot of noise. We ooooown the place.

# FRAGMENT I

H E CATCHES UP WITH HER by the Barnhus Bridge. The Bloated Woman's Emissary doesn't walk so fast these days. Since she last came back from China the years have caught up with her. She limps. And walks with a stick. It makes her look old. Fredman finds it disturbing. He always imagines her gliding along on skates. For some reason. Skating on Riddarfjärden. It must have been in the early fifties, more or less.

But now she's just old. And if her stick doesn't slow her down, the swans will. She loves swans. She always has bags of bread in her pockets. And she recognizes the different birds.

'Look, there's that big male with a very dark bill. And his family.' She doesn't say hello, doesn't even look up when he stops beside her. 'They have a nest on the other side of the water up that way. Just below the Bonnier building.' She points with her stick, swaying slightly. Fredman takes her arm. Gently.

'Don't worry.' She gives him a sidelong glance. 'I'm not that old.'

'You're older. But it suits you.'

'Nonsense.'

They wander north. Along the water. Under the Barnhus bridge. An elderly couple taking a walk. Two old friends talking about old times. The weather. Children and grandchildren. The Bloated Woman's Emissary loves to interrogate him about his grandchildren. Although the youngest of them is almost twenty. Frida is really the only one who gets in touch now and then. Frida, who's twenty-two and wants to be a painter. Who has a blog about art. Fredman is proud of the blog. Both because it's Frida's and because he managed to find it.

'Is she never curious about what you do?'

'Now?'

'What you used to do.'

'I don't shout about it.'

'Maybe you should shout a bit.'

'Just because she has a soft spot for an old man? You're getting empathy confused with aptitude. Do you think the home care aide who cleans your flat has aptitude just because she shows empathy?'

'I don't have a home care aide.'

A train applies its brakes on the other side of the canal. The shriek of the brakes echoes between the houses. Sends birds flying up and drowns out the sound of traffic.

'Who cleans for you, then?' asks Fredman.

'A black boy. Cleaning service, once a week. Jona from Ghana. Works for Norrmalm's Social Services. He's polite and thorough and incredibly bored. The bloody pigeons on the balcony are more concerned about me.'

'Isn't that the same as having a home care aide?'

'Oh, no.'

Fredman smiles. 'Well I have various teenage girlies from a private agency. Anything but thorough. But pretty to look at.'

'I wonder if there are regulations about old men having young girls running round their homes, and vice versa.'

'What do you mean? To keep us happy?'

They reach the long stairs up to the St Erik's district. The large round pool at the foot of the stairs is filled with dead leaves. Reeds grow in the shallow water. Fredman has wondered for a long time why the water in the pond is so still. Why isn't there a fountain? The way it is now, it's reminiscent of a dead lake. A sacrificial bog. There used to be one of those outside Wasa in the olden days – towards the end of the 1960s, at least. A death pit full of water. And corpses. Some believers threw people in now and then. And supplemented it with slaughterhouse waste and molasses. The water was almost alive. And stank something rotten.

The Bloated Woman's Emissary slows down and looks at a bird. A seagull. Entirely uninteresting. It irritates her that her eyes are starting to go. New glasses are expensive.

'Having that black boy Jona rooting about in my dirty laundry only makes me feel old.' Her voice lingers, as if she's thinking out loud.

'Yeah. Some of those girlies make me want to . . .'

'Wish you could get the knife out again?'

'Oh, no.' Fredman smiles. 'Those days are over.'

'And all the rose petals have floated away on the stream.'

'The skin of the young maid is rough as leather now.'

They walk on. In silence. Look at passersby. Joggers fighting middle age. Couples with expensive strollers. Cyclists. Young, healthy people. Two drunks sit on a bench staring into infinity. Fredman takes in their dirt and decrepitude with a kind of joy. They make him feel younger. And cleaner.

'Tanuddsen called,' she says suddenly. As if she only just happened to think of him.

Fredman nods. He's still thinking about the sacrificial pit. It would be a brilliant joke if Stockholm's City Council built a sacrificial pit in the middle of a playground.

'He says he knows where Konrad Landin is buried.'

'Really? How did he find out?'

'He found a relative, somehow. On the Internet.' She makes it sound as if Tanuddsen has been reading coffee grounds. The Bloated Woman's Emissary has only just got used to having both a telephone and a radio at home.

'I thought Landin was a dead end.'

'He's dead all right. But maybe not dead enough.'

'How did it happen? He disappeared. When was it?'

'Nineteen-eighty-nine. In May. He went back to his

mother's cottage in Kalmar and hanged himself. It seems that it took weeks before anyone found him. Some cousin.'

'He was cremated.'

'That's what we thought.'

'Everyone did.'

The Bloated Woman's Emissary stops and looks out over the canal. By the thickets on the other side a couple of swans come gliding on the water. The pair whose nestlings were taken by a dog last spring. A subway train thunders past on the bridge above. Under the overpass. Fredman remembers the vaulted bridge that used to run across. In the days when Vasastaden was just a mess of factories.

'He must have left instructions. They all did. Burn my body. Dissolve the ashes in acid.'

For some reason Fredman remembers Lohrman, the Lunatic King. Dr. Sondén's assistant and jester. He incinerated himself on a pyre. So he wouldn't have to meet The Bloated Woman's Emissary. Another one who knew what was coming tried using lye. He looked appalling when they brought him back from the dead. His mouth was completely destroyed, so they got no sense out of him.

'It could work,' she says.

'Where's he buried?' Another subway train thunders past. Fredman notices that he's not concentrating. His head is so damned slow these days. Is this how it feels growing old? Like drowning in syrup.

His thoughts wander off at the thought of syrup. Remembering a couple of years ago. A group of young people found Lohrman's temple under the Konradsberg Asylum. They played music down there. And things took their course. Incredible.

'Outside Kalmar.'

'Do we know anyone in Kalmar?'

'No one. Not even in Småland.'

Fredman doesn't say anything. One of the cleaning girls

suddenly crosses his mind. Amanda. She has a big tattoo at the base of her spine. You see it when she leans forward. It looks a bit like a Nazi eagle.

They start walking again. A wiry old man in a cap and steel-rimmed glasses. A chubby little lady with a fur-lined collar. Everything sounds funny under the bridge. Concrete foundations and parked cars. Teenagers on skateboards. Strange echoes. It sucks getting old.

'Shall I go down and take a look?'

She nods. Doesn't even say thank you. Fredman shakes his head. Why is he still doing this? He should join the Association for Retired People instead. Wine tasting for seniors. Play fucking bingo.

'I'll get in touch when I'm back,' he says.

# GRANDMA'S JOURNEY

G RANDMA'S GOING ON A JOURNEY. To the new land far
up north. At last she'll get to meet Armada and the
children. All the new little ones. The ones she's never even
seen. Who miss her all the time. Always and ever. Loshie and
Kinda. Simon and Jan. Zami's kids. All of them. And together
they're all moving to the house Uncle Tanic bought. The
house outside Hammarstrand, a little town up north. Near
Gesunden. Gesunden doesn't mean anything in Swedish. But
it's a lake. You can see it from the ridge next to the house, like
a big blue sea in a valley of green spruce. It looks beautiful,
serene. No humans. And quiet.

The house is big. Big and old. Brown, two stories. With
a cellar and a barn and a garage and a lawn. Big trees the
children can climb in. Space for the whole family. They're
going to be together again, all of them. And no one will have
to worry anymore. That's the best thing. They'll finally be
together again. In a big house. Completely undisturbed.

The family is filled with expectation. Restless and nervous. A lot of unnecessary arguing. They're all having trouble
sleeping. They're all thinking about Grandma. And Uncle
Tanic. Thanks Uncle Tanic for figuring all this out. Thanks for
understanding this disgusting country, Sweden. And thanks
Linecka for helping him. Those of us living in the two apartments would never have survived without you. We would have
starved. Died. Without you, we were prisoners in the horrible
land of Rosengård. Surrounded by people. Dangerous, loud
people. The kind who hate. The kind who destroy. The kind
of people the family has fled from, time and time again.

Grandma's going on a journey. Zami and Janoch will go and pick her up. The family's two finest boys will make the journey to the old country. That's what Uncle Tanic decided. He's planned it all very carefully with the boys. Practiced. For months. Learned English. With Linecka as the teacher. Memorized things. Checked maps. Learned things by heart. Neither Zami nor Janoch is good at reading, so they have to mem-or-ize. And Uncle Tanic has arranged driver's license documents. Taught Zami and Janoch about traffic. Practiced driving on the streets of Rosengård. Learned how to talk to the road. The impatient children have howled for Grandma, but Tanic has hushed them. Grandma's so old and decrepit that nothing can be allowed to go wrong. And on a long journey a lot can happen. She could die. In a lot of different ways. The police could start causing trouble. Custom-men. Some immigration authority or other. But she wants to see her children so badly. And her children want to be with her. They're going to be happy together in the house by Gesunden. When it comes time to leave, Linecka and Armada's children have already moved into the new house. The same day that the boys are setting off, Zami's younger brothers and Jan are heading north. Jan drives them all in a big blue car. The journey takes a whole long night. By the time the boys arrive in Gesunden with Grandma, everyone except Uncle Tanic will have already moved from Malmö.

They pack things in a bag for the boys. Booze. Money. Several mobile phones. Lots of cigarettes. Food from the shop in Rosengård. Real food that Linecka and Samina have carried home. It's important. So the boys won't have to eat rubbish in the Eurozone. A pistol Linecka brought with her when she came up from Albania. Bullets for the pistol.

Grandma's going on a journey. Malmö station is messy and scary, but it's time now. Zami and Janoch take the train from Malmö. Janoch has never been on a train before. He's so frightened he's shaking. When the train starts moving he closes his eyes. The train rolls through towns and tunnels and over the long bridge to Copenhagen. They look at the view, terrified. The open water frightens them. They almost hold their breath.

Copenhagen is big and noisy. They step off the train without looking at each other. In Denmark, people hate Arabs and everyone who's not Danish. That's what Linecka said. An Arab is a person who doesn't eat pork and who's angry about Danes loving it so much. Danes look like Swedish people but they talk funny. Zami and Janoch are careful. There may even be racists among these Danes. Like the ones Linecka has heard about on the television in the big apartment. Swedish democrats who are racists. And if there are Swedish democrats there might also be some Danish ones.

They find the Odense train. Watch each other out of the corners of their eyes. Janoch walks slightly behind Zami. Zami reads the signs and leads the way. They're dressed normally. Baggy jackets. Soft run-shoes. Jeans. Well dressed but normal. Two boys from abroad. Immigrants. They've washed themselves carefully so they won't annoy any dogs. Janoch stinks of apricot soap. Both are wearing sunglasses.

They find their seats. Without looking at them, Kinda comes up from behind carrying the big duffel bag. She arrived in Copenhagen several hours earlier. In the car with Linecka. She doesn't look at the boys. She just puts the bag in the compartment's luggage rack and gets off again. No one knows the bag belongs to Zami and Janoch. It's labeled with a Swedish name: 'Björklund'. And there are a few Swede-things inside. A book. A Swedish newspaper. A can of raw fish. If the police or the custom-men find the bag the boys will just pretend it isn't theirs. Look stupid and surprised. Act like immigrants. Avoid looking anyone in the eye.

The journey takes forever. Ninety minutes. Each one as long as an hour. Over another bridge. An unfathomably long bridge. Zami and Janoch stare straight ahead. Seeing the ocean out of the corner of their eyes, they break into a cold sweat. They keep an eye on the bag and watch all the people running on and off the train. A man sits next to Zami. He reads his book without looking up once. He smells of beer and tobacco. The conductor who checks their tickets swears at Janoch when he doesn't hand over his ticket right away. Janoch doesn't say anything. He looks down at the floor with mumbled apologies. 'Fucking Arabs,' says the conductor and walks out.

Grandma's going on a journey. Zami and Janoch hurriedly disembark in Odense with the bag between them. The station is almost as big and noisy as the one in Copenhagen. They keep an eye out for dogs. And democrats. And the man they're meeting, a friend of Uncle Tanic's cousin. From the Nine Gates pack in Podgorica. They walk slowly along the platform, waiting for him. If he doesn't show, it's all over. Then they will have to leave the bag somewhere. And take a train back to Sweden, if that's possible.

The friend stops them and says their names. He's fat and black-haired. Wearing a tatty dark-blue suit. A nylon shirt. Cap. He's got a hairy neck. Smells of tobacco and sweat. Janoch bares his teeth but Zami calms him down. Offers his hand to the friend. Their hands are similarly hairy. Firm handshakes. They mutter their greetings. The friend indicates that they should follow him, through the mess, all the people who don't see them. Three men and a big bag. It must look odd. Very suspicious. They'll be stopped at any moment. The democrats will get them. And Grandma will never get to Gesunden.

The car is white and huge. A van. A Renault with space for three in the front seat. A large storage space with doors in the back. You could fit a small car in there. Or a cow. Or a bed. Janoch climbs inside. He can take four steps in there. There are no windows. They put the big bag in. Zami gets out a wad of money and gives it to the friend. Thanks for the car. Zami nods. Smiles. Go now.

The friend gives the ignition key to Zami and leaves with some hesitation, as if wondering whether they want something else. Maybe they want to buy something. Their kind hardly ever have money. So they're easily duped. He almost turns around but changes his mind. In the corner of his eye he sees the big one, who smells of apricot. He's staring at him. The friend remembers. Don't mess with the big one. Uncle Tanic has warned him. No funny stuff, nothing unexpected. Just go.

They climb into the car. Zami is in the driver's seat. It takes a while to start it, to turn off the radio, which is pumping out awful music. To find the pedals. They have to back out of the parking area. Zami has only reversed once before. And the car he was practicing in was an ordinary compact car. A red one. Not a massive van. It's difficult to see what's behind. And Zami doesn't have the nerve to send Janoch out to guide him. He's sweating before he's even got the car out of the parking area. He backs into something. Another car, maybe. But no one seems to have noticed. Janoch nods at Zami. 'Drive.'

Grandma's going on a journey. It takes them an hour and a half to find their way out of Odense. An eternity of cars with blaring horns, and road signs in Danish. Driving is difficult. Changing lanes is lethal. Every roundabout-circle is a nightmare. But finally they're on their way. Zami and Janoch drive the Renault van towards Hamburg. First to the mainland. Eighty kilometers. A short bridge. Takes them an hour, more or less. The driving is going well. Along the E20 and the E45. Ninety kilometers to Germany. Staying in the right-hand lane the whole time. The road goes over Danish hills. In the hollows there are clouds of rainy haze. The trees are yellow and brown and red. There are tall spinning things here and there. Over Fredericia and Flensburg. Zami has learned the route by heart and it's easy finding their way. The German border and a light rain. Custom-men. Janoch sits moaning. Uniforms terrify him. The German custom-men have peaked caps that remind him of Luchany. And a lot of bad things. Pain. Sitting for days on end in the dog cage. Taking beating after beating after beating. Being the circus dog that has to eat off the ground. And getting a kick in the head if he doesn't run fast enough on all fours.

Another forty kilometers. Dusk is falling. It's getting easier and easier driving. Zami smokes and smokes. They stop to fill up outside Schleswig. A self-service pump. Always self-service. It's a bit difficult figuring out how to do it, but they manage. They eat in the car. Sausage from Rosengård. Sleep for a while. Janoch has nightmares and wants to go home. But they can't let everyone down now. They all want Grandma to come to them. And Zami and Janoch are the ones picking her up. The family heroes. The best in the Pack.

One hundred and fifty kilometers of German motorway. An hour and a half. Cars everywhere. They stay in the right-hand lane. The whole time. The slow one. Nice and easy in the right-hand lane. In the left lane come the Germans, who are in a huge hurry. Sometimes they pass so close to the Renault that it shakes. All the roads in the world seem to lead to Hamburg. The traffic moves along slowly, sometimes it's almost stopped. They get there late at night. Find the port. It's enormous, bigger than the whole of Malmö. Finding the right warehouse takes them half the night. They navigate by Uncle Tanic's sketches. Slowly reading German signs. *Veddeler Damm. Brandenburger Strasse.* Big docks. Barges by dark quays. Tall cranes. They have never seen anything like it. The port is like a living being, a threatening monster. Zami and Janoch are impressed. Frightened, but impressed. They could live in a place like this. Right in the belly of the beast. Better than Rosengård. More alive than the forest. More pulsating.

The warehouse is like hundreds of others. Green roller doors. A concrete loading dock. A broken sign on the roof.

Zami takes out one of the phones. Calls the pre-programmed number. Mumbles: '*Von Schweden. Öffnen*' when someone answers. After a while one of the doors rolls open. Two men can be vaguely seen in silhouette. Waving at them. Zami waves back. Throws the telephone on the ground. Reverses towards the loading dock. One of the German men helps him get it right. It's still difficult reversing the big van but Zami is starting to feel like he's got the hang of it.

Janoch gets out. Steps on pieces of cell phone. He sniffs the air. Looks around. Sees dark houses. Containers. Chimneys. The city lights hide the stars. He hangs around by the car while Zami turns off the engine and goes into the warehouse. His skin is almost free of the scent of soap now. It no longer dulls his sense of smell. He picks up the scent of the port. Water and rotten seaweed. Oil. Rust. Rotten fruit.

On the loading dock they open the back doors of the van. Zami hands out money. The German men laugh. The German men get a bottle of schnapps. They laugh some more. Shake hands. Talking some weird mix of German and English that Janoch doesn't understand. He's never spent a day in school. Linecka has taught him to read a little Swedish. Say a few words. Count to ten. After that it feels like he hasn't got enough fingers. They roll a big gray plastic trough from the loading dock into the van. He jumps up to have a look. The German men stare at him. He stares back. Without his sunglasses. They look away.

The trough is long enough to stretch out in. Wide enough for three. It reaches up to Zami's waist. The plastic is stained and smells of slaughter. Blood. There are piles of chains and wheels inside. 'Winch.' A word Zami taught him. You hoist up heavy things with a winch. Hang it from the ceiling and pull on a chain. The German men load a lot of things inside. Two mattresses. One of those things you lift cars with. A sack with metal stuff inside. Manacles, padlocks, chains. The German men show them and laugh. Some tools. Janoch smells things. More iron and oil. The beery, sweaty smell of the Germans. And something else. Beyond the stink of apricot there's some other smell.

Janoch walks into the warehouse. Looks around among the loading pallets and auto parts. It takes him a moment to find the dog. The Germans have shut it in a little room. It starts barking when he comes closer. He opens the door. Catches the dog as it leaps. Breaks its neck. Smashes its head into the wall. Drives the loathsome animal straight through the door. There's blood and flesh and wood splinters. Planks and bones breaking. Behind him, the German men shout. Run towards him. Zami shouts. Janoch turns to the German men. Shows his teeth. The German men stop. One of them has a big knife in his hand. They hesitate. Shout at Zami. Zami shouts back. They all shout and shout and shout. All except the dog.

At long last they're sitting in the van. Without anyone else getting hurt. The Germans got lots more money. Janoch wasn't allowed to bring the dead dog. Even though he wanted to. Zami scolds Janoch. No trouble. No fighting. You silly thing. Why do you forget? Why, why, why? They cry together. Hold on to each other.

Grandma's going on a journey. But the boys are tired and scared. As they drive out of Hamburg they're trembling with tension. Zami runs red-lamps twice. But there aren't many cars out driving at night, so they don't crash. Once out of the city, there's a moonlit motorway. They're overtaken by cars driving at insane speeds. Big juniper bushes grow in the fields alongside the road. To someone with night vision they look like staring people. Custom-men. Democrats. Racists. All sorts of nasties. The boys don't get too far. Only to Hannover. A hundred and thirty kilometers, then Zami can't take any more. He's driving too slowly, the German cars honk at them. 'Stop if you get tired,' Uncle Tanic said. 'If you drive badly you'll get pulled over by the police.' And we don't want to meet the police. Or custom-men. Or immigration authorities. They stop at a rest area outside the city. Zami changes the registration plates on the van. Throws the old ones into the bushes. Now they have a German van, that's what their registration plates say. Janoch feels bad. He's hungry and he misses the children. He's angry at the dog. He didn't mean to. Zami consoles him. They sleep curled up together. In the big trough. On top of Grandma's chains. Grandma's padlocks and keys.

The morning brings rain. A dog barking like mad outside. Growling. Throwing itself repeatedly at the car until someone stops it. When it's gone they rush out, get into the front. And drive off without looking around. To the next service area. One with a view of a wooded valley. They eat smoked ham from Rosengård in the car. Watching as the haze over the valley breaks up and disperses. Have a pee in the ditch. Then drive south. Nice and easy in the right lane. Zami is brave enough to drive really fast now. A hundred and fifty kilometers from Hannover to Kassel. Two hundred and twenty to Würzburg. The A33 becomes the A7. They smoke like madmen. Zami knows all the numbers of the roads. He doesn't get confused even once. The A7 is also known as the E45. They drive through autumn-red woods. Past fields with white cows. On motorways full of shiny, pristine cars. The gas stations are called Ar-al and To-tal. People in Germany seem to be rich. They all have nice, shiny cars. Janoch wonders if some of the people in the cars belong to the same pack as the German men at the warehouse. The dog's blood on his clothes has dried and turned a reddish brown. He no longer smells like apricots.

Grandma's going on a journey. Another hundred kilometers. Filling up outside Nürnberg. Light rain, afternoon. Soft hills and rusty red leaves. They pull off at a deserted rest stop and rest for a bit. They eat more sausage. But there's nothing to drink. The water ran out earlier that morning. They have loads of meat and sausage and three bottles of schnapps, but no water. Their throats are burning. Zami thinks it through. They have to go shopping. Go to the shop, however you do that. It's usually Linecka or Uncle Tanic who does that kind of thing. They're not afraid of people. They can talk.

Zami looks out the window. Rain. Houses far away. White, pretty houses. Not a human in sight. Just cars and fields. There's a ditch along the side of the road. There's water in ditches, especially when it's been raining. Zami collects the bottles on the floor. He gets out of the van and climbs down into the ditch. The water at the bottom is muddy. Stagnant. They'd get sick right away.

Zami gets back into the van and thinks. He has to buy something to drink. Has to has to has to. He drives on into the dusk and tells Janoch. Again and again. Do it like Uncle Tanic. Nags at him. You have to me-mor-ize. I'm getting out of the car to get water. Buy water. You have to stay in the car. Janoch growls. Uncle Tanic said: 'No shops.' Petrol in self-service stations. No talking with anyone. Don't walk around where there are people. But they have to drink. Don't they?

Five kilometers later a gas station shows up in the haze. It's the kind that has a shop. Zami drives in. Careful and attentive. No sign of dogs. No police. Not too many cars. He parks along the side of the building. Rolls down his window and sniffs the air. No dogs. Gasoline. The smell of warm engines. Cooking fumes. He looks at his face in the rearview mirror. Wipes off a bit more blood. Wipes again. Smiles at his reflection. Almost looks human. He tells Janoch again. Stay in the car. Whatever happens. Promise.

There are ten people in the shop. Ten too many. No one looks at him. Except perhaps the boy at the register. Zami looks around. Picks up the smell of food and cleaning products. There are bottles of wine on the shelves. And chocolate and lots of newspapers. Things everywhere. More things than in Rosengård. Nicer things. Bigger. Where's the water? Coca-Cola? He sees the drinks section. There's a woman standing there looking at various bottles. She puts one of them in a basket on the floor. Zami takes a deep breath. Goes over to the drinks. Avoids looking at the woman. Looks down. His shoes are stained brown with dog blood. The woman's shoes are shiny. Pointed. She smells of soap. She puts two bottles of water in her basket and walks off without looking at him. Zami goes up to the mountainous piles of soft drinks and beer. Looks around for water. There are some big bottles wrapped six by six in plastic. He takes one and then another. They're heavy. Heavier than he thought. He looks around for the Coca-Cola. There. Even bigger bottles. They're packaged in pairs. Zami sighs. They're really big. He should have one of those baskets the woman had.

He goes over to the register, with a double-pack of Coke under each arm and a six-pack of water in each hand. Really heavy. There are two people in front of him at the counter. A big man and an old woman. They both give him a look, then turn away. The man pays the boy behind the counter. Zami watches how they do it. The big man shows the things he wants to buy. The boy counts them. Says how much money. Takes the money. They smile. Doesn't look very difficult. He'll manage.

The woman pays for something and walks off. It's Zami's turn. The boy behind the counter smiles at him. Says something in German. Zami nods. Tries to smile. Mumbles in Swedish. He puts all the bottles on the counter. The boy does something weird that makes a beeping sound. Then says something in German. And smiles. Zami gets out some banknotes. Lots of them. Hands them over. The boy smiles even more and takes one of them. Zami gets money back. Nods. Says 'Thanks.' Takes all the bottles. Turns around and walks straight into a German. A big German in a leather jacket, with a motorcycle helmet in his hand. Zami drops a bottle on the floor. And another. The German laughs and helps him pick them up. First one, then the other. Zami says 'Thanks' again. He clamps the bottles under his arms. Smiles. Goes to the door, thinking how Janoch would have killed everyone in the shop by now. But not Zami. Zami is the one who dares. Zami is the one who can do the hard things. Zami is the one who jumps out of his skin when the shop doors slide open by themselves. He almost stumbles. Almost drops the bottles. Almost has a fit of panic. The thirty steps to the van feel like a thousand. Is someone following him? Did he do something wrong? The man standing over there smoking by his car. What can he see? A human carrying a lot of bottles? Anything else? Something he's never seen before? A beast. Something from a nightmare.

Janoch opens the door for him. There's a stink of piss in the car. Janoch has pissed himself with fear. These things happen. Zami throws the packs of bottles into the van and climbs in. His whole body is shaking. Drink, he says. Closes the door. Starts the engine. Janoch tears off the plastic wrapping around the bottles. Mumbles thanks, thanks, thanks for a long time as they head down the motorway. Zami can fix anything.

Grandma's going on a journey. It's raining in Bavaria. The hills around them are red and yellow. It's safe in the right-hand lane. They spend hours behind the same truck. They have their dinner, sausages from Rosengård. Smoke Polish cigarettes from Möllevången. Drink German water. They only stop to rest for a while. In a dark parking lot. No dogs in sight. Eighty kilometers to Regensburg. Slow traffic for a long time. Men working on the roads. A hundred and thirty kilometers to Passau. It grows dark as they drive through a large forest in red and brown autumn colors.

They cross a huge river surrounded by mountains. They drive into Austria in heavy rain. By Passau. Janoch has a fit of panic again. But there's no sign of custom-men. Just empty machine-gun turrets and switched-off spotlights. Signs everywhere. Blue signs with the ring of yellow stars. The sign of the humans. Huge trucks and shops. No one's looking for them.

Zami keeps driving. The road twists into the mountains. In long curves. You have to look out the whole time. And Zami's getting shaky. He sweats and sweats and sweats. Drives badly. Janoch starts whining about his steering. Shouting that he's not looking where he's going. As if he knew anything about driving. They shout at each other. Drink Coke and take headache tablets. Zami reels off place names. Passau. Towards Linz. A3 becomes A8. The landscape more mountainous. The roads more winding. White houses with black planks. Seventy kilometers to Wels. Then comes the hardest part. Over the mountains. Zami has learned that by heart too. It's the only way when you can hardly read. Recall. Mem-or-ize: A1 towards Salzburg before Linz. A1 towards Salzburg before Linz. It might also say E60 or E55. Then A9 towards Graz.

Grandma's going on a journey. The Alp-mountains have started. The hills get higher and higher. They see other headlights climbing up and down the mountains around them. The van climbs. Fights its way up the hills. Zami steps on it and steps on it. The Renault engine screams. Sixty kilometers to Liezen. Mountains on both sides. They drive through a long tunnel. Five kilometers of booming noises and yellow lights. Janoch has lived in a cubbyhole for years. But he has a panic attack in the tunnel. He screams all the way. Zami tries to calm him down. Think of Grandma. Grandma, we're coming. We have the keys. We have to be strong enough. Not afraid. Not afraid. Not afraid.

They stop at a parking area outside Liezen. Turn off the car. Stare into the night and let their eyes get used to the darkness. Cover their eyes every time a car passes. At home they keep the windows taped up. Never turn on the lights.

They can see anyway. Everyone in the Pack can see in the dark. And they play in the dark. And mess around and argue and fight. Eat Rosengård sausages. Because they can't hunt for real. You're not allowed to go hunting in Sweden. You just wait. Wait and wait in the dark. In the two flats. With a hole connecting them. The girls' flat and the boys' flat. They whisper about home. Smoke more cigarettes. They're homesick. Janoch cries again. They go to sleep leaning against one another. Zami dreams about red tail-lights turning into hovering spheres of light. The lights ascend towards the sky like bubbles in water. It's really beautiful.

They're woken by pouring rain. It's cold. They have no blankets. The car stinks. Piss and empty bottles on the floor. It's still dark when Zami starts driving again. Seventy kilometers to Leoben. Downhill now. The moon breaks through the clouds. Illuminates the mountain peaks. They drive through another long tunnel. Janoch's too tired to get scared. Their faces shine in the yellow light. They look crazy. The Pack's finest on their way to pick up Grandma.

Zami calls the Serb at dawn. From a parking area just before Leoben. Rain clouds creep along the slopes of the mountains as they talk. They arrange to meet in Maribor. The Serb speaks quickly and nervously.

'*Geld.*'

'Money.'

'Women.'

He's greedy. And hard to understand. But at last they're agreed.

'Maribor.'

'Yes.'

'Meet at containers.'

'Yes.'

'*Fünfzig* thousand euro.'

'Yes. Yes.'

Uncle Tanic and Linecka have prearranged the business with the Serb. Soon it'll be time. Zami throws away the phone and drives south.

Down mountains, through tunnels. Up another mountain slope. Sometimes you can see a really long way. Zami starts getting used to driving in the mountains. He learns quickly. But the van sounds tired. Fifty kilometers to Graz. Graz is a big mess. Nasty roundabout-circles everywhere. The road passes through the city center, more or less. Zami is afraid of taking a wrong turn among the jumble of people. Look carefully. Turn using the blink-stick. A9 towards Maribor. In the land of Slovenia. A new country. Zami wonders how it happens when humans decide to make a new country. Do they slug it out, like you do in a pack?

More mountains and forests and rain. More shiny cars with big red tail-lights. More sausage and cigarettes. Another refueling stop soon after Graz. Janoch says the car is starting to smell. He wants a new one. It's not possible. They only have one car.

The border is scary. Again. Humans everywhere. Big red, blue, and white flags. Soldiers. Police. Shops. Humans selling things. Humans trying to avoid the rain. Trucks. More big signs. Drive under the picture of stars in a ring. Women in short skirts. Get out the two pass-books. Show them if anyone asks. You come from Denmark. Don't be afraid of democrats. Slowly they roll past sentry-boxes with tired custom-men inside. Zami waves. He has the window rolled down and his arm resting in the gap. An experienced car person. Janoch pretends to be asleep. They have a pile of money and a bottle of schnapps on the seat in case some-one wants a present. The pistol is under the seat. If they get caught, Uncle Tanic decided Zami must first shoot Janoch and then himself. Janoch doesn't know about it. Linecka decided he shouldn't be told. He's easily frightened. Two women tap on his window. Janoch flinches and growls. Zami has to pull him away and smile and smile and smile. Wave at the women. They wave back.

Grandma's going on a journey. Twenty kilometers to Maribor. In light rain and deep puddles. It's afternoon when they find the place. An industrial plot in Maribor. They park and wait. By a sea of containers. Grandma's grandchildren take turns sleeping in the stinking van. One of them rolled up on the seat. The other staying awake and smoking. Sleep. Wake up. Keep an eye out. Wait. Sniff for enemies. Maribor stinks. Like Rosengård but dirtier and more dangerous. And no matter how hard you try to put your own smell on things it's difficult. 'Probably a lot of democrats live around here,' says Zami. Janoch doesn't answer. Zami tries to remember his childhood. Before Rosengård. In Yugoslavia. The land that disappeared. However a land does that. Grandma still lives in the monastery. The children live down in the valley. Play in the forest on the ridge. No humans to disturb them. They can hunt at night. Mate in the moonlight. It's beautiful and Zami doesn't really have any memories of it. He was too young. All he really remembers is what Uncle Tanic has told him. How they fled when the soldiers got too curious. First to the monastery where everyone starved. And then further. About his mother. Tereta. Who starved to death in a crate on the way to Malmö. Zami wasn't there. He was with Linecka in another country and on another road. Romania. All his childhood memories involve hiding. In trailers, in tunnels, under bridges.

The only thing Janoch remembers is Luchany. He remembers nothing before the men from the camp caught him. Nothing.

The Serb gets there late. In a green truck with 'Carlsberg' written on it. He's brought three big humans as guards. They come in their own car. A black one. They get out a short distance away and stand there looking threatening. They smell of smoked sausage and tobacco and sweat. And fear. They stay by their car. Good. The Serb comes towards them. The boys get out. Zami goes up to the Serb. They shake hands. The Serb is nervous. Shaky and twitchy. He smokes. Stinks of booze. Asks in English. Zami answers: 'Yes, from Sweden. You have women?' Janoch hisses behind him. The Serb stares at Janoch. Janoch makes him uneasy. It's hard to talk to someone when there's a big something growling behind him. Janoch has stopped even pretending to be human. From his place in the shadow of the van only the Serb can see him. Not the other three men. They only see the Serb and Zami. They see Zami take out lots of money and a bottle of schnapps. They see them making a toast. The Serb drinks first. Then Zami. They laugh when Zami coughs. Then Zami laughs too. He takes another big gulp. Asks: 'Women?' Gets out the bag of handcuffs and chains. And keys. The Serb nods and points at the Carlsberg truck. Zami gives him money. Laughs even more. Slings the bag onto his shoulder. Points at the Carlsberg truck. 'Come,' he says in Swedish.

The Serb looks at Zami. And at his guards. At the money in his hand and at Janoch. Then he follows Zami. The three men watch. Don't see Janoch. Only see the Serb and Zami with the bag. Watch them squelching through puddles.

There are four girls sitting on the flatbed of the Carlsberg truck. The Serb says something and laughs. The girls look scared. Zami hands him the bag. Tries to look composed even though there are eight people staring at him. He signals to the Serb. Get started. Move them out. He lights a cigarette with trembling paws. Steps aside. And prays. A key to heaven. And heaven opens. All the rain in the world pours down over them.

Janoch is up on the mountain of containers. Under cover of the rain, he climbs silently and quickly. Soaked through without realizing. Doing what his body is meant for. The reason he's come on this trip. The Pack's best warrior. Uncle Tanic and Linecka have told him. Again and again. The men you'll be meeting were in Luchany. They're from the same pack as the ones who tortured you. Janoch looks down between the two vehicles. Sees the three men standing there getting wet. They would love to get under cover, but they have to stand guard. And stare at Zami, who stands there staring back at them. One of the men has one of those patch-jackets. A soldier-jacket. A Luchany-jacket.

Janoch sees the Serb put handcuffs on the girls. Sees all the keys and locks. Holy signs. One of the girls is tall and blond. The other three are shorter and dark. They shiver in the rain. One of the small ones looks a bit like one of Linecka's sisters. Or children. Janoch smiles and forgets Luchany for a moment. Then he remembers the girls. The guards in Luchany have a disco house. They drag girls inside it and play loud music. By the time they've finished dancing the girls are really upset and bleeding everywhere. Some of them die. Janoch hates the disco house. He's afraid the guards will drag him there.

The Serb slaps one of the dark girls. Janoch gets angry. When he hears the men laughing he gets even angrier. It rises up in him. You're not going to the disco house. He growls. Shakes off the raindrops. Digs his fingers into the container he's sitting on. Bends steel plate out of pure anger. When Zami takes the chain and leads the girls away towards the Renault he's ready. Raging.

Zami leads the girls to the van. With his back to the Serb. It's hard to pick up scents in the rain. And hard to hear. He hears one of the girls sobbing, but he can't hear the Serb's steps. They could be coming after him, all four of them, without him hearing anything. He opens the back door of the van. Peers over his shoulder. The rain has turned everything gray. The Serb is slowly coming towards him. With his hand in his pocket. His right hand. The three men come behind him. Slowly. He takes a deep breath. Signals for the girls to climb inside, into the back. He wants them inside the van before the killing starts. The first girl has curly hair and a sopping wet yellow sweater. She looks down at the ground. He half drags her, half leads her into the van. The chains rattle. The girl stumbles. Falls to her knees and pulls the next girl down too. They whisper to each other. The rain against the roof of the van drowns out their words. Zami fastens the chain to the wall. Tugs a little. Come in. All of you. He points at the mattresses. Sit there. Hurry. People are gonna be dying out there soon. Don't look.

He drags the last of the girls into the van. She falls over and can't break her fall because her hands are bound together. Hits her head. Outside there are cries. Someone whimpers. Like a cat being tortured. Zami helps the girl up without looking at her. She grips his arm hard. Something makes a bang outside. Someone cries out. Someone barks like a dog. Something is thrown against the side of the van. The girls scream. Shrill and hysterical. Zami yells at them to be quiet. Then something slams into his head. His temple explodes.

Zami never finds out. What happened there in the parking lot remains a mystery. A long time later, when he's the only one left who's not dead or mad, he will start wondering: what happened there in the pouring rain? Janoch kills two of the men. Just as Uncle Tanic had decided. The third man is allowed to run. Just like when they stole all the money in Malmö. You always let one of them run. So he can talk. Because when the boss of a gang of thieves describes a beast like Janoch no one actually believes him. And so he never comes back.

The Serb also dies. Zami never finds out how. Or who fired the gun. But one of the men had a gun. He shot twice and one of the bullets hit Zami. Much later he finds the holes in the side of the car. He's out cold for a long time while Janoch carries him out. Shuts the girls inside. Reclaims their schnapps from the Serb. Fixes things up. Rummages around. Collects all the keys. Cleans up. Starts the engine. Zami regains consciousness in the driver's seat. He's covered in blood and next to him sits Janoch, shouting that they have to get going. They must, must, must. There are three humans outside and they're dead, dead, dead. But Zami is dizzy, dizzy, dizzy. He takes great gulps of schnapps. Frightens himself into waking up. Rinses his face with water. Soon he can see through both eyes, only with a bit of double vision. There are no other cars in sight. The Renault jumps when he tries to change gear. Slowly it lurches onto the road. He accelerates and almost collides with a tanker. He slams on his brakes. In the back the girls are screaming.

Grandma's going on a journey. Zami vomits on the side of the road. On a forest road, next to the van. He has no idea where he is. Or how he got there. It's the middle of the night. He's seen himself in the rearview mirror. His right cheekbone is broken. Swollen and red. The bullet tore open his temple and ripped off half his ear. His eye actually sticks out a little. No problem. They'll be there soon. Zami takes a gulp of water and passes out again.

They drive on. Early morning. Through haze and cold. But no rain. Zami is still dizzy. He blinks and blinks and blinks. It takes an hour to find the right road again. The road known as Three. Janoch is crazy. Really frightened and really frenzied. He sits there clawing at himself, then claws at the car, then himself again. Soon they're on the right road. Towards Virovitica. They cross a border. Without even slowing down. Zami forgets. He drives past the custom-men who are waving, but he pretends not to see them. And Yog-Sothoth protects them. No one pursues them.

Zami reels off signs and roads. Petrified that the bullet may have erased something in his head. He smokes and eats sausage. Mumbling. They almost run into a motorcycle. Zami brakes hard. The girls scream. Zami hears them falling down in the back. He accelerates, then slams on his brakes. Again and again. Until they're quiet. Janoch wants to get in the back with the girls. Talk a bit. You can't talk so they understand, says Zami. You have to sit here and keep me awake.

They have to fill up. They don't pass any self-service places, so they have to stop at a little gas station. There's just one car outside and no dogs around. Zami has washed his face and put the gun in his pocket. He's not afraid anymore. He gets out. Fills up the car without looking around. He hangs the nozzle back up and goes inside the little shop. Two people. They both look at him. At his mangled face. He smiles. They smile. He picks up a couple of packs of cookies. Pays. Smiles and mumbles in Swedish. The woman behind the counter smiles back. His face makes her look away. She mumbles something in a language he doesn't understand. It doesn't matter. Because he's Zami and he'll be meeting Grandma soon. He has the key. His head feels like it's about to explode. But he isn't scared.

Zami goes back to the car. Opens the back and peers in. The girls are lying on the mattresses in the trough. Half asleep. Like a litter of kittens. They squint at the light. There's a smell of piss and terror about them. The curly-haired one says something and waves her manacled hands. There's a rattle of chains. Zami smiles and tosses her the cookies. Shuts the door and thinks how they've been sitting there all day. It would be stupid if they died. Before they can meet Grandma. He throws them a bottle of water too. They should have brought blankets for them. But you can't think of everything.

Grandma's going on a journey. It's a long way to the monastery. Over Nasice and south. Towards Slavonski Brod. But you have to turn off before. It's cold now. A few degrees colder and the rain will turn to ice. But Zami drives and drives. With a pounding head. Sixty kilometers in one long, long drive. Before his memory quits on him. Off the big roads. Janoch half asleep beside him. Through ghost-lands. Narrow roads. Dark roads. Roads twisting across hills where no one wants to live. He drives slowly because the road is hard to make out. They meet few cars. Just the odd one. And an old tractor. A horse and cart. A man on a moped. Janoch snores. Zami smokes. It's quiet in the back. He rolls down the window. Feels the chill of the air. Like an ice cube against his forehead. There's a smell of land and forest. It's different than in Germany. It smells of home. Childhood. The smells bring out hazy recollections. Soon they'll be there.

On the hill leading to the monastery they're stopped. One of the Akasi brothers jumps onto the road and waves a flashlight. Zami slows down and the brother comes up to the car. He has a pungent smell. Cellar and earth. He hides his face in shadow. Swept up in a big brown coat. Pretending to be a holy Jesus-man. A good disguise. Pretend to be a worshipper of a dead god and humans leave you alone. Zami thinks about the other gods. The ones Uncle Tanic has taught them to pray to. The great gods, the old gods. Yog-Sothoth who shows the way. But you don't worship him in Rosengård. You pretend to believe in Allah instead. So you can walk among humans with your face hidden. Linecka could never have gone to school if anyone had seen her face.

Zami growls a greeting to the Akasi brother. The brother answers. The growling wakes up Janoch. He throws himself out of the van. Embraces the brother and howls. Zami sinks down behind the wheel. Waits for them to get through their greetings. Starts to roll towards the monastery. Slowly, with one arm hanging out the window. He can drive the van without fear now. He can do anything. However much his head is hurting. He stops the van outside the stone house with the veranda and the little tower. It's been almost a lifetime since he was here, even in his dreams. He cries.

He makes it into the hall before he passes out. In the midst of the chattering Akasi spawn. He falls down among them. And they lift him up. Carry him down the stairs in jubilant triumph. Down to Grandma.

★

Grandma's going on a journey. Zami sits on the little veranda. Half unconscious, half sleeping. The Akasi have put him in a torn red armchair. Licked his wounds clean. Chattered a lot. Happy as puppies and totally unintelligible. They rush round, round, round. They're curious about Zami and scared of Janoch. When they caught the scent of the girls and wanted to get in the car, Janoch gave a few of them a beating. Then Janoch put them to work. All while Zami rests. Zami has a long way to drive. As soon as they're done here.

Zami smokes to counteract his hunger. And drinks schnapps for his headache. The Akasi are poorly stocked with food and have no medicines. The sky is clear and starry. Behind him he hears noises from the cellar. Janoch and the Akasi brothers are working. They've dragged the trough downstairs. And the winch. The girls screamed like mad when they saw the Akasi. Zami had to calm them down and almost lift them out of the trough. And Janoch had to subdue the Akasi. Fairly heavy-handedly. One of them broke an arm.

Apparently it'll be hard lifting Grandma. Janoch comes up now and then and growls. It's not easy talking to the brothers. They're not much used to talking. With anyone. Or working. They're excitable and loud-mouthed. And stupid. Zami doesn't want to think that way. But that's the way it is. The Akasi are stupid. They've been in the countryside for too long. They're not used to humans. It wouldn't work bringing them to Gesunden. There's too many of them and they could never go on the train. Or drive a car. Zami wonders if they even know what they're helping Janoch do down there.

He wonders if Grandma understands. She was so different. It was like meeting Yog-Sothoth himself when the Akasi carried him down to the cellar and put him on the floor in front of her. She was wonderful. Big and mighty. Frightening. And utterly incomprehensible. He hardly understood a word of what she said. Maybe she was speaking in a strange dialect. With a strange mouth. But the Akasi seemed to understand.

They laughed and squealed. No matter what she said. And they cheered when she embraced Zami. Zami almost passed out again. Enveloped by her scent and warmth. He had missed her so much. Weeping, he tried to explain. While she licked his wounds. But she didn't understand. Or listen. In the end he gave up and just lay there in her arms. Home. He was home. Home.

He lay there for a long time. In the cellar of the monastery. The place where his family was born. Where the Pack had its roots. His beginning. The place Uncle Tanic had spoken of so many times. The place where he and Janoch were born. The place of the Agreement. Long before the war and the flight. The place Grandma had to leave if she was to go on living.

Zami remembers a year ago, when Uncle Tanic went to visit Grandma. He said she was alone with the Akasi. Everyone from her pack had left her. Almost all of them had gathered in awful Malmö. But some were dead. Or just gone. Disappeared in Luchany. Abducted by other families. And worst of all: Linecka's sister, Uoni, went off into the world. Alone. And no one had heard from her in three years. Uoni was tired of the Pack. Tired of the feuding. Tired of the cramped apartments. And tired of her sister. She had a brood of children in her belly. Zami's or Uncle Tanic's. But she left before they were born. Zami misses her sometimes. Maybe she went to the Norwayland, which she spoke about. She wanted to live in the mountains, she said. She wanted him to go with her. Start a new pack. But Zami stayed. He couldn't let Uncle Tanic down. Or his little brothers and all the children. Without Uncle Tanic and Linecka and Zami they'd die. All of them. Starve or kill each other. Or attract the curiosity and rage of humans. He really can't stand humans. They're everywhere and so numerous. And so hateful. But everything will be better in Gesunden. In Gesunden things will work out. And if Grandma gets there it really couldn't get any better. Ever.

Grandma's going on a journey. And Janoch slaves away. The important thing is to lift Grandma. And get her into the trough. And get the trough out of the cellar. Into the yard. And into the van. Even though Uncle Tanic has measured it, it'll be tight. And the Akasi are stupid. They don't think. Or talk. Janoch gets irritated. He has to point and growl. Winch on the ceiling. Above Grandma. Planks under Grandma. Lift her up with the jack. Look. Show. Bang someone's head. Look, stupid Akasi.

Grandma watches. She doesn't really understand either. Janoch knows that. He's told her 'home' and 'Uncle Tanic' lots of times, but she just seems tired. Her big dark eyes watch and watch. She recognizes him from his scent, he can see that. But she doesn't say anything. Not to anyone. Mostly she sits there sleeping. Now and then she wakes up and mumbles something. And the Akasi shout with joy. She shits on the floor. And the Akasi shit too. It takes a while before Janoch understands that's what's covering the floor. Shit. Things won't be like that in Gesunden. Zami and Linecka and Uncle Tanic would never allow it. Grandma will be washed. And she'll get clothes. And real food. Because the Akasi mostly eat rats.

He struggles on. It takes hours to get Grandma into the trough, using chains and the jack. He has to lift and pull. Lift and push. Calm Grandma who's upset and mumbling. Shove and tug at the Akasi to make them help. Hold the chain, you idiot. Or I'll take you to the disco house. Almost done, Grandma. Just hold on. Grandma will hurt herself if you let go. Hold on. Roll the trough over. Stop there. Stand still. Stop chattering!

It's morning by the time Janoch has transferred Grandma to the mattress in the trough. She makes herself comfortable among the blankets. And craps herself. Janoch goes up to have a word with Zami. It's early morning outside. Cold. The smell of fur and shit in the cellar turns to spruce and dew.

Zami sits sleeping in the red chair. Black and blue in the face and wrapped up in a brown coat. A bottle of schnapps in his lap. Zami, the hero. He who me-mor-ized the way to Grandma. Janoch pats him on the head. Zami mumbles something. He tells him he gave the Akasi's clothes to the girls. So they wouldn't freeze to death. Janoch nods. Good. You think of everything. You'll get all the girls when we get home. All the children in Gesunden will be yours.

Janoch goes down into the cellar. Grandma has fallen asleep again. The Akasi are messing around. One of them plays with the crane. Climbs and does somersaults. Time to start rolling the trough out. But first they have to put out planks for the wheels to roll on. It takes time and it's difficult to figure out. He's not so good at figuring things out. Especially not with the curious Akasi all over him. They're a hindrance as much as a help. And he's getting very hungry. He can't remember when he last ate. He drinks water from the bottles Zami bought, but there doesn't seem to be any food left. Maybe Zami's saving it. Or hiding it from the Akasi. They'd steal it right away if they saw it. Little thieves. They need to raise someone who can go to the shops. Or they'll starve in the end. Or start eating each other. All the time. Not just when someone dies. Like they do in Malmö.

Towards evening it starts raining. Zami is woken by rain splashing against his face. The veranda roof leaks. His head is throbbing and his mouth tastes of cigarettes. Behind him, he hears Janoch growling and hissing. He looks. Grandma is on her way up. They're tugging and dragging the trough up the stairs. Janoch does most of the pulling and the Akasi help. And get in the way. Zami waves at Grandma. She sits in the trough looking surprised. She can't understand what's happening at all. But she waves back. And drools. He smiles. 'You're going to be so happy with us, Grandma.' Then he goes to pick up the pistol in the van. He tucks it into the waistband of his pants. When he closes the door someone shouts inside the van. The girls. He had almost forgotten about them. They must be hungry. But they'll have to wait. There's not going to be any food now, not with the Akasi around. He bangs the side of the van. 'No food,' he calls out in Swedish. 'Quiet!'

Janoch and the Akasi drag the trough onto the veranda. Push his chair out of the way. Grandma looks around curiously. Zami wonders how long it's been since she was last above ground. Ten more steps to the car. Then they're on their way. Ten steps. With the Akasi swarming everywhere. And the girls in the car. Zami gets a headache again. This is going to be tough. He looks at Janoch. He's thinking the same thing. It could get dangerous. Very dangerous. Janoch goes up to the van. Measures the ten steps with his eyes. The courtyard's made of concrete. Good. But they have to get the trough down the steps from the veranda. And into the van. Ten long steps.

Janoch lays out the planks. Gives Zami a short length of plank to hold on to. Brings up the crane and puts all the chains next to the van. Puts all the locks and keys he found in the cellar in a sack. Throws it into the front of the van. The Akasi run after him. Five of them, all the time. Zami watches and understands why he has the plank. Janoch points and shows them how. Growls and starts toiling. 'Harder,' he hisses in Swedish. They get the trough down the stairs. Grandma rolls out into the rain. She looks at the sky. Smiles at the drops of water. Her eyes are shining. It's clear she doesn't understand anything. Has she been living in the cellar since the Agreement? Might she even be the Agreement? Janoch pats her on the shoulder. Walks around the trough. Mumbling to himself. Looks at the car. They have to open the back doors. Open them and lean some planks up there to roll the trough on. Try it out and measure. Strain and pull. Lift over the edge. Keep it balanced. Simple. Everything will go well as long as the Akasi don't start wondering where Grandma's going. Or unless Grandma gets scared. Or someone picks up the scent of the girls in the van.

Grandma's going on a journey. Everything progresses slowly. Slowly. Slowly. Zami smiles at Grandma. Lights a cigarette. Don't be afraid. Yes, look it's raining. Water from the sky. Who would have thought it? And Janoch? What's he doing? Zami moves closer to the trough. Chitchats with Grandma in Swedish. Look. Now Janoch has gathered all the Akasi together. He points and points. Now they're going to roll you into the van. That's right. That white thing is called a van. Vroom. Vroom. With that van we're going to Gesunden. In Sweden. It's going to be really nice. And here comes Janoch. Now they're going to push you into the van. Are you ready?

It all goes smoothly until Janoch opens the doors. Until the Akasi see the girls. And the girls see Grandma. And Grandma starts screaming just because everyone else is screaming. His head really hurts. Zami screams too. And raises the plank like a club.

An hour later things are quieter. Zami parks on a gravel road about twenty kilometers from the monastery. Checks everything. He's alive. His head is throbbing. He's bloody everywhere, but it's not his blood so it doesn't matter. Janoch sits doubled up. They stabbed him with something. He killed half of them. And Zami two more. With his plank. Then they got Grandma into the car. And realized she'd start on the girls as soon as the boys weren't standing in her way. She heaved herself at the girls. Tried to reach further than her body would go. Hissed and growled. Wheeled around with her claws. And the girls screamed and tried to get out of the van. In spite of the chains and in spite of the Akasi and Janoch outside. Zami gave Grandma a little taste of plank. The girls got some too. He shouted at them all. Turned around and smashed one of the Akasi clawing at the girls. Shouted some more. Hit Grandma on the head. Shouted at the girls. Around. Around. Around.

Janoch had chased the Akasi into the house. They put the winch on top of Grandma. Tangled her up in the chains. Gave the plank to the blond girl. Closed the doors and drove off. On their way down the hill Zami wondered about the Akasi. What would they do now? Keep living in the monastery? Drift somewhere else? Make another Agreement? Die off?

Zami steps out of the car and listens. Nothing can be heard except the rain. There's nothing to be seen on the road to the monastery. He lights a cigarette. Smokes in the rain. Feels the rain rinsing the smell of blood from his hands. They made it. Grandma's with them. Now they just have to get home. He has six cubs now. Grandma, the four girls, and Janoch. Janoch is wounded. And Grandma is buried in a pile of chains. She's hungry, the poor thing. And the girls too. He has to get them all some food. And he has to examine Janoch. Zami, who can do anything, is going to pull it off.

There's a yell and a bang from the back. Grandma wails and one of the girls screams. The blond one, Zami guesses. He wonders what language she speaks. He's going to teach her to talk in a way people can understand. And if she's a democrat he'll try and cure her.

Janoch is pale. He has wiped his face, but his mouth is still bloody. His own blood. They try to talk, but Janoch slurs his words. He lifts up his sweater and shows him the little hole. A small hole in his hairy chest. High up. Right between two ribs. Almost no blood. Janoch doesn't understand. How come it hurts so bad if he isn't bleeding?

'Why, Zami? Why? Can you fix it, Zami?'

Zami gives him a hug.

'We're gonna make it. I just have to clean up a bit in the back.'

The truck bed needs tidying up. Washing out. It stinks of piss and Grandma. The only light in there is from a vent in the roof. Grandma is lying in the trough, wrapped in chains.

The girls are pressed up against one of the walls. The blond one is kneeling with her bit of plank raised. Teary-eyed and furious. When Zami opens up she starts talking. She points and snarls. Zami understands. She can put up with the chains. And has understood that Janoch is good. But Grandma is too much. Grandma is hungry and not so particular about what she eats. Zami climbs inside and tries to talk to Grandma. Grandma is angry. She wants to eat and get free of these chains. Zami says no. They screech and growl. The blond girl keeps her eyes on them. Looks at Grandma, looks at Zami. Tries to understand. Then she understands that Zami and Grandma don't understand each other and she starts talking as well. Soon they're arguing, all three of them. The other three girls, who have just woken up, watch them drowsily. They try to understand what's happening. What the others are arguing about.

When Zami closes the doors they're agreed. No one is going to eat anyone else, no one is going to hit anyone else, and Zami is going to sort out the food. Janoch has fallen asleep in the front seat. He needs medicine. Or maybe just sleep. Zami is not so good with clocks, but he's been up for a very long time. Awake for several days. They're all tired. He could sleep forever.

Grandma's going on a journey. Zami doesn't know a lot about cars, but the van feels tired and heavily loaded. It sways and the engine feels weak. And it stinks of blood and family and shit. The sausages are gone. The water is gone. Slowly he drives down deserted hills. Meets no cars. The sun rises in a sky of gray clouds. Koprivnica. Janoch snores. They meet convoys of green trucks. Soldiers or custom-men. Maybe they are looking for the people who killed the Serb and his friends. But they don't see them. They're just another vehicle on the road. They pass the border he forgot earlier. A custom-man waves him on. He doesn't even get scared. They pass Maribor in the morning. With his eyes still wide open, Zami drives on. He almost runs over an old man on a moped.

Another border pops up that Zami had forgotten all about. He's so tired. He doesn't even know which border it is. He snatches up the pistol and a wad of money. Just in case. But no one notices them. All the guards stand hunched up in the rain. No whores bang on the window this time. Janoch wakes just after they've passed through. Sits up and looks around with his bloody face. Zami shouts at him. Down. Out of the way. Hide. Janoch no longer looks like he understands. His eyes are feverish and empty.

Grandma's going on a journey. Zami hears a commotion in the back as they cross the E66. Plank-whacks and Grandma-screams. Soon after, his cigarettes run out. And Janoch falls on the floor. Graz looks like a black field of sparks in the pouring rain.

He's got to talk to someone.

Zami calls Uncle Tanic from an abandoned farm a short distance past the first tunnel. Tells him Grandma's in the van. That Janoch is wounded. That they must have food. Uncle Tanic is calming. You have to buy food somewhere. Go nice and easy. How are the girls? They're all alive. One of them is fighting with Grandma. No problem. Zami doesn't tell him how tired he is. Or how much his head hurts. He'd like to finish the last bottle of schnapps and go to sleep. The whole bottle. But he can't give up. Not now when he's the only one left. He throws away the phone and starts driving again.

Grandma's going on a journey. They drive across dark mountains in drizzling rain. The engine roars and roars. The girls scream from the back. Zami shouts back. Bangs the wall. You're going to get food. You're going to get water. Stop causing trouble.

Many miles, mountains and miles. More tunnels and more mountains. More miles and afternoon. Zami stops at a filling station outside Liezen. He forces Janoch down on the floor. Tells him, 'Don't move.' He roars at everyone in the back to be quiet. Brings the pistol and money. Gets out and fills up. Like a human. One of them. He walks into the shop. Grabs bottles of water and sausage and cookies. Two bottles of schnapps. There are four people standing at the counter. They're watching television. Some kind of competition. Football, maybe. Zami smiles at them. Points at the car and the items he's buying. Mumbles in Swedish. Smiles. Points at cigarettes. Indicates 'Five packs.' Gets out a big wad of money. Gives the man behind the counter three big banknotes. Gets a lot of money back. Smiles and smiles. The man stares at his forehead. Zami catches a glimpse of himself in a mirror and understands why. Half his face is black and blue. He looks worse than ever.

There are no other cars at the gas pumps. And Zami has parked so that no one in the shop can see directly into the back of the Renault. Two of the girls are sleeping. They're pale and silent. The blond girl and the yellow sweater are awake. The blond girl looks angry and defiant. Grandma is asleep. Or pretending to be asleep. He throws in water, sausage, and cookies to the blond girl. Points at Grandma. Points at his mouth. You feed everyone. The blond girl points at herself. 'Lena,' she says. 'Le-na.' Zami understands. Says 'Zami' and points at himself. Smiles. Lena smiles. Says 'Zami' and points. They smile at each other. Zami explains in Swedish. Feed Grandma. Grandma nice. A bit further to go.

Janoch comes to life when he gets water. Zami talks to him as he drives away from the filling station. Janoch is tired. It hurts when he breathes. He wants to lie down. He wants to sleep and sleep and sleep. The great warrior is tired. He has a few mouthfuls of sausage before he goes back to sleep. Zami starts to realize that he's on his own. Janoch may not even make it to Gesunden. He may have passed through the gates by then. Zami is alone in the land of Germans. With another two days of driving. He thinks. Grandma and the four girls have to be guarded. He must sleep. Before he can't sleep any more.

He finds a parking area outside Heining. Dusk has fallen and the rain is pouring down again. Zami explains to Janoch. Last watch. One more task. You have to be strong enough. Then I can drive. All the way home.

Janoch keeps watch all night. He looks at the rain and feels his life ebbing away. Looks at the tractor-trailers swishing by in clouds of spray. While he collects all the keys. The keys to all the chains and handcuffs. Keys belonging to the Serb and his men. Janoch puts them all together. He removes them from their keychains and puts them in a pile. Along with all the keys he found in the Akasi's cellar. Amid Grandma's shit. All while he feels the numbness slowly spreading through his body. He learns to recognize the pattern. First pain and heat. Then it fades. Until there's nothing at all. His feet. Calves. Thighs. He understands what's happening. He's dying. Slowly, but inevitably. Those little vermin got him. He'll be going to the One who waits in the dark. Alone, but without fear. His pack will remember him. And pray for him. Grandma will be thankful. Zami too. The girls will remember the brave warrior who saved them from the Luchany men. He's going into the dark. With the key in his hand. The key to the gate. It no longer hurts.

Grandma's going on a journey. Zami wakes with the morning sun. It's the first time they've seen the sun in days. Shiny eighteen-wheelers are rolling along the E56. The forests gleam with green moisture. Beside him Janoch is sleeping. He's snoring and there's a little blood running from his mouth. There's a gurgling sound when he snores. The loading bay is silent.

Zami looks around. They're alone in the little parking lot. He goes to the back. Lena flinches when he opens up. Then both she and Zami see the legs sticking out of the trough. Lena screams. Zami jumps inside. The trough is full of blood.

Torn bits of clothing and nastiness. Grandma is sleeping with the yellow sweater behind her head. Grinning with bloody lips. Zami tries to understand how it happened. How did Grandma get the girl into the trough? Why didn't he hear anything? Why didn't Lena wake up? He shouts at Lena. Lena shouts back. They shout and shout. The two other girls wake up. Grandma wakes up. Everyone who's alive is awake and shouting at everyone else. Lena hits Grandma with the plank. Watches out for her claws and hits her and hits her. Soon Grandma understands. Lena's in charge. Rules. Again. No one eats anyone else in the back of the van. Lena, you stop hitting. Everyone be nice. You two girls stop shouting. Lena, you watch over them.

Zami steps out of the van. Lights a cigarette. The sun dazzles his eyes. It's a long way to Gesunden and his hands are shaking. One of the dark girls has a small nose and big eyes. The other has very bad teeth and seems very tired. She has to eat and drink more. He smokes five cigarettes and eats a thick, spicy sausage before he dares to get back behind the wheel.

Grandma's going on a journey. A hundred kilometers to Regensburg. Janoch is pale and sweaty. He keeps dropping off and mumbling funny stuff. He talks all day with Uncle Tanic while Zami drives and drives. A hundred and ninety kilometers to Würzburg and ninety to Fulda. Janoch talks about the key and the gate. In Yog-Sothoth's voice. Or Uncle Tanic's. Voices from other worlds. The sun is covered by black clouds and when they cross Route 51 it starts to rain. Yog-Sothoth's rain. The rain that will protect them on their journey. 'You serve me well,' says Janoch's body. 'You are the thorns of my briar-bush. When the time comes you will get your reward. A key to the gate. A path to my side.' Janoch talks about the girls too. 'Lena will be good in the pack,' he gurgles. 'Eat the other two. Eat them.' Zami can't understand how he knows the girl with the yellow sweater has been killed. He didn't tell him.

Just before Göttingen the thunder starts, at dusk. Zami has driven all day. He's hypnotized by the road. His legs have gone numb and he sees red tail-lights when he closes his eyes. His heart beats in time with the windshield wipers. Near Kassel, police wave them past the scene of an accident. The traffic crawls forward. He doesn't even get nervous. He's smoked three packs of cigarettes and the water's almost gone again. Janoch sleeps. Pale and sweaty. It's quiet in the back. He thumps the wall. Twice. Someone thumps back twice. He thumps once more and someone thumps once. Lena. He must get her some food. She's going to be one of the Pack. He thumps three times and smiles when she answers.

Grandma's going on a journey. Zami drives onto a forest road outside Seesen. Opens the back and borrows Lena's plank. It takes a long, long time to get Grandma to let go of the remains of the girl with the yellow sweater. She hits him in the face. Right where it hurts. He hits her back. Too many times. Then he hauls out the remains of the girl. All the bits. Drags them into the woods. Covers them with brushwood. Feels nothing.

He throws the last of the cookies and the schnapps to Lena. Her eyes are huge. Beside her sits Big Eyes. She's holding Tired Girl's head in her lap. Zami shouts 'Don't die!' and slams the door. He drives for another two hours. The German motorway past Hannover. Finally he almost runs them off the road. Slams on the brakes. The girls scream. Janoch hits the floor. Without waking up.

Grandma's going on a journey. Zami sleeps over the wheel in a parking area outside Soltau. It rains and rains and rains. And Zami dreams. Dreams about Janoch. Janoch's on his way to the gate. He travels through other worlds and hears the flutes around the throne. A servant on his way home. A servant with a deed yet to be done. One last thing. Before he can go through the gate. Janoch can give the Pack one more thing. One more thing. A wedding.

When Zami wakes up he knows. And he knows it's right. He tries to talk to Janoch. Shakes him. But he doesn't answer. Zami collects himself. You can't have a wedding in a parking lot. They have to keep moving.

Grandma's going on a journey. The night is rainy and Hamburg shines like a carpet of lights. Zami buys more food at a petrol station on Route 206. He smells really bad now, people stare. He smells the stench himself. He buys the usual: cookies, schnapps, water, sausage, and cigarettes. Everything feels like repetition. He smiles. Points at the cigarettes and puts down money. Walks out and hears the whispers behind him.

A hundred and ten kilometers to Rendsburg. Zami changes license plates. The van becomes another German car. He stands for a long time in the rain trying to get clean. Rinsing away the stink of the car. Because the van, Janoch, Grandma, and the girls stink like garbage. The whole floor at the front is covered in empty bottles and sausage wrappers. He scrapes out as much refuse as he can. Janoch smells dead. Zami forces him to drink water, but he won't eat anything.

Grandma's going on a journey. And the night is long and without moonlight. Zami drives into a forest before Schleswig. Gets out of the car and drags Janoch with him. Tries to get him to talk about the countryside at the night. The way it smells. Do you smell it? The scent of rain and forest. And sea. Far away. He gives him a bottle of schnapps. Blesses him and sits him down on the roadside.

He thumps the side of the van. Lena answers. He opens the back. And recoils at the stench. Grandma growls welcomingly. Lena says something in her language. The dark girls are sleeping. No one wants to fight. Zami climbs in and unlocks Lena's manacles. Leads her out of the car. She gives a questioning look. Suspicious. Dirty and hunted. Zami gives her a bottle of schnapps. Pats her on the shoulder. Smiles. Tries to act human. She smiles back. Zami shoves her into Janoch's old seat.

Zami climbs into the back of the van. Time to prepare for the wedding. He talks to Grandma in the old language. Says the holy words. She looks at him with eyes that understand. There's wisdom in there. Something primeval awakens. She looks expectant. Covetous. Worked-up.

Grandma's getting married. It takes time to prepare everything. Getting the girls undressed takes time. They're limp and heavy. Zami pours schnapps into them and tries to calm them down. First he gets Tired Girl into the trough. She whines and makes herself comfortable against Grandma. Without opening her eyes.

Grandma looks at her with curiosity. Licks her face. Growls deep in her chest. It's a bit more difficult getting Big Eyes into the trough. She weeps and struggles. Weak and clumsy, like a kitten. At last Zami gets her inside. Grandma grabs hold of her. Presses her down on the other side. Firmly but carefully. Big Eyes squeals and writhes. Drunk and exhausted she may be, but she wants to get out of there. Grandma watches her thrashing with a smile. Her eyes are suddenly shining, full of purpose and will. As if she's woken from a long sleep.

Zami thinks. They ought to have flowers too. And loads of keys. He has some keys, but they're needed for something else. And the forest is dying because it's autumn. He wanders off into the bushes beside the road and scouts around. He picks up armfuls and armfuls of golden leaves. Spreads them over Grandma and the girls. Puts the Serb's car keys on Grandma's brow. All three of them are looking at him. Grandma smiling and the girls perplexed. They look so small next to Grandma. Even more so now that they're naked. They're white and bony. Zami wonders how old they are. What it would be like being their male. He'll try it in Gesunden. But first they have to get there.

Janoch's getting married. But he's sitting on the roadside without a clue. Zami shakes some life into him. He's soaked. And full of schnapps and weird dreams. Nothing he says sounds quite right. He's delirious, talking in a language Zami doesn't understand. He points at the stars and tries to say something. Zami doesn't listen. He hugs him. Realizes how warm he is. And how he stinks. Illness and dirt and death. He starts taking off his human clothes. They've stiffened with dried blood and piss. Here and there his fur has gotten stuck to the clothes. It's hard getting Janoch out of his clothes. Zami struggles in the rain and the dark. All the while Janoch mumbles to himself. Occasionally he loses his balance. It's heavy keeping him on his feet.

At last he's standing naked by the side of the road. Zami throws his clothes in a ditch. Wipes some of the stains off his body. Pours water on the worst of them. Makes sure that he drinks more schnapps. He can see Lena at the front of the van. She's staring at Janoch. She doesn't look scared anymore. Curious instead. Maybe so much has happened that she's no longer frightened. Maybe she's gone mad. Zami doesn't know anything about how humans think. Only that they are always either scared or dangerous.

At last Janoch is ready. Naked and splendid he stands in the rain. Even though he's dirty. Even though he's sick. In spite of his wounds. Zami sees the little hole in his chest. That such a small, small wound could lay low a mighty warrior. Zami finds it odd. It doesn't quite add up. But there's a little strength left in Janoch. Enough energy to get married. Zami slaps his face a couple of times. Janoch flinches and opens his eyes. For the first time in ages. A growl deep in his throat. Zami smiles at him. His pack companion. Janoch blinks and blinks. Zami says, 'You can leave soon. But first Grandma and the girls want to meet you.' Janoch blinks again.

'The girls?' he says.

'In the car.'

'Grandma?'

'In the car.'

Janoch grins. Sluggish and complacent. He licks his mouth.

Laps up the raindrops. Tries to be the one all the females in the apartments always had their eyes on. What he was a few days ago. How many days? Zami doesn't have a clue anymore. He lets go of Janoch's shoulders. Opens the door to the back of the van. Invites him to step up. Without saying anything more, Janoch shakes himself. His hackles rise. Everything rises. The key will open the gate. Grandma growls when she sees him. The girls titter. They already sound totally crazy. Grandma makes a hissing sound. She sounds like a snake. A big snake. She hisses louder and louder as Janoch starts climbing into the trough.

Lena could sleep for years. She sits in the front of the van. Two gulps of vodka away from sleeping. But it doesn't matter. Because she's not afraid of Zami. However he may look. And she has to sleep. Far away she hears the back doors closing. How the nasty sound cuts off. How someone laughs. Barks like a dog.

She listens to the sounds from the back. Tries to hear over the roar of the rain. It sounds horrible. Like pigs rooting around. She really doesn't want to know what's going on. She's just glad she's not there, with Sasha and Nina and that big, horrid, repulsive thing. She's glad it's not her shrieking in there. That it's not her slamming against the wall. She covers her ears. Hides her head between her knees. The stink of the mess on the floor makes her nauseous. It smells of dog piss and apricot. She's almost fallen asleep by the time Zami climbs into the van. He starts the engine. Pats her on the shoulder. Says something in his weird dog language. Lena starts crying. For the first time in months.

Grandma's going on a journey. Carefully, Zami drives out of the forest. Finds his way back to the main road. Lena snores beside him. Behind him someone is shrieking. The rain is pouring over the car, stronger than ever. The windshield is like a waterfall. Zami leans forward. Drives slowly with his nose against the window. His whole world contracts to water and red tail-lights. Now and then they hear noises in the back. It sounds as if they are fighting.

Zami crosses the Danish border in the gray dawn. With wide-open eyes and a throbbing head. It's silent in the back of the van. Lena woke briefly, looked at the rain and then fell asleep again. Zami counts the kilometers. Three hundred and fifty to Malmö. Then eleven hundred to Gesunden. Almost to the bridge. To the gate. To the road to Gesunden. By the bridge is a road. Through the sky to Gesunden. Janoch used to sing that. While they sat with Uncle Tanic and memorized. He'll make it. He has to. He can't stay among the democrats in Denmark. Just drive. Drive. Drive. The signs say Fredericia and Odense. A long way to go.

Grandma's going on a journey. And Yog-Sothoth makes the rain pour down to hide her from people's eyes. They smoke and smoke in the car. Talk in a new language of their own. Making it up as they go along. Mixing Swedish, the old tongue, and Lena's language. Zami tells her things. About the Pack. How they used to live in the old land. With Grandma. How the war came and made them flee. About the Luchany men. How Uncle Tanic and some others came to Sweden. How they got the apartment from the humans. About the Swedes helping them. The democrats. Rosengård.

They have to shop. They have to fill up. Zami has to sleep. Just before Kolding he almost drives into a ditch. Lena shouts. Scolds him. He tries to apologize. Doesn't want her to be angry. He knows no signs for 'sorry'.

She calms down but continues talking. She points at her stomach. At her mouth. Pretends to eat. At the bottles on the floor. He nods. Tries to explain that the rain could stop. That he's afraid of Danes. Uncle Tanic has told him they're dangerous. But Lena is obstinate. At last he leaves the motorway by Fredericia. Lena looks around. Scouts out the territory. Then points. A little gas station. Hidden in some trees.

No humans in sight. The rain thunders against the roof over the pumps. Zami gets out and starts filling up. He doesn't even notice that Lena gets out of the van and goes into the little shop. His thoughts are slow as if wallowing in mud, he decides that he must finish refueling before he goes in to fetch her. A lot can happen. If she makes trouble he'll have to kill everyone inside.

She's waiting for him inside the little shop. Dirty and soaked with rain. She's piled up food in a basket. Bottles, tins, and little packets. She gives him a fierce look. Zami tries to smile, but all he can think about is that he left the pistol in the van. He forgot it. And all the doors are unlocked. Anyone could open the back door and chance upon the wedding. He hauls out a big wad of money and gives it to Lena. She stares at it. Zami says 'Cigarettes' and goes out to the van.

Grandma's going on a journey. And Lena climbs into the van with a plastic bag full of things. She gives Zami a big piece of chocolate. Puts the money next to the pistol. Zami gobbles down the sugar. Imagine, he never thought chocolate would taste so good. There are even cows and Alps on the chocolate's wrapper. He munches and smokes and starts the van at the same time. Lena mimes a question. Should she feed them in the back? Zami shakes his head. Leave them be. Those who are still alive will eat the ones who aren't. They coast onto the motorway and the rain starts up again.

Seventy kilometers to Odense. The day is steel-gray. The sky trails close to the ground. It's time. Zami throws the first key out of the window. Lena gives him a quizzical look. He smiles back. This will turn out really well. Trust Zami. No democrats are tailing them. No one tries to stop them. The Renault is just another car ploughing its way through the pouring rain. Like boats in a storm. Zami tries to remember what Odense looks like. Remembers the man they met, but can't remember his face. Lena fiddles with the pistol. She points at a little thing on its side. A switch. You have to press it down so you can fire it. Like a lock. Zami had no idea about that. He throws out the next key. And thinks the right thoughts. The wiper blades sing along to his sacrificial offerings. The rain drums the beat.

Grandma's going on a journey. Odense is a distant clump of stars in a sea of rain and haze. They drive slowly. You could run faster than these cars on the motorway. If you can run in a rainstorm, that is. Zami throws out a key, then another. They pass a car accident. A van lies in the ditch. A police car has pulled up alongside, its lights flashing. Zami makes the final call. Tells Uncle Tanic that it's time now. Uncle Tanic blesses him. There's a faint answering mumble. It comes from the back, from the engine, and from the screeching windshield wipers. At first Zami thinks he's the only one who can hear it. But he notices that Lena hears it too. Even though she's listening with her feeble human ears.

Grandma's going on a journey. A hundred and thirty kilometers to Copenhagen. They pass another accident. And another. An overturned truck. White boxes lie scattered like large sugar cubes. Zami sings quietly. The song of the spheres. Throws out a key. Big twigs fly across the road. Something hits the van with a bang. Lena shrieks. They don't stop singing in the back. Zami wonders if Grandma taught the girls the song. Or Janoch. He wonders if Janoch is even alive. He doubts it. He throws out another key. Lena tries to ask something in her language. But he isn't listening anymore. He has to drive the car. And sing.

Grandma's going on a journey. They head for the long, long bridge. Gusting winds try to overturn the van. The sky is black, although it's only afternoon. Right now they're chanting in Gesunden. All sitting on the grass. And chanting and singing. The song of the spheres. The song Grandma's grandmother sang when she was still a pathetic human. Before she met Yog-Sothoth. Before the Agreement. Before she learned to make herself different and have children who

were even more different. A long time ago. The windshield
wipers screech. They're overtaken by an ambulance. It's driving insanely fast and sprays lots of water over their car. Zami
throws out a key. He asks Lena to do the same. She throws
out a key. As if just to be friendly. A hurricane wind forces its
way into the van.

Grandma's going on a journey. A journey through the
gate, a journey through the spheres. Journey. Far. Grandma
has a key. Grandma is a key. Zami is a servant bearing keys
to the gate at the end of the stars. Far ahead the ambulance
skids off the road in a volcano of black water. It plows up the
ground and tosses human bodies in all directions. Zami tries
to get Lena to sing along with him. But she doesn't understand. Doesn't understand what is happening. Where the
road is. Where the voices are coming from. The voices chanting with Zami. The voices coming from outside the van. The
voices from the engine. It's the Pack chanting. The family in
Gesunden. Grandma in the back. They chant together now.
Across the universe they hear each other. They build a bridge
of voices.

Grandma's going on a journey. Zami roars. The Pack
answers. A terrific storm hurtles across the land of the Danes.
Obscures the sun. Obscures the day. Night sets in. The darkness is endless. Unreal. Abnormal. Zami puts his foot down.
The car lurches. The engine wails. The water on the road
strikes the underside of the van. Whipped up by the tires.
It sounds like a torrential rain from below. Zami floors the
accelerator. Drives like a madman through the water. He
puts a key in his mouth. Swallows it. Screams. Lena screams
too. Because she's scared. Because she's terrified. Because the
ground just disappeared under the car. She can hear it. The
rain from beneath just stopped.

Grandma's going on a journey. Zami throws fistful after
fistful of keys out of the window. Over the roof of the van.
He opens the gate. The sky cracks open. The rain becomes

thick as tar. The right-hand windshield wiper breaks off with a snap. The wind intensifies. Almost overturns the car. They career along on two wheels. Leaning like a sailing ship. A girl's voice in the back is screaming. It gets hard to see anything outside. The headlights of other cars are like stars in a black universe. Far away and far below. Everything falling. In all directions. Zami gives praise to Yog-Sothoth. He who opens a way. A way to all places. For Yog-Sothoth has seen everything. He asks for the car not to overturn. He asks for them to fly.

Grandma's going on a journey. The choirs turn to flutes. The pack calls out 'Come.' Come to us at the end of the sky. Come to the gate. Zami and Lena sit in a dome of eternity. Locked in by the rain and the car doors. It's quiet in the back. All that can be heard are the flutes. The whining car engine. And distant voices. Someone knocks on the roof of the van. The windshield wiper creaks. It is no longer sweeping water away, but the actual storm clouds. 'Malmö!' says Zami and points. 'Malmö.' A little patch can be glimpsed far below on the right-hand side. Lena nods sleepily. He doesn't think she understands. She doesn't understand that long thin thing down there is the bridge to Malmö. Either that, or she does understand and that's why she's fallen asleep. Zami understands. It's a lot for her. A lot to understand. A ragged piece of cloud hides the lights. Turns them off. The last fixed point. Now they've left the human world. Something big and black flaps past the car. A rag or a bat. Zami laughs. A frightened laugh. He lets go of the wheel.

Grandma's going on a journey. Zami takes a big gulp of schnapps and leans back. 'It worked,' he marvels with one part of his brain. Another part wants to curl up and never open its eyes again. A star is shining beside the van, filling the cabin with chalky white light. Everything starts leaning. Forwards. As if they're heading down a long slope. He catches sight of the moon in the rearview mirror. It's huge.

He lights another cigarette. Wants to throw out another key, but doesn't dare roll the window down even a little bit. He swallows one instead. Looks at Lena. The car leans even more. He holds on to her. So she doesn't get hurt. Stares into the abyss. They fall. The engine splutters and dies. They fall down towards something big. The earth? A sea of clouds? An infinite universe filled with stars?

Zami will spend the rest of his life trying to explain those last moments in the car. He'll tell Lena's and the two lunatic girls' and all of his and Janoch's children how he made it to Gesunden with Grandma. How everything went black. About the flutes and the spheres. Everything he shouted. Everything he heard and saw. And how suddenly the van was driving along a sunny road. Outside Hammarstrand. A little town in northern Sweden. Near Gesunden. Gesunden doesn't mean anything in Swedish. But it's a lake. He saw it straight away. Like a big blue sea it lay there in a green valley of spruce. Then he saw the house on the ridge. Big and brown. It looked beautiful, serene. No humans. And quiet.

# FRAGMENT II

No ONE ON BOARD HEARD THE EXPLOSION. But everyone felt it. The minesweeper's stern suddenly shot upwards. Her bow cleaved the surface as the whole vessel pitched forward. The prow disappeared underwater, and on the bridge, the helmsman and Ensign Larsson were thrown into the windshield. Everyone who had been working on his tan on deck lurched forward. Elvis, who had been sitting on the bow, vanished for a moment underwater. The davit on the foredeck broke loose, its arm swinging violently. Hundreds of things slid off tables and shelves. Tools, plates, pots, books, and ashtrays. Everything that was not strapped down crashed to the deck and flew forward. The whole crew screamed as if with one mouth.

Down in the engine room, machinist Simonson fell head-first into the diesel engine. He slid half-conscious across it, scalding, charring, and tearing his flesh before hitting the ground. A sledgehammer missed his head by an inch. A bucket of oily water did not. He watched the ceiling lamp swing back and forth at an insane angle. Heard the propeller speeding up. High above the water. 'Twenty degrees,' he managed to think. That, and 'Jesus H. Christ,' before the stern fell back into the water.

More crashing noises. More screaming and wailing. The boat rocked savagely as the waves slammed into it from behind. The wooden hull creaked ominously. Water flooded the deck. On the bridge, Ensign Larsson attempted to steer. 'Fucking mine!' he screamed. Over and over again. 'Fucking mine! Fucking mine! Fucking mine!'

The waves ebb away. The lesser noises remain. Distressed

seabirds. Echoes like after a thunderclap. Chatter on the mine-sweeper.

'What happened?'

'Are you okay?'

'Is anyone hurt?'

'Are we sinking?'

'What happened?'

'A mine?'

'One of ours?'

'Are we going down?'

'What in God's name was that?'

The petty officers rush to and fro, in their petty officer way. Trying to sort things out. Check what's working and who's present. What's broken? Is anyone missing? Is anyone hurt? Are we taking on water? The engine's running and the power's still on. People are soaked, but everyone's on board. So far, so good. Get the crew in order. Clear the deck. Why the hell are there potatoes everywhere?

Lieutenant Wikman steps out of his cabin, his uniform stained with coffee. He spilled it when he fell backwards out of his chair. He hit his head on the safe, too. Blood is running down his neck.

Two sailors are standing by the railing. Wet, bare-chested. They straighten up when they see him.

'We hit a mine, Lieutenant.'

'Don't be silly, boy. If we'd hit a mine, you two wouldn't be standing here jabbering.'

The sailors nod. I jabber, therefore I am. They hear screaming and shouting from below deck. Someone's shouting for a flashlight. And fresh light bulbs. Ensign Larsson calls down from the bridge. 'What do we do now, chief?'

'Heave to!' Wikman bellows. He needs time to think. 'And get me a damage report.'

'Look aft.' The sailor named Ljusberg points his finger. 'It's still bubbling.'

Lieutenant Wikman squints. His neck hurts like hell. There. Half a nautical mile aft. Bubbles in the water. As if a large vessel had just sunk. Could someone else have hit a mine? There wasn't anyone behind them. And there aren't supposed to be any mines around here. Maybe some scrap from the war had drifted in here. It's possible. A fucking vagabond mine. They must have sailed right over it. Could there be more? You only get this lucky once. And what was it that set it off, if not us? The detonator could have triggered itself somehow, but that didn't sound likely.

'Ljusberg, climb the mast. I want to know what you can see, over by where the mine went off. Check for debris.' Ljusberg nods. 'And where's my mine specialist?' Wikman continues.

'On the poop deck, chief,' someone says.

'Bring him here.'

One of the corporals rushes past and says something about a broken arm. He slips on the wet deck and falls on his butt. Keeps sliding, through wet clothes and potatoes.

'Chief?' Mine Specialist Kjellman is red in the face.

'Kjellman, tell me. Do we know if there are any minefields around here?'

'No chief, none whatsoever. They'd been planning fields farther up the coast at Svenska Björn before the war, but they were never deployed.'

'Did you see the explosion yourself?'

'Only the spray, chief. It did look like a mine explosion.'

'How deep is it here?' Wikman shouts towards the bridge.

Larsson's head pokes out, disappears again. 'Ten fathoms or more down the whole route, chief!' he shouts.

'Have you seen anyone else? Could a fishing boat or tourist have set it off?'

'We saw a skiff to the south about fifteen minutes ago,' Larsson replies.

'What about that?' A sailor, Ahlgren, points straight

ahead. Three or four nautical miles towards Högfjärden is a fishing boat.

'Son of a bitch. We're going to need all hands. Kjellman, get the boys out here and keep watch on all sides of the ship. And dig up everything you've got on Russian and German mines.'

'Chief!' Ljusberg shouts from up by the smokestack. 'There's something in the water over there.'

'What do you mean something, what is it?'

'Tough to say, looks like a skerry, just under the surface.' He points. 'Right there, under all those gulls.'

Wikman looks aft. There's a flock of seabirds where the bubbling had been. As usual after a mine explosion—the mine kills a ton of fish and the gulls have a party.

'Get a telescope up to the lad. Ensign Larsson!'

'Chief?' Larsson pokes his head out again. He says 'chief' like he and Wikman were dressed in zoot suits in some jazz dive in Stockholm. College kids. Good heads, strange manners.

'Round up the damage reports. And prepare to sail back towards the explosion. Send a wire to Vaxholm. And Berga. MUL 10 reporting, suspected mine detonation in Skarvleden. Something like that. Investigating the situation, will report back. Kjellman! Notify me when the lookouts are in place.' Wikman takes a deep breath.

'Ahlgren.'

'Yes, Lieutenant.'

'Do you have a smoke, sailor? I spilled coffee on my tobacco. Tough titties, as the ensign would say.'

Wikman stands on the quarterdeck smoking as the crew get in order. He stares at the bare, nameless islets all around them. Tries to look composed. Reports come in. No one is seriously hurt. Bruises and sprains, that's all. One of the mine specialists broke his arm, and a machinist cut himself pretty badly. No one went overboard. No one took a davit

to the head. The cook was on deck smoking when ten gal-
lons of boiling soup went flying. Lucky devil. The hull was
unscathed. An accumulator bit the dust. The radio's cutting
out more than usual, piece of shit. They should put it out of
its misery, then maybe they could get a new one.

Otherwise they've just got a lot of cleaning to do. Nothing
more. Dumb luck. Thirty seconds earlier and they would have
capsized. Ass over tea kettle. A full minute and they would
have been stone dead, every last one of them. Shit. Shit. Shit.

Ensign Larsson reports back that the men are in position. In
ten minutes. Excellent. Good work boys. Wikman gives the
order to get moving. Two knots. Towards the seagulls. Look
damn carefully in the water, boys. Full astern if I so much
as cough. He goes to stand on the bow. On top of a cable
drum. Behind sailor Nilsson. The one the boys call Elvis. He
thinks about Warrant Officer Björkman at the naval officers'
academy. Björkman the Bomb. Five tours to Murmansk with
the American merchant navy. *Yes, sir. Achtung Minen,* and
you're damn right he had a story or two to tell after a couple
of drinks. Mines. Mines, gentlemen. A mine will break both
the legs of any man standing. Push your shinbone through
your thigh. Nasty business. They stand on spring mattresses
up on the bridge. One guy, a Canadian, gets obsessed about
not standing on deck. He starts jumping. And jumping and
jumping and jumping. As long as he's airborne, he'll be all
right. They eventually have to sedate him with opium. And
tie him to his bunk. Wikman thinks about the Canadian
every time they handle live mines. He too wants to jump and
jump and jump.

The gulls squawk and squawk. There's hundreds of them.
Thousands. All out of their little bird minds. Wikman gets
the feeling that something's wrong. Something about those
gulls. It takes three boat lengths for him to see why. It isn't
fish they're fighting over. They're just flying in circles, frenzied. Terrified.

Then they're in among the seagulls. In a cloud of hysterical birds. The squawking overpowers everything else. They get a glimpse of what's in the water. A dark mass floating, just under the surface. Half a cable length in front of them. A mess of bubbles and oily water. Wikman shouts to kill the engine. He gets the impression that there's wreckage floating just below the water. Or a hot spring. He saw one off the coast of Iceland once. They drift into the eye of the seagull storm. Then they see it. Everyone on the bow can see. The chatter begins again. Loud enough to drown out the gulls.

'What in the hell?'

'Jesus Christ.'

'Are those jellyfish?'

'What the hell is that?'

'What a fucking mess.'

'Are they squid, lieutenant?'

'A whole school of 'em?'

'Look at the eyes!'

'Holy shit.'

'There's no squid that size in the Baltic,' says Lieutenant Wikman. Nobody's listening. They inch forward slowly. The boys lean over the railing and stare.

'What is that?'

'Fuck, it's moving.'

'Where?'

'There.'

'No fucking way.'

'It's coming towards us.'

'Look out!'

Elvis Nilsson drops his boathook. Stumbles backwards into Wikman. The mine specialist knocks over two sailors. Someone screams. A pitiful, plaintive howl. Screams along with the screeching gulls. Something strikes the hull. Once. Twice. Like an axe against a tree trunk.

'Full astern! Full astern! Larsson, for Christ's sake!'

# THE BROKEN MAN'S WISH

THE FIRST SOLDIERS CAME TO TYDAL ON THURSDAY. It was late afternoon. Just as the sun was breaking through the clouds. They came riding up the road from Haltdalen, soldiers in gray cloaks on scrawny horses. They paused at Tord Gudmundsen's farm and looked around. Surveying in their soldierly way. Cautiously. First for militiamen. Then for food. Taking their time. Then they rode on. They're like wolves, people say. Like wolves sniffing for weak animals. And shouldn't they be down near Trondheim anyway? That's where the war was, after all. Yes, that's right. King Karl sent a host to take Trondheim. Granted, it takes time for news to reach the valleys, but surely we would have heard something by now if things had changed.

The horsemen came back the next day. More of them this time. Led by an officer with a wig. The officer spoke and the horsemen listened. He gave orders and pointed. Sent them in different directions. Some rode down towards Haltdalen again. Others rode off to the nearest farms. Some stayed with the officer on the road. Siv spied on them from behind Agnes's chalet. She wondered if they were Danes or Swedes. Maybe they were some of Nordenfelt's men, the ones they talked about in the villages. Nordenfelt who battled the Swedes from his hiding place in the woods. There was no man the Swedes feared more than Nordenfelt.

That's when the soldiers saw Per Halte come waddling down the road with an armful of firewood, singing to himself. Everyone in the village knew to keep their distance when there were soldiers around. But not poor Per. He was too dumb to hide. He walked straight towards them. Later, Siv recounted how they stopped him and beat him down. Maybe he said something impolite. Then one of the soldiers dismounted and started kicking him. So Siv ran away. With Per's screams echoing behind her.

They should have fled. As soon as Siv came back to the farm. But Bjarne hesitated. Was Siv sure that the soldiers were on their way? What were they supposed to do with the cows? And the pigs? The hens and the barrels full of rye? It had been a pretty good year, and Bjarne wasn't about to leave it all to the marauders. And if it really was Nordenfelt's men coming, maybe they had no reason to flee at all. He hesitated. Then again, Lene was down in the village. His youngest daughter worked as a servant for Per Brand. The richest man in the village. And a widower. A good man. Maybe he'd grow fond of Lene when she got a little older.

Bjarne looked up at the sky. It was a beautiful day. The sky was a pale blue. It would be light for a long while. They had plenty of time. He spoke to Nana. What did she think? His mother-in-law was a wise woman. Despite being a Lapp. When Máret died, she remained on the farm. Helped him with the girls and the cooking. Nana said her people always took to the mountains when the lowlanders rode in with swords in hand. No matter if they were Swedes, Danes, or just from Trøndelag county. But her people didn't have a farm to worry about. Maybe she should go and fetch Lene in the meantime? So that Bjarne and Siv could pack a few things. Bjarne took her advice. And so Nana headed to the village. She walked along the road, tripping over the hard frozen earth. But what if the soldiers get her, said Siv. Nana is not such easy prey, said Bjarne. If she needs to, she can always take the form of a grouse and disappear.

Bjarne walked to the woodshed. Maybe they could hide in the mountain forest for a time. It hadn't snowed much yet. Although it was quite windy. Only the mountaintops were covered with thick snow. The midnight hours could get really cold, but they would survive a night or two. They should have had a sleigh, he thought. And a horse, of course. All they had was a sled. And Bjarne would have to pull it. He wished he had a stableboy. Or a son. Someone who could help him with the heavy labor. His only son, Karl, died three hours after Máret. That damnable winter in 1712 was when Bjarne had stopped believing in the goodness of God Almighty. He had dragged them both to the cemetery himself. On that very sled.

He called for Siv. She came running when she heard him. She had just been out with the animals. He asked her to pack some food and firewood for a night in the woods. She set off right away. Without argument. Little mother Siv, he called her. She had a mother's way, though she was only fourteen. She would be a fine housewife some day. A woman who could sew and slaughter animals and cook too. Who was strong and happy and dependable. Siv, who had inherited her father's blond hair and ruggedness, and her mother's stubbornness and clarity of mind. She would inherit the farm too when the time came. Mrs Siv of Bjarne's farm. That had a nice ring to it. Soon he'd teach her to dance like her mother. He smiled to himself as he towed the sled out of the woodshed.

Siv gathered two baskets of food. Bread and a little bit of pork and dried fish. A little cheese and a flask of schnapps. She put the baskets by the door for now. Bjarne walked inside. He pulled out the flintlock rifle and the three wolf pelts. Siv packed some extra clothes. Mittens, scarves, and hats. Socks. Where were they going? she asked. Does Nana know a place in the mountains? Otherwise they'd be sleeping outside. Siv wanted to know. Her father didn't have a good answer. Who was coming? Were they Swedes or Danes? What if it's as windy as it was the other day? That night it got really cold. And it would be worse up in the mountains. And were they bringing the sow, the hens, the cow? He hadn't decided yet.

While Bjarne pondered, he carried the smoked meat from the Christmas pig up to the loft. The loft was small and narrow and the door was hard to spot. He carried up both barrels of rye as well. And the sausages they made at Christmas time. The turnips, the last of the cheese, and finally the dried trout. Then he closed the door to the loft. Hid the edges with bits of moss. Brushed away his footsteps and put the step-stool away.

They heard the first gunshot in the early afternoon. It echoed through the mountains. There was another, immediately after. Bjarne and Siv stopped and listened. Two more shots. No hunter shoots four rounds. No one scares off a wolf with four rounds. The soldiers were shooting at something. Or someone. Bjarne tried to make up his mind. When would Nana be back? He couldn't go to the woods without her. They had to wait. They stood next to each other for a long time, looking down the road. There was yet another shot. A faint cloud of smoke rose up from the valley, hanging over the sun like a veil.

Then Siv said she could see the soldiers on the road. Over there. Where the road emerges from the little forest. More and more and more of them. Like a long worm of blue and gray, she said. Swedes. The Danish king's men wore red and white. And Nordenfelt's men wore gray. Soon Bjarne could see them too. Marching men and banners and muskets. They stood watching the procession march up the hillside. More men than had ever been in Tydal. They could see the fatigue in their steps. Men tripped over their own feet.

Then came Nana, bounding over the fence to the south. Like a limping ball of brown and gray fabric. With her breath like a cloud around her head and her hat in her hand. As fast as her legs could carry her. Stumbling and wheezing. She pointed toward the road. Couldn't get a word out. She fell to her knees at their feet, coughing. Swore in Lappish. 'Swedes,' she said finally. 'The Swedes have come to Tydal. The whole army. They're marching up towards the mountains. To

Essanden. They came down from Bukkhammeren yesterday, riding on the mountain winds. And they're half-mad. Starving and mean. And the general has ordered them to take the villagers hostage.'

'Did you see Lene?' asked Bjarne. No, but Brand's farm was teeming with horsemen. Hundreds of them. Nana coughs and coughs. She had run into one of Ante Karlsen's stableboys. The one with the bent ear. He said that the soldiers were like devils. Ante had been badly beaten. And they had slaughtered both his cows. Nana had hidden in the bushes, trying to see what was happening. She falls silent. Coughs again. Her breath bubbles like her lungs are full of mud. Bjarne wants to shake her. Get her to finish the story. But she just coughs and coughs. Finally, she says what he doesn't want to hear.

'I ran when I heard the shooting at Brand's place. In the barnyard.' Her eyes are full of tears. 'I could hear the screams. From the womenfolk. I think they're all dead.'

A knife twists in Bjarne's stomach. It feels like he's falling and falling. He looks down towards the valley. The smoke is thicker now. Two distinct pillars rising skywards. The two large farms. Karlsen's and Brand's. His eyes well up. Lene. Lene who's almost thirteen. Who's shy and doesn't say much. Just like her father. And who's just as beautiful as her mother. Dark Lappish eyes and narrow shoulders. His most precious treasure. Was it she who screamed? Did the soldiers kill her? Or something even worse? Sweet Jesus.

'Did you see Lene? Answer me!'

'Father, you're hurting her,' says Siv. But he can barely hear her. He's grabbing Nana by the shoulders. Shaking her. Screaming and scolding. Why didn't she do something? Why didn't she run and get her? Why didn't she save his child? Her grandchild?

Siv grabs his arm. Screams 'Father!' in a shrill voice. Bjarne stops shaking Nana. Lets her go. She falls over in the snow. He looks around. Siv points. Right and left. Says 'Get the rifle, father. Get it now.' Her voice is tense. As if she has stopped breathing.

They come from the road. From the field and the forest down by Assar's heath. Fearless as wolves, they come. Slow, but unyielding. A dozen of them on the road. Carrying muskets, a few carrying pikes. The afternoon sun flashes off their bayonets. Those coming from the field and the forest are also a dozen strong. Spreading out as they approach. Wolves on the hunt. They point and shout. Set their sights on Bjarne's farm. Three gray-blue rows of plunderers, with blue and yellow caps and legs wrapped in rags. Siv stares at them as Bjarne runs inside the house. She mumbles a prayer that they won't come any closer. It's like praying to stop an avalanche. She tries to help Nana up from the ground, without taking her eyes off the men.

The soldiers come closer. Thirty men against a little girl and an old woman. Siv can see them. Clear as day. They're dirty and tired. Many of them are mere boys. Their emaciated faces are fuzzy with facial hair. They're wearing peasant mittens and brightly colored scarves. Their bandoliers are dirty gray and the yellow fabric has lost its luster. Only their muskets are clean and polished. The sun glitters across the black iron barrels and steel bayonets.

The line of men is thirty steps away when Bjarne comes rushing back. With flintlock in hand he shouts, 'What do you want?' His voice cracks. Siv looks up at her father. Sees how afraid he is. She wonders if the flintlock is loaded. If it makes any difference to the soldiers. She can see how calm they are. Businesslike. Indifferent. They plan to simply do what must be done. Like slaughtering a cow. Or taking an egg from a hen. They are neither angry nor hateful. Only exhausted. They will never stop. No matter how much Bjarne screams and threatens. They tilt two long pikes towards him. Cock their muskets. Still approaching. One of them shouts: 'Food!' Another: 'Hungry!' A third: 'Please, sir!' With a begging voice. But they are not begging. They are demanding.

Siv looks at the closest soldier. Tries to catch his glance. But he's looking at Bjarne. The boy has white-blond hair and pits for eyes. No older than eighteen. His cap is too big for him. When he shouts, she can see his black, broken teeth. She looks up at the line of soldiers on the road. Searching for help. For someone to see. But the soldiers march onward without looking up. There are more of them now. With wagons here and there. A couple of cows. An officer on a horse. One of the cows has a white head. Brand's prized heifer. Beate, he called her. Siv understands. Everyone at Brand's farm must be dead. The soldiers will take everything.

Bjarne also sees the cow. And raises the flintlock. He should have shot one of them. Right then and there. If only to show them that he would. As if that would help. The tall toothless one, maybe. Or the pikeman with the white scarf. He should have done something. Before the pikes reached his chest, pushing him almost playfully backwards. He takes a step back, and another. A pike stabs towards his head, another goes for his leg. The first jabs him in the throat, the second catches the hollow of his knee and he falls. Without even having cocked the gun. Siv screams, 'Father!' He drops the flintlock. Hits his head on the ground. He writhes, gets a pike in the face. And one under the chin. He lies still. Powerless. Bjarne, protector of the family. He has just enough time to hate himself for a moment. Then they hit him on the head. His eyes go dark. All he can feel is snow on his face.

The soldiers get to work. Thorough and carefree. Two of them keep watch over Siv and Nana. The rest search the farm. Lead the cows out into the yard. Overturn the sled. Drive out the sow. A few of them root through the cabin. Others take the woodshed and barn. Everything they find is investigated and appraised. Can you eat it? Can you burn it? Can you wear it? Is it worth something? The hens are killed immediately. Anything they can't use is tossed aside. The quilts from the beds are divided among them. As are the pelts from the hunting chest. They search through tools and utensils. The baskets Siv packed are rationed out. Henchmen cut the pork into bite-sized pieces. The schnapps is passed around, as are the loaves of bread hanging over the stove. The late mother Máret's dowry box is dumped out. The fabric that was being saved for Siv and Lene's weddings is snatched up. The embroidered cloths will be turned into scarves and bandages. The bonnets are thrown on the floor.

Siv watches it all. Without daring to do anything. Her whole life, pillaged. The house she was born in. The house her mother died in. And she doesn't dare do anything. The soldiers bicker, and she can't understand a word of it. Swedish sounds so strange, she thinks.

One of them shouts to the men on the road. An officer shouts back. Siv will be getting no help from the officers. Instead, more soldiers come down from the road. A couple on horseback. They slip away from their commanders. Siv knows why. It will be dusk soon and they want to avoid a cold night outdoors. That's why they're dragging things out into the yard. Chairs, logs, the dowry chest. A soldier in red pants chops them apart. With Bjarne's axe. The chest takes several swings. When the lid cracks, so does something inside Siv. She screams. And runs towards the soldier.

The shot makes everyone freeze. There's a hole in the back of Siv's sweater. She falls to the ground. Hard. One step from the chest and the chairs. Her legs twitch a few times. Then she's still. Mrs Siv of Bjarne's farm will never learn to dance. The soldier who shot her stands at the door to the woodshed. The smoke from his musket rises slowly skyward. Like a cloud on its way home. His mouth hangs open. He looks surprised. Flabbergasted. As if he didn't expect the musket to actually work. He's not much older than the girl he just killed. The soldier with the axe reprimands him. Not angrily, though. More like scolding a dog. Nana screams. High-pitched and wild. The soldiers shrug their shoulders. Mumble to each other. And keep plundering. It'll be dark soon and there's much to be done.

Bjarne crawls along the ground. He knows that Siv has fallen. That she's most likely dead. But he doesn't remember how. Or why. His head just hurts so much. He hears chopping, far away. And that wailing. He was supposed to protect them. Siv. Nana. Far away, at the other end of a tunnel, he watches the soldiers take Siv's boots and socks. They look under her skirt and snicker. He gets to his knees before he is hit again. He falls down into a deep dark hole. All he can hear is the screaming. After a few seconds, even the screaming stops. The soldiers got tired of Nana and beat her into silence. A while later, they shake him back to life. Pull him up onto his feet. Three soldiers and an officer with a rapier. Bjarne blinks and blinks and blinks. It's almost dark. His feet are freezing. Someone has taken his boots. There's a large fire in front of the barn. And two more some distance away. Soldiers everywhere. They sit around the larger bonfire. Some awake, some sleeping. Rolled up in capes and blankets. They look utterly exhausted. There are weapons and clothes and people all over the place. Over there a scrawny dog is running around. And over there some soldiers are butchering Bjarne's cow. But no Siv. Has she recovered? Resurrected like Jesus himself and walked away? For a moment he believes it. He knows it. Almost. Then he sees her naked feet sticking out of the cabin door. She's only been moved out of the way. Two soldiers walk past. Without looking at her. They're dragging Bjarne's sow. Leaving a trail of blood in the slush. Those bastards. They don't know how hard he toiled to get that pig. He wants to fight. But he can barely stand.

'Where did you hide the food?' asks the officer with the rapier. In Swedish. Bjarne stares at him. The officer slaps him in the face.

'Where did you hide the food?'

Bjarne shakes his head. The officer speaks to the soldiers in the soldiers' language. They discuss something and let Bjarne fall to the ground, where he remains. The earth is wet, muddy. The fire has thawed it. Bjarne lies there a while, listening to the chatter around him. His head aches. He thinks about how he and Siv had joked about her wedding. One beautiful day, father, I shall be a bride. And you'll be the prettiest in Tydal, Siv. And you'll be so proud, father. And then we'll marry Lene off too.

Memories of Lene and Nana flit through his mind before the soldiers come back. Lene is probably dead. Nana too. The soldiers lift him up and drag him away from the fire. So that he won't be a disturbance, he realizes. They throw him on the ground. Two of the soldiers sit on his arms. The third kicks Bjarne in the groin. With all his might. Bjarne cries out loudly. Swallows bile. One of the soldiers on his arms asks: 'Food?' Patiently and without anger. Bjarne shakes his head. Two more kicks and he's unconscious.

They wake him up by throwing snow in his face. They crush his foot with the blunt side of an axe. His axe. Bjarne screams and screams. Writhes and flounders to and fro. But he says nothing. Not even when they crush his other foot, too. He clenches his jaw until a tooth snaps. Then he faints. It's as if the sky is falling down on him. Everything turns white. And then black. He thinks about Lene. Did she make it? He's going to need the food when the soldiers move on. He and Nana will die otherwise. Somewhere in the darkness where his feet don't hurt, he makes up his mind. The soldiers will never get the food. Bjarne is going to save them.

The soldiers talk amongst themselves. What can they do? The Norwegian is stubborn, and maybe we've found all there is to find? The pig and that skinny, lousy cow? There must be more. Farmers always make the soldiers' lives more difficult. Well, then. What do we do now? They discuss torture methods as casually as they would the weather. In the sky, a half-moon breaks through the clouds. It lights up the snow and the pale faces of the men. Four frozen boys. Finns from Österbotten. The oldest is twenty-one. The youngest sixteen. The Norwegian on the ground could be their father. Crush his thumbs with the butts of our muskets, suggests the youngest. Pull out his teeth. Burn down the house, says another. Where will we sleep if we burn down his house, idiot? Put him in the bonfire.

They pull open Bjarne's mouth and have him bite down on a piece of kindling. Then they take turns clubbing his knees to pieces. Some men by the fire shout over at them. Ask them to keep it down. They bicker about what's more important. Sleeping or eating? An officer asks them all to shut up, please. Mind your business, he says. He then continues to help himself to Nana's cheese and bread.

Bjarne is in a deep, dark well. At the bottom of the well is a little meadow. It's summer. High up in the mountains. You can see so far from here. All the way to the Sylar mountains. Just below them, the Ennare river breaks into rapids. And Bjarne, Siv, and Lene are walking through the heather. Nana is not far behind, leading a herd of reindeer. The reindeer have tiny red Lapp hats, every one of them. They are beautiful. In a funny, colorful sort of way. Bjarne smiles. He knows that he's dreaming.

They try to wake him. Bjarne can feel them cramming snow in his face again. But he doesn't wish to speak with them any longer. They slap him. Shake him. But it's someone else's body now. There is someone else lying there in the snow. Bloody and barefoot. Bjarne is in the mountains. With his family. A golden plover is singing from a grove of birch and willow trees. The cottongrass covers the ground in small, white clouds. Siv walks beside him. Lene is running up ahead. Veering to and fro like a restless calf. She's singing one of the ballads Nana taught her. A song in Lappish about a swallow that flew so high that the summer sun set its wings on fire.

The soldiers are getting bored. They break Bjarne's hip, mostly because they're already standing there with an axe. Might as well. Maybe also because they're hungry. And because they've done nothing but starve in God-forsaken Trøndelag. And because it's cold. Then they leave him.

The night is cold. The sky is clear. The soldiers stock their bonfires. Dry their clothes and try to cook what they've stolen. They bicker with the band of camp followers who have caught up with them. Begging widows, bony whores, and peddlers without anything to sell. The soldiers are just as poor as they are. They beg from one another. And bicker. Over bits of food and places by the fire. Over the nasty rumors that King Karl has been shot dead. There are children running about now, too. They peer down at Bjarne. Laugh at his broken legs. People sleep in piles on the ground, wrapped in clothes and rags. Wolves howl in the distance. The air stinks of charred meat and dysentery. They take beams from the cabin to use as firewood. Two soldiers find the food that Bjarne hid. They try to hide it from the others, but are discovered. A much larger boy beats them both half senseless with a cudgel. Then they divide the food equally. And curse the greedy farmers in God-forsaken Trøndelag. The soldier who killed Siv is sleeping by the big bonfire. He trembles from the cold, not thinking for one second about the girl he killed. He dreams about his mother and the cottage back home. In Kokkola. Mother has been baking. It smells so good. And it's warm by the oven.

Morning comes. The sun turns the mountains into blood-red teeth. Bjarne is awakened by the sound of drums. He's never heard a drum before. Yet he knows what it is. Although he can only see sky from where he's lying. On his back and as stiff as a log. The soldiers are gathering. They trample around his body. Quarrel over the last of the food. Piss. Look through the house one last time. Two soldiers didn't get up. Consumed by hunger and dysentery, shoeless and covered in their own shit. Their bodies will remain where they died. Just like Bjarne and his family. Half sunken into the mud as it thawed, and then half stuck in it as it froze. Bjarne's nose and cheeks burn with cold. He's surprised to still be alive. He can't feel his legs anymore. They could just as easily be gone. He can't feel anything below his navel. Not even the cold, or the ground.

He tries to look around. Turns his head slightly. His hair is frozen to the ground. He can see the soldiers walking towards the road. Their steps are stiff and still half asleep. There goes the boy who shot Siv. With heavy steps, rigid body, and dizzy with hunger. Bjarne wishes him to hell one last time. Wishes the whole of the Swedish scum to hell. Because they killed them all. Bjarne, Siv, and Nana. And the smoke from Brand's farm is still rising from the valley. Still hanging over the sky like a veil. He hopes that Lene didn't suffer as much as her sister. Or that she had the sense to flee down to Haltdalen. It's an idle wish. Lene is much gentler than her sister. Pious and cautious too. The poor child. She wouldn't get far on a road full of soldiers and scavengers. Bjarne cries.

Suddenly someone speaks to him. Nana's face is only an arm's length from his. Her eyes are red, her face beaten. Her ear is blue and swollen. She's on her knees, croaking in Lappish.

'They're dead,' she says. 'Both of the girls.' And then something in Lappish. Over and over again. No one but Bjarne cares about her. The last of the soldiers have hurried off to the road. The scavengers remain. Still searching for scraps of food. Before Bjarne came to his senses, she tried to chase them away. But they just laughed. Some vagrant children threw rocks at her and made taunting faces.

He tries to look her in the eyes, tries to move a hand. Slowly, slowly, he manages to lift an arm. Clasps her hand. He cannot speak. Can only pat her a little. Like a kitten. Bjarne has become a wretch. They have broken his body and spirit. He is nothing but a cripple lying frozen in the mud.

'I want to kill them,' Nana says, putting her hand on his. She looks at him with calm earnestness. The face she uses when she wants him to listen. Despite the fact that he's a man, and a Trønder.

Bjarne nods. He wants to ask how Nana knows that Lene is dead, but he cannot. If she knows, she knows. Maybe she met someone from Brand's farm. That must be it. Someone else who had time to hide. Before the bastards came to slaughter and steal. Bjarne swallows a mouthful of blood and God knows what else. He too would like to see the Swedes dead. Every last one. And their women and children. All of them.

'You shall help me.'

'I can't even walk,' Bjarne croaks. His voice sounds hoarse and faint. He screamed his throat raw last night. 'I'll be dead soon. And I have no gun. Or sword.'

Nana nods. And nods again. She looks around. Bends over him. Whispers. A deadly secret. Colder than the ground and the icy mud.

'Ittakkva!'

Bjarne blinks without understanding. The Lappish fairy tale? Why is she talking about that now?

'Ittakkva!' Nana whispers. Quiet so the scavengers don't hear her. A wind sweeps between the houses. As cold as the north wind in February. The scavengers gather together. Look up to the road. Better hurry. Soon they're gone. The children run ahead towards the soldiers. A woman shouts after them.

'Ittakkva.' Nana nods. 'He who wanders on the wind. My father taught me.'

Bjarne wants to tell her that she's delirious. That the thrashing she received went to her head. That no matter what tales her father told her, they're still only tales. There are no trolls in the woods. No grims in the river. No long-legged ice giants striding over the mountains. And Jesus doesn't live in the church in Trondheim. For if he did, he never would have let Siv and Lene die. It's just like Per Halte says. God has not forgotten Tydal. Because God has never heard of Tydal.

Bjarne tries to speak, but nothing happens. It feels like there's a lump of porridge in his throat. He looks up at the sky. At the mountains. At what's left of the cabin's roof. The morning is cold and clear. The world is a pale gray. It's as if the sun hasn't yet woken up all the colors.

'Ittakkva came to me once. Do you remember nine years ago? The great storm in May?'

Bjarne nods. Máret was still alive and the girls were little. So much snow fell in one night that they could hardly leave the cabin. Nana was living with the Lapps then. He remembers that. She and Máret were not speaking.

'My father did that. My father and Ittakkva.'

'What did he do?' Bjarne remembers Nana's father, the shaman. A leathery, one-eyed little Lapp. And a curmudgeon, too. They only met twice and exchanged few words. The shaman spoke very little Norwegian. But he was satisfied with the lowlander his grandchild had married. Or at least that's what he told Nana. That Bjarne was a good man. And that his family had always been kind to the mountain people.

'The storm.' Nana grins. 'He sent the storm. He asked Ittakkva to come. And Ittakkva came. I saw it. My father blew the whistle and Ittakkva came. Ittakkva's eyes were red like embers. And the fools that called my father a witch and a demon, they didn't get far. They were going to the church in Duved. To drink the blood of Jesus and be forgiven of their sins. The half-wits.' She laughs quietly. The woman who cradled Bjarne's children and cooked his food is gone. The woman leaning over him is a stranger. Crazed. Terrifying. Her Lappish accent breaks through more and more. 'The sin of being friends with my father. They didn't get far. Ittakkva feasted on their frozen flesh. For a whole night. All that was left of them was their bones. And their eyes. Ittakkva always leaves the eyes.'

Nana laughs again. Cruelly. 'Father wanted so badly for you to have a son. Ever since the Swedes killed my brother. Those scoundrels in Åre hanged him. Said that he had stolen a cow. Liars.' She lets out a lengthy curse in Lappish. Bjarne knows the story well. The Swedes used to hunt Lapps when he was young. They could choose between being baptized or killed. That's how their fathers met. When the Lapps fled to the Norwegian side of the mountains.

'When Máret died . . .' Nana pauses. She remembers that day. The day that everything changed. A raven glides through the pale sky behind her. Large and powerful, searching for food. Ravens always start with the eyes. What if Ittakkva leaves the eyes just for them? Bjarne feels his mind quicken. His feet feel warm. Like he's warming them by a fire.

'Father's only grandchildren were girls, and I was the only child he had left. When the Swedes set fire to the camp, he lost all he had. What was left to inherit? He was old and useless. All his power had faded away before he could pass it on. The last of it burned up along with his drum. It was all over.'

'What about you?' Bjarne asks. 'And the girls?' His voice sounds like a crow's. Nana looks surprised. Like she hadn't expected him to say anything ever again. She becomes herself again for a few moments. Her eyes begin to well up. What have they done to her son-in-law? Her dear, strong son-in-law, who was always so good to her and her daughter. She blinks to keep the tears at bay. Then she sees Siv and Lene in front of her and sobs. She leans her head against Bjarne's icy chest and cries. Cries until she's shaking.

The drums up on the road fall silent. 'Only a man can be a shaman,' Nana says finally. 'That is how it has always been. I found him up on Baltintjakk that autumn. When the first snow fell, he walked up into the mountains to die. Without saying goodbye to anyone. Alone, starving, and brokenhearted. No matter how proud he was of Máret, and that she'd found you, he was crushed that he couldn't pass on the art of drumming.' Nana is lost in her memories. She never speaks of these things. The kind of things you plan to talk about some beautiful day. A day with nothing to do but sit in the sun, surrounded by your grandchildren, cleaning fish. She talks about Siv and Lene. Life in the summer camp. About the Swedes, and the shaman drums. About how Máret, little Máret with her black troll's hair, came running through the heather saying she met a Trøndelag boy down in the fields. His name was Bjarne and he was eleven years old. Bjarne is lying on the ground beside her now. Crying and praying to Jesus. Jesus who's probably never heard of Tydal.

Nana starts speaking Lappish. She's in a trance again. Some kind of fever dream. Bjarne wonders who she's speaking to. Her father maybe. Or Ittakkva. The cold has driven her mad. Bjarne knows that both of them are as good as dead. He has known it for some time now. Since he came to his senses. He just hadn't thought about it until now. He wonders if it's like they say. Does it feel warm and cozy when you freeze to death?

'We're going to kill them,' says Nana. She turns to Bjarne. Her eyes are black. Bjarne imagines that she must have been very beautiful once. Like Máret. And he's having trouble listening to what she's saying. She starts unbuttoning her cardigan. For a moment she really is Máret. Then Lene. Then Bjarne realizes she's gone insane from the cold. He's heard that when people freeze to death, you often find them undressed. They strip naked before they die. He tries to lift a hand to stop her, but the hand doesn't obey. Nana digs inside her blouse. Swears to herself.

She takes out a tiny piece of wood. A flute or a whistle. She's had it on a string around her neck. Bjarne strains to look at it, but his eyes have gotten weaker. And his legs are warm now. He wonders if Lene died quickly at least. If they should try to get a goat this summer. His head spins and spins.

'Ittakkva's whistle.' Nana grins maniacally. The kind old

woman is gone and the witch is back. 'Look! You can call him with it. All you need to do is blow. Father did it. I followed him up to Baltintjakk and found him there. Dead and frozen solid. He had taken off his clothes. And lain down in the snow. It looked like he was taking a nap. Ittakkva didn't eat his eyes. Ittakkva gave him a gift. A flute.'

Nana tugs the string off her neck. And shows him. A flat gray thing. As long as a finger and as wide as two. Made of stone or bone. Maybe that soapstone you can find over by Duved. It has a little hole in one end. Two in the other. There's something carved in the middle of it. Bjarne tries to turn his head. He looks closer. The carving depicts a man cloaked in snow. With long legs and icicle fingers. He's racing over the snow, almost like he's on skis. Bjarne knows who it must be. Ittakkva. Though he's never seen him before. But the eyes should be red. You can see them from far away, even through a blizzard. Bjarne knows. To his surprise. He's heard the stories.

'Blow.' Nana's voice is like a whisper. Something in the wind. A winter morning haze. A gloom over the valley. It obscures every other sound. The shouts from the road. Squeak and creak. Stomp stomp stomp. Everything else drowns in that single word. 'Blow.' Bjarne tries to roll over. To look at her. He twists his neck and meets her gaze. Her eyes are burning. Glowing coals in a face that's already dead.

Nana takes his hand. Lifts it. Bjarne feels like a ragdoll. His limbs have no will of their own. 'Take it. Blow.' He fumbles for the whistle. His fingers feel like someone else's. He feels the flute. It's warm from lying against Nana's breast for eight years. It's been waiting for him. Waiting for someone who wants to kill. Someone who wants the men stomping down the road fifty paces away to march straight into hell. Every last one of them.

'Blow.' She guides his hand up to his mouth. 'Only men can summon Ittakkva.' Bjarne nods. He knows it is so.

There are rules. Just like the stories. Goblins can't walk over salt. Trolls crack open in sunlight. Ittakkva doesn't listen to women. The goat in the swamp doesn't listen to men. That's how it is. He feels the flute against his lips. Stone. Which tastes like skin. Smells of Nana. Máret's mother. Siv and Lene's grandmother. His family. Who let him in to hers. A lowlander. Because he was a good man. A man who would protect them. But who failed and became a broken pile of flesh and bones in the snow. A broken man. No man at all.

He blows the whistle.

Bjarne Arnesen blows the whistle.

The sound is thin. Shrill as a wailing cat. It hangs for a second in the wind. And blows away. He blows again. And again. A scavenging man by the cabin looks around. What is that sound? A soldier's whistle? The soldiers who were farm boys a year ago look around. What a strange bird. It sounded like a . . . sounded like a . . . never mind.

A weight falls over Bjarne. He thinks about how pathetic it is that blowing a whistle almost killed him. Then he feels it. In just a few seconds it's gotten colder. Much colder. The chill stabs into his fingers and nose. Chews on his naked, lacerated legs. A wind of ice sweeps in from nowhere. The frozen father of all ice ages sweeps through the valley. Hissing and whispering, they clear the path for what will come next. The bonfire in the yard notices and quickly fades away. Surrendering before a force it cannot fight.

Bjarne's hand falls down to his side. He drops the flute. He can see Nana's face in the corner of his eye. Her eyes are gleaming. With pride. She's proud of her kin. Her daughter's husband. The father of her grandchildren. Her blood.

'Ittakkva is coming,' she says. 'Ittakkva fattagh gana'ck. Ittakkva with the red eyes. The wanderer on the wind.' She closes her eyes. Falls forward beside him. The farm is suddenly still. The fire dies out, as if it got tired of burning. High up towards the mountain, where the road becomes a path, the soldiers stop marching. They gaze down into the valley. See the black clouds rising towards them. As if birthed from the sea far below them. And they're coming quickly. It's like the storm is rushing after them. Maybe we should turn around, someone says. Well, sure. But the officers know best. They say we should go on. So we go on. Up the mountain. Towards Duved. Homeward, away from God-forsaken Trøndelag.

Bjarne turns over on his side. It's hard, like dragging a log over stones. And it feels as though someone's pulling an oxcart over his hips. But he wants to see. To watch the Swedish devils marching into the mountains. Row after row after row of them. They stomp and stomp and stomp. And snow-flakes whirl around their heads, more and more and more. You hear that? Ittakkva is coming. You're dead, you bastards. Bjarne wishes he could see the man with the long legs and the slender fingers walking behind them. Wishes he could see the eyes. For it was Bjarne who blew the whistle. He should get to see him. To greet him.

Then he sees her. Up on the road. Maybe sixty paces away. Among the scavengers walking between two groups of soldiers. Lene is up there, walking with the Swedish women. She's wearing a mantle that Bjarne has never seen before. She's speaking to the other women. As if they were friends. She looks down at the farm, but only once. Almost as if by mistake. Bjarne wonders if she even sees her father and grand-mother lying there. Maybe they're just two more bundles amidst the scrap in the farmyard. Two more piles of flesh and rags.

He wonders what she's thinking. If she's chosen to follow the army to avoid freezing. If she's chosen a life with the army over a hard life in Tydal. Once, he remembers, she said she wanted to travel. See the world. Kristiania. Copenhagen. The king's castle. Jerusalem. Sweden. They hadn't even been to Trondheim. Only seen the city from the mountains. Same with the sea. They'd never seen it up close. Maybe the crazy girl has fallen in love with some young soldier. Someone who's made her his concubine with promises of gold and voyages to foreign lands. Maybe he's a fine gentleman. A good man who plans to make an honest woman of her. Bjarne doesn't know, and he never will know. A snow shower hides her from him. Forever.

When the snow dies down, she's gone. The road is full of new soldiers. Other soldiers struggling up into the mountains. With their scavengers and their officers. In amongst them rolls a cannon. It must be a cannon. Bjarne has never seen one before. He's amazed at what power and might King Karl has sent to little old Tydal. Such magnificence. Such splendour. With horses and banners and drums and muskets. So stupid, all of it. There was nothing to fight over here. Just woods and mountains. And no one to fight against. No one but Bjarne and his children. He cries again. So stupid. And now they're all headed up the mountain. And that's where they'll die. For the cloud is over them now. He can see how a pair of officers on horseback have stopped in their tracks. They're pointing down to the valley. Watching the black wall of clouds coming up from the sea. Ittakkva is coming. And it was he, Bjarne, who invited him. To feast on frozen meat. To kill the Swedes. And Bjarne knows that Ittakkva will not be merciful. Not to man nor beast. Soldiers and officers and camp followers will all be treated equally. And young girls from Trøndelag. Bjarne knows that Lene will die. And that Ittakkva will enjoy her flesh the most. And neither Bjarne nor Jesus nor anyone else can stop him.

The sun didn't shine all afternoon. It was New Year's Eve, some people remember. The final day of a year of misery and unrest. In just a few hours, 1718 would be over. Six thousand soldiers marched through Tydal. All while the wind rose and darkness fell. And this darkness chased clouds of ice and snow up and down the mountain. Nana died at nightfall. Without a sound, and without waking up again. Soon her eye sockets were full of snow. Just before midnight, Bjarne Arnesen died too. Alone. Frozen solid and praying until the very end to gods that did not listen.

They didn't find Bjarne until March, when the snow finally melted. The bodies of his mother-in-law and eldest daughter were never found. Perhaps the Lapps came down from the mountain to fetch them. Perhaps the great wolf found them first. The same wolf that devoured Bjarne's body, taking everything but the eyes. Straight into death they stared. Stubborn and powerless.

# FRAGMENT III

THE MAN IN THE LEATHER VEST stops in the doorway to Azalee. Looks inside the bar, taking in every detail. Sizing everyone up. Gangsters everywhere. Old friends and new ones. He stares through his sunglasses at the three black guys by the bar. Two of them get up. Easy does it. No sudden movements. Hands where I can see them. They walk into the next room. Followed by dozens of eyes. One wrong move and the shit hits the fan. The bartender already knows where to duck and cover. Between the refrigerators. Janne from Småland over by the pool table thinks he'll take the big black guy first. Barrel one of his shotgun. And barrel two to black guy number two. Akki – Black Guy Number Two - is going to snuff out the two bikers outside. Uzi through the window. But the bikers are ready, with Glocks and a couple of hand grenades. They'll let loose on anything that moves. Akki's brother sits in a car across the street. AK-47. Ready to blow them all to kingdom come. Sitting in the surrounding cars are two pairs of police officers, three investigative journalists, and ten other gangsters. It's a regular office party. A who's who of the Malmö speed trade. And in the midst of it all, two clueless thirty-something women, drinking lunch and talking shit about their bosses.

The man in the leather vest walks up to the bar. The black man stands up, revealing a Rolex and Nikes. Makes a gesture that could be a bow. Or something from a rap video.

'El Presidente.'

The man in the leather vest nods.

'Hussein.'

They both hesitate. In the movies, bosses hug in situations like this. Italian bear-hug style. But neither El Presidente nor Hussein is Italian. And hugging is for homos. They shuffle their feet a little. Don't bother shaking hands. Look around for their boys. Check out the two women. Hussein sits on a barstool. El Presidente plays with one of his rings. Sits down. With one barstool between him and Hussein. He lights a cigarette. The bartender hurries into the kitchen.

'It wasn't us,' says Hussein. 'You know that.'

'Oh, we know.'

'Trust me on this.' Hussein does a Godfather gesture. Both hands over his heart.

'I said I do. If it was you, I'd be drinking coffee out of your skull by now.' El Presidente talks slowly, quietly, and clearly. Stone-faced to the max. Sunglasses and no expression. Only Hussein can hear him. 'I don't think much of you and your gang, but this I know.'

'So? Why are we here?'

'Because I don't want to end up at war over something neither of us did.'

Somebody shouts something over by the pool table. A whole lot of hands reach for a whole lot of weapons. El Presidente doesn't flinch. When everyone who's anyone in Malmö is looking at you, you can't sweat the small stuff.

'Just some guys playing pool,' Janne and Akki whisper to each other. 'Polish construction dudes,' Akki's buddy clarifies.

Hussein nods. 'We have peace, you and me.' A new Godfather gesture. 'But maybe we have a mutual problem?'

'Someone robbed us. Us. So *we* have a problem. *We*. Why would it be your problem if you weren't involved?'

'Because if somebody new's trying to crack the market then it's our problem too. And if they're trying to send you a message, show how tough they are, then it's us or the Yugos who are the next target.'

'It wasn't the Yugos either.'

'How do you know that?'

'I called Milan and asked.'

'How do you know he's not bullshitting you?'

'I've known Milan since your daddy was in diapers. Keep yourself alive another fifteen years and I'll start calling you too.' El Presidente takes a long drag. Lets the words hang in the air. 'It's some freelancers. Total psychos.'

Hussein nods theatrically.

'I want to warn you. Against doing business with them, for one. Because we aren't going to appreciate people doing business with them. That's our money they're using.'

'Of course. We'd feel the same way.'

A meter maid walks by outside. She wonders why half the cars on the street have someone sitting in them. Five guns are discreetly aimed at her.

'But also – ' El Presidente watches a guy come rushing out of a doorway yelling at the meter maid, ' – because I want to warn you . . .'

'About what? I said we won't do business with them.'

'You did.'

'You have my word.' Godfather gesture on 'word'.

El Presidente crushes out his cigarette. Leans slightly forward. 'I want to warn you about *them*.' He takes off his sunglasses. Looks Hussein in the eye. Cinematic timing. He whispers. 'They're dangerous. Real dangerous.'

Hussein looks into the calm, gray eyes. Searches for El Presidente's soul. He finds nothing that he can understand. No mutual gangster nerve. No mutual friends. Only sincerity. 'Do you understand what I'm saying?' says the most feared man in Skåne. 'They're dangerous.'

Hussein nods cautiously to coax an explanation. 'You need help taking them out?'

'Huh?' says El Presidente. As if the thought hadn't crossed his mind.

'We'll help you round them up. Find them and take them out. No problem.'

'You don't want to find them. Don't you get it? I just want these bastards to leave town.'

'You're going to let them get away?'

'You've got to know when to cut your losses. You haven't learned that yet, and one of these days you're gonna get yourself whacked.' Hussein tries to say something, but El Presidente continues. 'A piece of advice. Don't mess with zealots, political or religious. They have no nose for business and can be fucking dangerous. Unpredictable. These guys are in that category. There was a ton of speed and weapons at Johan and his girl's place, but they only took money. Get it? They rob our fucking warehouse, but only take cash.'

Hussein theater-whispers. 'Was it Muslims?'

Out on the street, two cops joke about provoking a fire-fight. A lot cheaper for the justice system if the gangsters just kill each other, they laugh.

'Peter Lorentz, who survived, said they were either Arabs or Yugos.'

'Those aren't the same thing,' Hussein says without thinking.

'That's what Milan said too. It's like saying "either a Finn or an Indian". South-European then. Some damn Mediterranean. Not black, not yellow. Three or four of them. One woman. That's what Peter Lorentz thinks. An older guy did the talking. Bad Swedish. Two of them had some kind of masks on. The woman and one other. They looked like dogs or something.'

'Dogs?'

'Or pigs. Peter was a little out of it.' He'd gone on about bats and werewolves too, but El Presidente keeps that part to himself. He doesn't want to shame poor Lorentz completely.

'We can take three or four guys, easy.' Hussein has already started planning. El Presidente knows. And raises the stakes.

'We haven't found one of Lorentz' legs yet. They cut it off below the knee and took it with them. With a hacksaw.'

Hussein doesn't bat an eyelid. He's already chasing them down in his mind. To do El Presidente a favor. To show he's not afraid.

'So they go to Johan's late one night. Him, his girl, Peter Lorentz, and Josef Lesniak are there. They ring the doorbell, break down the door, then break Lesniak's neck, and the necks of Johan's two big fucking pit bulls. Johan's crazy Russian bride, Vanja, flips out and jumps into the fight, so they beat her to death too.'

'What kind of guns did they have?'

'No guns.'

Hussein makes a Godfather face, like, respect. Not just anybody can take on two dogs and an outlaw with a knife. El Presidente continues.

'Then they tie Johan and Lorentz up. And start demanding to know where the money is. Johan tells them to go fuck their mothers, and they start eating him.'

One of the civilian women lets out a shrill laugh at something on the other one's phone. Hussein thinks he must have misunderstood something. Swedo-Danish slang. Like when people from Skåne say balls instead of butt cheeks.

'They start with his arms and then his thighs. Gnaw on him like a couple of fucking hyenas. Then his chest. Johan passes out and the older guy continues talking to Lorentz. Tells him his bones are for dessert. Nobody can handle shit like that. I've seen people do some sick fucking things and I've seen people have some sick fucking things done to them, but this . . .' He shakes his head. He's not pretending.

Hussein shakes his head along with him.

'I don't give a shit about the money.'

'How much did they take?' Hussein has to know.

'About a hundred thousand. I don't care. Whoever can take it from those assholes can keep it.'

El Presidente stops talking. The word's as good as out. No matter what he says to Hussein about staying quiet, rumors will spread about the sick bastards that robbed El Presidente. And every small-time thug in Southern Sweden's going to try and find them. And it's not as though it'll do him any harm. El Presidente might have backed off a little, but he has friends. Friends who would gladly hunt down psychopaths for weeks at a time. And if Hussein gets in any trouble? Well, it's a tough business.

# HAPPY FOREVER ON ÖSTERMALM

DANIEL AND NADINE STRUCK IT RICH. And their life was filled with gay men. Suddenly they were everywhere. At least two of the antique dealers Daniel had begun working with were gay. Kooky old queens with nice things. They were like two little old ladies. In expensive suits, with smooth hands and floral-patterned silk on the back of their vests. Just the fact that they pranced around in vests was enough. Then they had to say 'risqué' and 'faux pas' on top of it. And talk like they were from the 1800s. Nadine couldn't understand half of it. Daniel didn't quite get it either, but he was a proper Swede and had a good poker face. Nadine saw through it though.

The broker in charge of the paperwork when they took over Kalim's apartment was gay, too. Only fruitcakes and bodybuilders look in the mirror that often. And only queers call other men 'dear'. Every. Time. The hairdresser on their new street was gay, and screamed it. And he loooooved Nadine's hair. He really did talk that way. Like on TV. He even flapped his hands and everything. Nadine wondered how they started talking like that. Did a guy wake up one morning, go 'daarling' and think, 'Well, guess I just might turn gay now?'

Anyway. Their new neighbor with the yappy little dog was gay too. 'Von Etterlin' it said on his front door. On an enameled sign. Von E wore a silk scarf with a checkered blazer. Östermalm chic. And he looked like he had botoxed his whole face and fallen asleep in a tanning bed. His dog had a rhinestone collar. Cecilia thought Nadine was joking when she told her. Rhinestone? Out in Hallunda, dogs have studs on their collars. Like punk rockers.

The interior decorators who came to fix up the apartment were *suuuper* gay. All three of them. Flaming, sizzling, smoldering gay. Move to Östermalm and take over a bunch of antique furniture, and you'll need an army of flamboyant decorators to sort it all out. Anybody can understand that. And then there was Love, who helped Nadine shop at NK. Her 'personal shopper'. Ridiculous but true. Love was nice, and too gay to last ten seconds in Hallunda. They'd kill him. Just to be on the safe side. Nadine knew. Her family was from Macedonia. Where they kept homosexuals on a short leash.

But not on Östermalm, no way. Here they stand on the street corners sipping lattes all day long. When they aren't cutting each other's hair or trying to sell furs and antique chairs to the people walking by. And Nadine had, in fact, just bought a fur. From a little old gay man of the 'vest with floral silk' variety. Just because she could. And because Daniel told her to. After all, they could afford it and were head over heels in love. The fur was sable and cost an insane amount. It would have been all the rage in Macedonia. Fur was hot there. All the money in the shithole Nadine's father was from couldn't pay for her new fur. She could buy her hometown with what it cost. And burn it to the ground.

Now the fur hung on her closet door. It shimmered in the light from the living room window. She could see it in the mirror on Daniel's closet door. All it did was look expensive. And unnecessary. And she could see it in the mirror on Daniel's closet door because Daniel wasn't in bed. Again. He was in Bern doing some job for Kalim. Again. Nadine wasn't even sure where Bern was. In Belgium, she thought. What the hell was Daniel even doing in that pedo-land. Couldn't Kalim be content owning property in Stockholm? She missed Daniel. And she was jealous of Kalim. She wanted her boyfriend all to herself.

She rolled around in bed. A Hästens, incidentally. Expensive and checkered. You can fuck like crazy in a Hästens and it won't even squeak. They'd tried it only once since they bought it. Four weeks ago. On a Thursday night. Before Daniel went to Prague for three days. And they had only done it once since then. On the new sofa. Following some pay-channel porn. Dirty and silly, straight out of *Cosmo*. She had joked to Cecilia afterwards. Five steps to drive him wild. One: Make sure he's home. Two: Get him out of his office. Three: Tell him you're wearing panties that cost 900 kronor. Four: Keep him awake. In case of emergency tell him what the bra cost. Five: Put on a sexy movie. *The Erotic Castle*. Pay-per-view, darling. Girls from Macedonia don't do that sort of thing. And if they do, they don't admit it. And if they admit it, then they say they were coerced or drugged and that it was all so disgusting.

The day after *The Erotic Castle*, Daniel left for Prague again. There was a lot of traveling in this new life. But he'd caught his big break, and if there were going to be wads of cash, there would have to be tons of travel. Wearing expensive suits and dragging a brand-new Samsonite. No more ten-hour days at the office. No more real estate insurance. No more risk evaluations. Daniel Engman was on the way up. A traveling business executive, darling. Making big money for Mr Kalim. Last week he almost flew a whole lap around the world. Atlanta. Cairo. Istanbul. He video-messaged her from endless identical terminals. Same ads, same couches, same tired men with expensive telephones, sharp suits, and acute homesickness. When he closed his eyes, he said, he didn't know where he was. He was so tired that everything blurred together. And back in a cab in a city he didn't give a single fuck about, it was her he longed for. He longed for her cooking. No matter how bad it was. He longed for their evenings in, with Xbox and red wine. He yearned for home, for making out, and Halo.

He bought her wine and perfume from duty-free stores that all had the same inventory. He never had time to buy anything real. And what did you buy for Nadine? Books? She never read. Another fur coat? Music you couldn't find on Östermalm? She mostly listened to the radio anyway. Jewelry? I have soooo much jewelry, darling. More than my whole family combined.

Nadine got up. Tiptoed through the darkness to the kitchen. Twenty-two steps. The light from the street lit the way. She saw the shadows cast by all their stuff. All their new stuff. They had been rich for two months, tops. And they had bought so ridiculously much stuff. New furniture that looked old and expensive. And a giant flat-screen TV. And an Xbox 360. And a microwave so big you could cook Cecilia's pit bull in it. It was the only thing in the kitchen Nadine could use. She was deathly afraid of the huge AGA stove. A thousand pounds and just as many knobs.

She lit a cigarette under the hood. Over by the kitchen table (the small one), a faint light glimmered in the crystal bowl with snakes on it. They had gotten it from Kalim. It could hold a basketball and felt like it was made of lead. Luckily, Kalim's kitchen table was incredibly stable. They had taken over quite a bit of his furniture. Pretty old things that looked like they had been stolen from a museum. The queer eyes for the straight guys loved them. They bought china and conversation pieces to match. They brought ideas and fabric samples. You've got to pick your curtains, sweetie. Five things you've got to get before you move in. Curtains, tableware, torchieres, oyster forks, and wireless internet. And there they were, in the middle of it all. A Macedonian girl from a high-rise in Hallunda. A Swedish boy from a high-rise in Jakobsberg. The apartment was full of things that didn't really go together. There were bags of clothes in the hallway that she'd forgotten to put away. Nadine had a new phone with way too many buttons. Daniel's had even more. They were thinking about buying a new car too. A BMW.

Not some drug dealer trophy car, or a midlife-crisis-mobile. Daddy would be impressed. He respected German cars, gold teeth, and not much else. He and Nadine rarely spoke.

Swedes are impressed by other things. Take it from Cecilia. Five ways to impress a Swede. One: Live on Östermalm. Two: Have a family with history. Three: Have old money. Four: Have a house in the archipelago. Five: Have a hot wife with a good job. Nadine scored one out of five. Not so great, darling. Sometimes she was afraid Daniel would get bored of her. Because she had only finished high school. Because she was just a receptionist. And also because she had been unemployed for four months. Suddenly he would find some substitute with good grades and table manners and a father who owned a whole island in the archipelago. Someone in the damned peerage book.

You could hear poodle noises from the stairwell. Von E was out on a nighttime ramble with his little monstrosity. Nadine's cigarette tasted terrible. Everything was just dumb luck. That's what she told Cecilia and Eva-Lena, Daniel's mother.

Daniel and Nadine had already been on the way over to Eva-Lena's place when she called. Mom-in-law had the stomach flu. Some daycare brat's fault. They were already at Central Station, so Daniel had decided they would play tourist for the day. They walked all of Kungsgatan. A beautiful late-summer day. Tourists and half-naked people everywhere. They walked over Stureplan. Straight through VIP country and up to Östermalm. They passed the border of Sibyllegatan and were suddenly in a different Sweden. Expensive outfits. No street clothes. Checkered blazers. Luxury cars. And poodles all over.

They had just gotten ice cream when they saw the sign for the showing. Six rooms, on Styrmansgatan. Insanely expensive. Why not? Maybe they'll have free coffee. Let's do it. Nadine was into it. We'll just say it's not really what we're looking for. Better yet, there was complimentary wine and the apartment was unbelievable. And Daniel got along really well with Kalim, who owned it. They talked for over an hour. Three glasses of wine. Nadine was almost starting to get restless when Kalim asked, 'So, you said you work in real estate?' Just a drive-by question. Two days later Daniel had a new job. Eight years slaving away in insurance and suddenly they were on Östermalm. And before long they started *looking* Östermalm. Distinguished, as the antique dealers would say. They dressed differently. Discreet. Tiny details that cost a fortune. Watches, handbags, shoes. You could spend 5000 kronor on shoes. And you'd never tell the difference.

She went back to bed. Her new lingerie itched against her back. It was expensive, black, and sinful and matched her long, black hair perfectly. The woman in the mirror was beautiful, wraith-like. The new Nadine. A ghost with expensive details. With perfectly crafted nails, a rock-hard ass, and pussy as smooth as a peach. She wanted some work done too. Fix her Greek nose, her tits, and her blossoming double chin. But Daniel said no. Her nose was distinctive. He saw no double chin. And C-cup was *lagom,* not too big, not too small. The Swedish way. The people who had a word for 'good enough'. Wine gets better with age. Furniture maybe. But not women. Nadine used to look at the other girls at the gym. They looked like dancers, all of them. Dancers whose slightly too large tits pointed straight up when they bench-pressed. Sure, Nadine was twenty-six, but hers had never looked like that.

She sat on the bed. Her phone wasn't blinking. No new message from some random airport. No 'Missing you in lame-ass Moscow'. Or 'Watching TV. Will Smith is speaking Italian'. She missed him more than ever. It was silly. They'd been living together for three years. Maybe one year too long, she admitted to Cecilia. But now when they never saw each other, they were suddenly super in love again. And fucked like rabbits. Those few times when both of them were awake and in the bedroom at the same time.

Nadine lay down and thought about masturbating. It wasn't her thing. It always ended with her feeling alone. She stared up at the queer-eye ceiling lamp. It was butt ugly. A lump of crystal. But it matched the sculpture things on the ceiling. The long, tangling formations that looked like snakes seemed to run right into it. At night the streetlamps cast insane-looking shadows on the ceiling. When it was windy, they moved. And the lamp made reflections like lightning. Only a gay dude could spend his time thinking about stuff like that. Östermalm, baby.

She fell asleep without taking her eyes off the lamp. She woke up, convinced she had to go to work. She made it to the bathroom before realizing that Aldecta had closed their Stockholm office. They didn't need her anymore. Thanks for your two years. She never thought she'd miss her co-workers. But she did. She even missed taking the subway every morning. There was just enough time to read *Metro* cover-to-cover from Gullmarsplan to Thorildsplan.

She showered and put on the new coffeemaker. She got dressed. Turned on the TV and realized it was Saturday. How could she not know that? She ate a kiwi and two crackers. If you're not allowed lipo, you'd better not eat much either. She decided to go to Nautilus and put on her new exercise clothes. Love, the personal shopper, said they made her look 'snappy'. She liked Love. Thanks to him she hardly had one piece of clothing left from Gullmarsplan. Whatever she hadn't tossed, she donated to thrift stores. They had gotten a whole bag of shoes. She drove by in a taxi, jumped out and left it there. Cecilia loved that. The whole thing was so insanely hip-hop diva-esque. It was fun doing bratty stuff like that for a few days. And it was fun teasing Daniel about Kalim. Kalim likes you, Daniel. He wants to bang you. Darling, isn't it exciting to be wanted by a dark, older man. Great fun when you felt like being chased around the apartment and wrestled down on the bed.

But mostly it just annoyed him. The Kalim subject was a little touchy. Daniel had always worked for banks and bigger companies. Never for one single person. And Kalim was the boss. The big, bald boss. No matter how nice he was. Piss him off and it's bye-bye to Daniel's new job and their new life on Östermalm. The whole fairy-tale castle could burn to the ground if Daniel didn't do a lap around the world every week. It was a bit tricky.

The sun was out. Everyone on Östermalm was dressed to kill. As if they had nothing better to do than strut around in Gucci clothes. But Nadine blended in. The trick was not to stare. And to carry your twelve-thousand kronor handbag like it was something you found on the street. And stand up tall like you owned the place. Also, be friendly in a casual way. Hi poodle guy, hi latte queen. Hi pricey pumps and even pricier tits. Hi old hag with Botox cheeks. Hi person I saw on TV, who was with that guy who used to be a pop star. Nice weather we're having. Yup, late fall this year.

The gym was full of desperate housewives. They ran and jumped and lifted. Burning fat and money. Time and anxiety. Nadine ran on the treadmill. Obviously, darling. Why jog for free in the park when you can pay an arm and a leg per month to run on a machine in front of the mirror. The housewives stood in a long row and stared at each other out of the corners of their eyes. Documented. Compared. Unmasked. Who'd had what done? Whose boobs didn't bounce naturally? Who ran long enough to earn milk in their coffee? The one nearest Nadine ogled her. She could feel it in her skin. Under it. Men stare like idiots. But women. Their stares are corrosive. They search for the smallest flaws. Look, varicose veins. Look, snaggletooth. Look, a callus. But they could stare at Nadine all they liked. Raven-black hair way down her back. Not dyed, darling. Brown eyes. Skin like light nougat. Her curves are real, her face 100% Macedonian mountain chick. Natural, all of it. Football and basketball in school. Älvsjö Park's ladies' junior team. Not for wimps. The stuff you don't find in the peerage book.

It was an old joke, but it made her smile as she ran. Kalim had been visiting. Checking what they had done with the place. They were celebrating Daniel's first trip abroad, he said. To Van Der Meulen in The Hague. Something with a book collection had gone well. Nadine didn't really get it. They drank wine and ate sushi. At the gigantic table in the dining room where a whole mafia family could fit. It was fucking ridiculous. They each sat at their own corner of the table and waved and shouted. How's the sushi over there? They had put a new, expensive, queer-approved candelabra in the middle of the table. With nine bright candles that filled the room with a fiery golden light. Made them look like three vampires. Nadine and Kalim, anyway. He also had a Greek nose and was probably dark-haired once. Now the candle-light just reflected off his scalp.

Kalim was in the best of moods, and he and Daniel told dirty jokes and work stories that only they understood. They tried to explain them to Nadine, but to no avail. They were shitfaced. But funny. It suddenly hit Nadine just how close Swedish Daniel and Kalim from, like Jordan or something, had gotten to each other. They were friends. Actual friends. Kind of like father and son, or something. It made her a little envious.

Anyways, peerage books. Books used by Swedish nobility to trace their lineages.

'One hundred and three families,' said Kalim, shaking his chopsticks. 'And they all have a pedigree.'

'Sounds like something for breeding dogs,' Daniel giggles. Like he always does when he jokes about sex.

'Can we breed a Von Knorring with a Ramel?' Kalim laughs.

'Yes, their offspring will have mighty fine fur.'

'And long tails.' Nadine makes her cerebral palsy face. The one her mom scolded her for doing when she was little.

They burst out laughing. And it's inbreeding jokes all night. Kalim and Nadine crack each other up with sick stories from back home. Cousins with six toes and cleft palates. The uncle who was a little bit special. Even before he rode his bike into that olive tree. They seem to be just as inbred in Macedonia as in Jordan, or Iraq, or whatever. They laugh so much together that Daniel feels a bit left out. He just sits and grins. With his mouth full of sushi and a wine glass in his hand. A tired little Swede, Östermalm style. She told Cecilia afterwards that it was then they became friends. She and Kalim. They understood each other. In some weird way. Next time they met, there was something there. A wink. A little joke. Silly little signs that they were friends. Not-from-Sweden-buddies kind of thing.

The text came late in the afternoon. While she was walking down Biblioteksgatan, doing nothing in particular. 'MISS YOU' it said. All caps. A short one for Daniel. He could write entire novels while he sat waiting for the plane. She saved the best ones. One where he described *Friends* on German TV. Dubbed so they all sounded like Nazis. Amazing. The one about Turkish toilets was good too. She answered, 'Miss you too. When are you coming home?'

The reply came late. When he should have been at Arlanda airport already. Nadine's sitting on the couch. Half asleep. In her expensive dressing gown. Watching a movie. Sharon Stone flirting with some hunk. Nadine is marginally interested. 'Emergency. Kalim very sick. Me too. Have to stay.' Daniel sounds different. It worries her. She calls and calls but no answer. Not once. All she gets are strange dial tones and messages in French.

She sleeps on the couch, phone in hand. She dreams she's on the subway in a tunnel that never ends. She comes to at five a.m. Sweaty and tangled in her dressing gown. She gets up and walks around aimlessly for a while. Because you know, Cecilia, you really can go for a walk in this apartment. She drinks a little water. Looks down at the street. She pretends she's the only one in the whole city. Everyone else is dead. Like in a zombie movie.

She eats a couple of crackers. Walks out into the office. Looks at the photos on Daniel's desk. Nadine swimming in Crete. Nadine naked and in love, in bed hiding behind the duvet. The second time they slept together. A late summer night. They had barely fallen asleep by the time the sun came up. She runs her hand over the back of Daniel's chair. There are two shirts hanging over it. Egyptian cotton. Crazy expensive. Only the best for a traveling business executive.

She looks at the piles of binders. Boxes that Kalim took with him when he moved, which Daniel later lugged back. Heaps of paper. Bookkeeping. Contracts. Lists of things. So dusty and so fucking much of it. It always smells dusty in here. But so be it. Mr Kalim was an analog dude. Lots of loose-leaf archiving. Databases weren't his thing. Bundles of paper with string or ribbon around them. That was his thing.

When they took over the apartment, Kalim had moved all his paperwork and most of his furniture to a storehouse in Årsta. The kind you rent and then put your whole life in. He himself lived at a hotel. Reisen in Old Town. Daniel had discovered it after a few weeks. Bizarre. Kalim who owned apartments in three or four cities. Daniel had seen several of them. They could even borrow the penthouse in Rome whenever they wanted. Swim in the fountains and wave to the pope. But first Daniel had to get up to speed. Kalim wanted to move to Istanbul and just sit and look at boats. That's why there were so many trips. They needed to get affairs in order. And Daniel always said, 'It's a lot now, but it'll settle down soon.'

Oh well. She walked out into the TV-room. The couch,

the new Xbox. *Sopranos* and *Friends* box sets. The floor lamp that looked like a vine. 'Jugend,' said Kalim proudly. 'Very expensive, hold on to it for now.' A flat-screen from hell. As big as a billboard. Some dead houseplants in the window. Wonder what sort of disease he's got. Some kind of tropical sickness? In Belgium? Food poisoning seems more likely.

The dining room. The giant table. The vampire-candelabra. 'Are you in the peerage book, little girl?' They should put more stuff on the walls. The gays said one piece per wall. But when the wall is twenty-five feet, it ends up looking a little empty.

The bedroom. The kitchen. The guest room behind the kitchen. Never used. The small dining room. Yes, we have another dining room. We use it for storage. Boxes. Kalim's fricking papers. Junk from the basement on Gullmarsplan. Stuff from when Daniel was little. Her eyes land on a package he came home with a couple of weeks ago. It's still sealed. In silky, baby-blue paper. 'Something special to share the next time I get home.' She was more than a little curious. She begged and begged. There's something about unopened packages that drives girls crazy. Then they'd fallen asleep in front of the TV. And the next evening it was time to go to Bern. Nadine hasn't thought about the package since then. The size of a shoebox and fairly heavy. A gift from Mr Adell in Cairo. 'We'll savor those when we have more time.' He said 'savor' in his antique dealer voice. 'Mr Adell promises we'll enjoy them.'

It's six-thirty when the phone rings. The sun is almost up. She's been walking around and around the apartment for over an hour. With her phone in her hand. The Macedonian ghost of Styrmansgatan. With a rock-hard ass. It's from a foreign number. She can hear him clear as a bell. Like he's calling from Östermalm Square. He sounds terrible. Dull and hollow.

'Kalim is dead,' he says. 'His heart stopped.'

Nadine feels dizzy. 'What happened?'

'He got sick. Caught a cold. Just like me. And then he just died. In his hotel room.'

'When did it happen?'

'Just tonight.'

'What about you? How are you feeling?'

'I'm sick too. Some kind of flu. I'll find out more from the doctor in a little while.' He tries to laugh. It sounds unnatural.

'Are you sure it's just the flu?' Nadine starts pacing really fast. Like she's going to walk to Bern.

'Yes, baby.' It had been ages since he called her baby. Years. He must be really scared.

'Did Kalim have the same thing?'

'I think so. We must have caught it on the plane. Or somewhere in the city.'

'You don't have a headache?'

'No.'

He starts coughing. It sounds like his lungs are going to explode. Nadine transforms into her mother. Old mother Kirovski. She starts thinking about doctors, medicine, and ways to get to Bern.

'When are you coming home?' she asks, finally. 'Do you need any help?'

'I want to sleep for a week.' He starts laughing. 'I'm getting on a plane first thing in the morning. So, tomorrow.'

'What are you going to do with Kalim?'

'With his body?' He sounds surprised.

'Yeah.'

'Some of his relatives from Amman are coming to get him. I talked to his aunt or something on the phone. Her English was really bad. I'll be taking over the company for the time being.'

'Only once you've recovered, please.'

She can hear him nodding. She sees it in front of her. Feverish eyes and sweaty clothes. The suffocating feeling eases off a bit. She turns into her mother even more. Orderly, caring, and unwavering. Nadine Kirovski will take care of you. You just get yourself home now.

'Should I meet you?'

'I'll take a cab.'

'When are you coming?'

'Around eleven.' He starts to cough again. 'I miss you,' he tries to say. That's what it sounds like.

They hang up without saying much more. Nadine goes for a smoke. Three cigarettes. Puts on some coffee. Daniel doesn't seem terminal. Everything's fine then. What does it mean that Kalim is dead? What happens with the 'company' later? It takes her ten minutes to remember to pour water in the coffeemaker.

She drinks coffee and smokes. And not under the stove hood. She texts Daniel. The message gets long and confusing. She changes it several times. Deletes and starts over. Finally she just goes with: 'Hurry home. Call if you need anything. Be very safe.'

She showers and thinks about all the things she planned to do. Tomorrow. Tomorrow is Monday. She had planned to look for a job. Find out if there's a career center on Östermalm. She's sick of shopping and exercising. Sick of spending money. Sick of having nothing to talk about over dinner. Today at work. I did something today. Something that wasn't just for myself. No wonder women who walk up and down Östermalm go out and get dogs and have kids. Or take up drinking or have affairs. They're just sick of running around and shopping, that's all.

But now there's other stuff to do. Mamma Kirovski is taking over. There's a life to save. Or two. Both Daniel's and her own. Because no more Mr Kalim means no more money, darlings. Who owns the big man's firm, really? Does he work for someone or does he just own a bunch of things that he sells to people? He must earn something from all the apartments. He pays Daniel's salary, and who knows what else?

Does Daniel know? Are there next of kin? She flies around the apartment fantasizing about women in burkas chasing her along Storgatan. Kalim's many sisters. Does the boss have any family at all? Besides this aunt in Amman? Can aunts in Amman be heirs? Where's Amman? Saudi Arabia? Syria? Jordan? She should have an atlas at home. Jordanian inheritance laws for five hundred.

She gets dressed and hurries outside. Time to go shopping. Eight-thirty on a Sunday. Good idea. Östermalm's not awake yet. The whole city's in bed watching breakfast TV. Wine tips and interviews with famous people.

She walks across Östermalm Square. There are pigeons everywhere. Two guys are loading boxes into a kiosk. Nadine heads downtown. Restless and full of ideas. She needs a plan. For what, she doesn't know. What is she shopping for, anyway? Food? What does Daniel eat when he's sick? Juice. Toast. Does he take aspirin? Cough medicine? Åhlens department store. There's a pharmacy next door. Effervescent tablets. A few different kinds. She bustles along. Daniel will be home soon. Thirty-six hours go by quick.

She's home by noon. With shopping bags and a stomachache. She forgot to eat. There's nothing in the fridge resembling lunch. She bounces around the apartment for a while. Straightening up. Making the bed. Vacuuming a little here and there. Moving stuff around a little. Dusting. She calls Cecilia. Cecilia's not home. Sunday morning. She must be sleeping over at a guy's house. Some piece of Stureplan nightclub ass. Nadine leaves some jumbled message on her voicemail. Smokes a cigarette. Drinks a glass of wine. Yeah, yeah, on an empty stomach. She finally decides to go out and eat. She walks down to Östermalm Square again. Light-headed. Jumpy and mechanical. Sushi? Something in the food court? She buys an expensive baguette with cheese on it. Exclusive cheese. How the hell else could a sandwich cost 60 kronor? Östermalm, darling.

She stands in the middle of the crowded food court, eating. Dead fish are staring at her from across the aisle. Someone screams and swears in Greek. She tries to start breathing. Daniel will be home in twenty-four hours. And he won't want to come home to a half-drunk, nervous wreck. No, no, there has to be sanity and common sense. She hurries home along Storgatan.

The day goes by at entirely its own pace. Sometimes time stands still. Sometimes she sits down and an hour flies by. She's home the whole time. Five signs that Nadine Kirovski is losing her grip. One: She changes her clothes four times and showers twice. Two: She's blown through almost two packs of cigarettes and almost two bottles of wine. Way more than usual. Three: She's not even really drunk. Four: She forgets to eat. Five: All the misery in the world is slowly creeping up on her. She starts crying for no reason. Everything on TV is so sad. She flips through depressing medical shows and docu-soaps of people crying. Injured puppies on shows about veterinarians.

She surfs the internet. For hours. Looks up influenza and inheritance law. Flus are dangerous. In 1918, twenty-five million people died from something called the Spanish flu. A killer influenza. Thank god we live in the 2000s.

And the all-important question. Can you take over a company that you work for? If the owner dies. And for lack of other heirs or employees. There's very little info about law on the internet. And what there is looks like it's been written by twelve-year-olds. And on top of that, most of it is American and all about suing people. Pay to find out more.

She dozes off. Tipsy in front of the TV. Wakes to the sound of rain. In the middle of the night. Gets up. Showers. For the third time. Goes and lies down in the Hästens bed. Sleeps like a log. Dreams about lawsuits and her hometown in Macedonia. Her triumphant return as a rich girl. Her dad says she should give a little money to her brothers. Her three unimaginative little brothers. One an auto mechanic, one a doorman, and one whatever he is this week. They rarely see each other and she never misses them. Then the snakes on the ceiling come and eat them up. All that's left is Nadine and a woman from Amman. They talk about Kalim's funeral. His casket will be pulled by seven black horses.

The taxi pulls up at eleven. There's a light rain. Nadine stands on the small balcony. A little hungover. Ever so slightly dressed up. She smokes and spies. Watching every taxi. Freezing. Cigarette ash falling down to the street. Looking down at the world from the French balcony, darling. An old cougar stares at her from the building across the street. You can see chandeliers in every window. And bookshelves. Where the fuck do people find the time to read all these books?

The taxi stops right below her. The driver steps out and opens the door. For a 29-year-old. From the third floor Daniel looks thin. Hunched over. His suit doesn't fit right. He needs to meet with Love and do a little personal shopping. Some fresh new looks for the newer, thinner me. He needs Mama Nadine.

She rushes into the apartment. Out through the door. Down the stairwell. Daniel's in the doorway trying to explain something to the driver. He's deathly pale. The driver doesn't want to carry his bags in. Nadine butts in. Screams at the driver crazily. Takes the bags. Helps Daniel inside. Reassures him. He smiles at her with a look of tired appreciation. Says he can walk. He sounds so hoarse. They shuffle to the elevator. In and up. She holds him hard around his shoulders. 'You're home now, baby.' It's been a long time since she called him that. She helps him over to the sofa. Helps him take off his shoes and sportcoat. She fetches some juice. Asks how he's feeling five times.

It takes five minutes before she's sitting still beside him.

'Hi,' he says and smiles. He sounds like a ghost. A very sick and wheezy ghost, at that. But the smile still works.

'Hey,' giggles Nadine. 'You're a mess.'

'I know. The bitch next to me on the plane wouldn't stop staring. I should have said I had AIDS or something.'

Nadine laughs until she's nauseous. She grabs on to his hand. It's dry and hot.

'Do you need anything?'

'That I didn't need a minute ago?'

'Yeah.'

'I need a shower.'

'Yeah.'

'Don't stare at me like that.' Daniel covers his eyes with one hand like he's embarrassed. Kalim did that constantly. 'I can sit up.'

Nadine tears up.

'And I don't plan on dying, babe.'

She starts crying. She falls into his arms. He falls backwards on the sofa. They lie like that for a long time. Nadine heaving against his chest. With his hands in her hair. He combs his fingers through it. She can hear his heart. It's beating too hard. He smells like sweat and spices and more sweat. It's a wonderful smell. She closes her eyes. Focuses on her senses. Enjoys holding his hands. Presses against him. Feels him getting hard. It presses against her stomach. He notices that she notices it.

'No way.' He laughs. It hisses inside his chest. 'I'll die from overexertion.'

'You can just lie totally still.' Nadine says, almost joking.

'Is cardiac arrest a turn-on for you?'

'You have no idea.' She turns towards him. 'Should I carry you to the shower?'

'As long as you don't try to violate me.'

'Violate? Is that some kind of Östermalm-ism?'

'Fine, how about "diddle?"'

He hugs her hard. She heaves him up and stumbles over to the bathroom. Nadine wants to help him, but he doesn't let her. He can do some things himself.

Nadine sits there drying her tears. Gets mascara on her sweater. Listens in on him. She sighs when she hears the shower. A long sigh.

She helps him out of the shower. Sees him wearing only a towel. Pale as a corpse. He looks like a skeleton. With an erection. He's always hard, Cecilia. And that strange bruising on his chest. Like he's been beaten. He smiles and says soon he'll be hotter than ever. He has no idea what the bruises are from.

She leads him into the bedroom. Puts him in pajamas. The blue ones. Tucks him in. Runs around fetching things for him. Want something to read? Drink? Sleep? Should she get a bucket in case he needs to puke? Do we even have a bucket? He asks for a glass of water. Smiles at her running around.

He gets her to sit down. Says that he doesn't know where or how he got sick. It's not anything he ate or drank. Not an insect. And not AIDS. He grins. Sick jokes for sick boys. Nadine shoves him. First of all, he's not contagious anymore. She doesn't need a mask when they make out.

Anyway. He tries to explain. With a voice that sounds weaker and weaker. The doctor in Bern said it's meningitis. A type of meningitis, anyways. The virus had a Latin name. He has it written down in his bag. It can last for weeks and there's not much you can do for it. Only rest and rest and rest. He has pills for the fever in one of his bags. Otherwise it's rest that counts. Drink a lot of water. Try to stay hydrated and eat as much as you can.

He stops explaining. His eyelids are getting heavy. Nadine wants to ask him about Kalim. Did he have the same thing? About the money. The inheritance. But Daniel is on his way out. He shuts his eyes. Nadine almost starts crying again.

She takes in all the details. The pale light from the living room turns everything gray. His sunken cheeks. His hair. The blotchy red spots on his neck. Daniel's nails look long. A little dry and yellow. He has more small bruises on his hands. They look very AIDS-ish. Fuck, imagine if he did have something like that. She could have it too.

She sits looking at him for a long time. Too tired and worked up to do anything else. He coughs. She jumps. He moves slightly. And she's ready to call an ambulance. Or start crying.

She lies down beside him. On her side of the bed. Holds his hot, dry hand. Sees that it's two o'clock. It starts raining outside. Beats against the windowpanes. Monday afternoon.

She wakes up to him falling out of bed. He tried to go to the bathroom but his legs gave out. He's angry and embarrassed. Teary-eyed. She reassures him. Nags him to go to the hospital, but he refuses.

'Just be glad I can still wipe,' he mutters when he's back in bed.

'You're not puking. Want something to eat?'

'In a bit,' says Daniel. And sleeps for another thirty hours. Nadine gets a little water in him a couple of times. And helps him to the bathroom. It's like trying to get a sleepwalker with a boner to pee. So fucked up, darling. Some parts don't get sick, apparently. She changes his sheets. For the most part, he's totally gone. She checks the internet to make sure you can't sleep yourself to death. And it takes a week to die of thirst. Thanks Wikipedia.

She sleeps a little beside him. Wakes up and runs around. Puts away his things. The computer bag with his laptop and a couple of notebooks. With rubber bands around them, Kalim-style. Ancient stacks of yellowed paper. His Samsonite luggage. More papers. Bundles and binders and books. A black coffer that can't be opened. A couple of candles. More presents from Mr Adell? Everything smells like cinnamon for some reason. Daniel seems to have thrown out a bunch of clothes to make room for Kalim's stuff. Maybe Kalim Inc. is saved after all? Good thinking, darling.

She carries all the papers into his office. As well as the

coffer. Peeks at Mr Adell's blue package. Tonight is not the night to open it. She throws all of Daniel's clothes in the laundry. Puts his phone and wallet on the bedside table. Puts his tickets and passport beside them. She finds the medicine in his computer bag. Yellow bottles with little pills in them. Brown and white. A bigger bottle with some kind of ointment. It smells like death and menthol.

The sky outside is gray. She goes and makes some coffee. Eats a sandwich. She goes and does this. And goes and does that. And goes and goes and goes and goes. Then she sleeps. Next to Daniel. Waking up when he coughs. Lies there listening to him breathe. She sleeps again. Wakes up without knowing what time it is. Falls back asleep. Wakes up from a strange sound in the hall. An alarm. She shuffles out into the hall. Finds a cell phone in Daniel's jacket. Must have been Kalim's. A Katanga was calling. Isn't Katanga a place in Africa?

She wakes up. Falls asleep. Falls asleep again. Wakes up again, rushes around the apartment for a bit. She changes clothes. Sweater and pants to sweatpants and a housecoat. Then sweatpants and a tank top. It's warm in the apartment. But Daniel's freezing. He sits in bed watching TV. You can pretty much live in a Hästens, as it turns out. She rests her hand on Daniel's chest. So she can feel if he stops breathing. The slightest cough wakes her.

'Are you taking your medicine?' she asks when he manages to change his T-shirt by himself. It's like he's moving in slow motion.

'Of course I am.'

'I don't know. Maybe you're hiding them under your tongue.'

'Hiding them from you? Why?'

'I don't know.'

'Why do you think I'm like this all the time?' He nods at his crotch.

'From the pills?'

'Duh, sweetie. Works like Viagra.'

She pours some juice in him and forces some kiwi and toast into him. Makes him go to the bathroom and take a shower. This time he can stand up by himself. He comes back in a bathrobe. Still pale, bruised, and with a boner. Smiles and jokes that he doesn't know what day it is. Nadine doesn't either. The sky outside is always gray, more or less.

'Really?'

'Yeah, I think it's Wednesday.'

'You really don't know?'

'No.' Nadine looks towards the living room. 'It's dark out though.'

'That doesn't help. Weren't you watching TV?'

'Just *Friends*. Phoebe is pregnant.'

Daniel looks confused. 'Phoebe?'

'Phoebe Buffay.'

'Buffay?'

'Yeah, from *Friends*.'

'Not ringing a bell. I'm sorry.' Daniel shakes his head. Nadine doesn't know what to do. Daniel, who can recite long chunks of *Friends*, suddenly doesn't remember who Phoebe Buffay is. Now that's scary.

'It's strange,' he says. 'It feels like I'm forgetting things. When I was in customs in Bern, it hit me that I couldn't remember my social security number. It's like my brain has shrunk.'

'Scary.'

'How do you remember what it is you've forgotten?'

They're quiet. Nadine tries to think of something to say. All she can think of is the retirement home she worked at after high school. The terror in the old people's eyes when they understood they were starting to forget things. That their brains were dying. That their memories, their identities, were dying. As if they were drowning. Trapped in an old, broken body.

Daniel crawls closer to her. 'I can lie here while you watch TV.' He puts his hand on her stomach. Gently, as if he's afraid she'll say no. His head against her arm. She strokes his cheek. He's asleep in a few moments. With his hard-on against her thigh. He smells like that nasty ointment. It tickles her nose.

A little later he tries to go to the toilet by himself. He makes it two steps before falling to the ground. His legs just give out. Nadine screams and throws herself towards him. Daniel swears and holds his knee. It's hard to hear what he's saying. He mumbles like he can't remember the words. She helps him onto the bed. Asks ten times how he's feeling. He promises to ask for help next time. They fall asleep holding hands.

When she wakes up again his hand has moved. To her breast. Under her top. It's rough and warm. And dry as paper. On TV there's a panel of judges discussing something. Dancing, maybe. His knee is on top of hers. She doesn't know what day it is. But he's rock hard against her thigh. Still. She presses her thigh against the hardness. Carefully. She thinks about men who die from too much sex. Retirees who marry models. She presses a little again. And again. Slowly, as if her hip is following her breathing. It tingles in her stomach. He presses back. Lightly. Nadine's heart starts racing. She wants him. Fever or not.

They lie like that for a long time. Slowly rocking. Everything smells like nasty balm and warm skin. She starts fantasizing. *The Erotic Castle* flashes by. Dark, stately looking men in cloaks. And a ton of fucking. They're sitting together on the sofa. Holding each other's hand and being very quiet. They're watching porn. Drinking white wine. There's fucking on TV. She can't bring herself to look at him. She's wearing her most expensive lingerie. And not much else. She hits fast forward. Until she's lying on the sofa. With her legs around his neck. On TV they're also eating pussy. She sips her wine and watches. Makes a wet spot on the couch. Comes so hard she almost breaks his neck. Swedish boys, darling.

They're not afraid to go down on you. Because they know what they'll get in return.

She tries to move. To move her hand down. Daniel coughs. And coughs again. He rolls away from her. Turns over. Nadine swears silently. She itches all over. She wants to scratch, pick, scrape. But she goes for a cigarette on the balcony instead.

The phone rings after a few hours. Daniel's phone. He doesn't answer 'Engman' like usual. Instead: 'Hello?' Then he starts speaking English. About books and deeds and wire transfers. He's picked up Kalim's weird accent. It happens sometimes when people work together.

He hangs up and takes a deep breath. Drinks some water. Nadine asks the big question. The one big question. The one that is linked to all the others.

'What happens now?'

'With what?'

'With the job. Does the company still exist?'

'Yeah.' Daniel looks as if he'd like to dodge the question. 'It's complicated. A bunch of paperwork that should exist, doesn't. Because Kalim wasn't his own company, legally speaking. He was just his own investor.'

Nadine nods. So far she's keeping up.

'And he wasn't so good with paperwork.'

'I can see that.'

'He didn't even have a real firm before I started working for him. You understand?'

'What?' Nadine has only heard Daniel complain that Kalim was lazy with paperwork. This is worse. Maybe a disaster. 'No firm? Who was paying you then?'

'John Kalim Aziz, the individual. His billing address is in Ankara.'

'That's just crazy.'

Daniel nods. His eyes are foggy with fever. He looks translucent. But still healthier than when he came home. Nadine wants to scream the question.

'So what happens now?' She sounds like she's asking if he wants more coffee.

'What do you mean? The stuff I've organized is still fair game. The rest will collect dust waiting for an heir. It's all kind of a mess.'

'The heirs?'

'All of it.'

'What about you?'

'Me?'

'Yes.' She wants to scream at him.

'I'll keep working for the company.' Her smile is reflected in his eyes.

'How long?'

'For now.' He smiles at her greed. 'So you can have more furs.'

Nadine squirms nervously. Is it that obvious? She feels embarrassed. And Daniel grins. In an unpleasant way she's never seen before. Triumphant. Deathly pale with splotches on his throat.

'If you're a good girl, I mean.' Daniel laughs. And coughs. Nadine doesn't know how to respond. He's never called her out before. Although he knows that she loves money. Although he knows that she likes to be the richest sibling, the sibling with the best clothes and the best life. She was like that already, long before Östermalm. She wanted to get far away from those idiots in Hallunda. Be rich and Swedish. Earn her own money. And Daniel was a perfect part of that plan. He knows that, even if they've never talked about it. And now he's falling asleep before she can think of anything to say.

She sits out on the sofa for a long time. Teary-eyed and angry. And with her future secure. As long as he doesn't leave her. As long as he doesn't die. Better make sure he survives and feels pampered. They should get married. Or else sign some kind of agreement. Civil union or whatever it's called.

She walks out into the kitchen. Makes tea. Goes to the

living room. Looks out the window. It's raining a little. She should call a doctor. She goes back into the kitchen and butters a couple of crackers. She crawls in next to Daniel again. Tea and crackers and horror movies on TV. Some lunatic slicing people up with a knife. So lame.

She wakes up in the middle of the night. He's coughing and drinking water. Mumbling to himself. Some kind of strange chant. It sounds like a nursery rhyme in Italian or something. He's delirious.

'Daniel?'

Daniel mumbles something. Starts to cough. Waves at her in the darkness. He lies back down and searches for her hand with his.

'No worries. Just a raging fever.' He laughs.

'How did he die?'

'What?'

'Kalim. What happened?'

'He got sick the day after we got there. A little after me. I got really bad that night. But he got way sicker than me. And then he died. I was pretty out of it then. So I don't know.'

'Were you there when he died?'

'No. They didn't even wake me up.'

'Were you in the same room?'

'Same floor. Nice rooms. Like a regular hotel. They had really cute nurses. And nice sheets.'

Nadine yawned. There was so much she wanted to ask. Weren't you at a hotel when he died? But it didn't seem important. She wasn't even sure she wanted to know.

'Did you see him?'

'Kalim?'

'After he died?'

'Yeah.'

'Was it scary?'

'He looked like a dead Kalim. An empty shell. The soul had sailed onward.' Gay voice and Kalim gesture.

'Huh?'

Daniel smiles tiredly. 'I'm really not funny anymore. Sorry. He passed away in his sleep, as far as I know. Without much pain.'

'Did he know he was going to die?'

'Kalim? I don't think so. Why?'

'Just wondering. It would be so awful to know, I think.'

He kisses her forehead. He smells like that horrible ointment. He asks her to light one of the candles he brought back with him. Some kind of aromatherapy. Sort of like incense. They suggested them at the hospital. Strange but true. She gets a little dish and a candle and puts it on his bedside table. The candle is grayish-black and smells like cinnamon. It smells even more when she lights it.

She falls asleep and dreams about Kalim. He's dead and lying on a stretcher surrounded by thousands of white lilies. Three signs that you're seriously losing your marbles. One: You dream about your boyfriend's dead boss. Two: You think that everything in your bedroom smells like cinnamon. Three: You look at the clock without really understanding it. She finally just turns it off. Pulls the cord out of the wall. And goes back to sleep.

She wakes up and sleeps and wakes up again. Once, Daniel's on the toilet when she turns over. It feels surreal. The second time he's sitting up and smearing his chest with that balm. A third time she wakes up and lies for hours staring at the snakes on the ceiling. She falls asleep again. She dreams Daniel's smearing the balm on her breasts. She wakes up with the stench still in her nose. The telephone had rung. Kalim's. Daniel had taken it into the bedroom. He was probably talking to someone about the funeral or something.

She gets up and goes shopping. More juice and toast and kiwi. She nags Daniel for ten minutes before she leaves. Call me if something happens. Call 911 if it's an emergency.

He's in the little dining room when she comes back. In

his bathrobe. On his knees, on the floor. Bent forward over a pile of paper. He looks up and seems dejected. He's opened several boxes. Like he's looking for something.

'What are you doing?'

'I just had to check something. A customer called. I'll be done soon.'

'Are you sad?'

'Right now, yeah. It catches up with you. I didn't care before. I just wanted some peace and quiet. And sleep. There's a bunch of Swiss people that want me to fill out a bunch of paperwork about him.'

'Swiss?'

'Yeah, they love paperwork.'

'I thought you were in Belgium. In Bern.'

'Bern is in Switzerland.' He does one of those Kalim gestures he's adopted. 'Everybody knows that.'

Nadine blushes. 'Public school.'

'Huh?'

'We didn't learn that in public school.'

Daniel stares vacantly at her. Nadine wants to scream. How can you forget that? It's one of our things. That we always say. If there's something Nadine doesn't know, we blame public school. Always, always, public school. Everything is public school's fault. If the bus is late or if Nadine burns the food. Public school. But Daniel on the floor in the little dining room has no idea. She can see it in his eyes. What happened to you? She has to call some kind of brain doctor.

She walks away. Leaves him with his papers and his binders. She walks around and around and around the apartment. It suddenly feels small. The ceiling is lower. Claustrophobia, darling. People need air. But Daniel's always freezing. He's curled up in bed, staring at the flame of the cinnamon candle. Everything smells like sickbed and balm and cinnamon. She wants to call Cecilia. But she can't find her phone. It's gone.

She finds Daniel in the bathroom a few hours later. He's

standing at the sink with his shirt off. He has a few of those horrible blotches on his back as well. Did he have those when she helped him into the shower? Then she sees it. He's swaying to and fro with his eyes closed. Drool coming from the corners of his mouth. She's got to get him back to bed. He's shaking all over. He's like jelly. Except for the erection. It never quits.

'I get nervous when you go out,' he says a few days later. They're eating toast and fruit soup in bed. Nadine hasn't worn proper clothes since she went shopping.

'We need real food. Now that you can finally eat a little.'

'We can call someone. I know a place. Kalim talked about it.'

'Won't that be expensive?'

'We have money. Don't you remember, baby?'

Soon it all becomes routine. The ghost taking care of the cripple. Sitting beside him, watching TV. Fetching him drinks. Daniel lives off kiwi, toast, and apple juice. Nadine off of small salads and crackers. It's a cinch getting food delivered. James, the cute black guy in an expensive sweatsuit, comes up from the fancy food hall. He flirts shamelessly. Calls Nadine 'cutie pie'. So ridiculous. He's a one-man operation who goes around shopping for people. The second time he comes, he says he can get wine and beer too. And go to the pharmacy. The third time he offers coke, speed, massage, and housekeeping. Östermalm, darling. Östermalm.

She calls Cecilia from Daniel's phone. Hers is broken. She found it in the bathroom. Smashed on the floor. She lies in bed next to Daniel, talking. Holding his hand. He's snoring and looks awful. She tells Cecilia the story. About Kalim's death. How sick Daniel is. She doesn't talk about the money. Cecilia has met a guy at the dog groomer's. A security guard. Kurdish. He has a Rottweiler and an Audi and lives in Sätra. Good work, Cecilia. Someone from outside Botkyrka. They should all get together when Daniel's better. Sometime soon.

Daniel's sweating profusely. Nadine changes the bedding and washes it in the washing machine in the guest bathroom. She hangs the sheets all around the apartment. Daniel refuses to take pain medication. He only takes the pills from Bern. Every time Nadine suggests they talk to a doctor, he gets irritated. But yet he can cough for half an hour straight. Any time of the day. Or suddenly have a sky-high fever. He lies still, mumbling and mumbling, with his eyes moving back and forth under his eyelids. And so it goes. Day in, day out. The phone rings a couple of times a day. Daniel answers and speaks English or German. German with the customs agency in Switzerland. English with Kalim's relatives. Time flies by. They pull the curtains closed and crank up the heat. Hide themselves under all the sheets. Sit and soak up the light from the TV or the cinnamon candles. Daniel says it's harder to ship a dead person to Amman than a living one. And he says Kalim's family doesn't seem to care much about him. Who is the relative?

'One of his mother's cousins.'

'Didn't you say it was an aunt?'

'Do I look like I speak Arabic?'

'Didn't he have anyone else?'

'Apparently not.'

The conversation dies off. Daniel doesn't like to talk about Kalim. He's probably just scared. If he doesn't talk about death he won't die.

She comes out of the bathroom. Naked, with only a towel around her waist. The fifth day or so. She'd forgotten her robe in the bedroom. The light on the ceiling is gray, so it's probably morning. She walks past the sheets that are lying across the dining room table. Daniel's taken several calls since she woke up. She lay beside him listening as he spoke. He's gotten really good at German. He just has to stop talking like Kalim. It sounds silly. Especially German with an Arabic accent.

The bedroom stinks of balm from Daniel and cinnamon from the candle. It's most noticeable after she showers. He's sitting up in bed. With half-open eyes. Half-watching TV. In half-darkness. She comes in. Topless. Walks over to the closet. He moves in the bed behind her.

'You're beautiful, baby.' His voice is like a whisper. A news anchor is speaking English on TV. Nadine can't remember the last time he called her 'baby'. Before he got sick, at least. Her bottom lip starts to tremble.

'Turn around. I want to see you.'

She turns around. Slowly and not as sensually as she would have liked. She hasn't worked out in a week. Only eaten and slept and washed the sheets. There's a skull peering up at her. Shadows hiding its eyes. Daniel has disappeared. Something thin and pale and starving is sitting in her and Daniel's bed. Something with yellow nails. It's smiling.

'It feels like I've never seen you like this before.'

'It's been a while.'

'Yes. Eons. But I've wanted to.'

Nadine is suddenly afraid. Something is very wrong. She doesn't want this skull looking at her.

'Lose the towel.'

She does as she's told. Relaxes the hands holding the towel. It falls around her feet. She has never felt so naked. The eyes in the shadows look closely. Study her. Curiously. Her eyes wander from the skull to the thing standing up under the sheets. And back again. She doesn't want this. She wants to turn the light on. To scare away the monster.

'Come here.'

She obeys. Crawls in next to him. Death's Head Daniel shows her the way. Gently and assertively. Lie here. Like this. Under the sheets. He pulls them over her. He's hot and dry. Wearing only an undershirt. And stinking of ointment. Menthol. What was it for? And when did he take his pajama pants off?

He touches her. Carefully. Slowly. His hands move over her skin. Exploring. And for a second she's sure. Those are not Daniel's hands. But her hands recognize his body. It's emaciated, but it's his. Warm and menthol-scented, but Daniel all the same. Right body, wrong hands.

His hands examine her breasts. Not aroused. Not arousing. She lies still with her cheek on his shoulder. She can hardly hear his heart. Death's Head Daniel has no pulse. God, so fucked, darling. She's being examined. Back. Shoulders. Waist. Slowly and breathlessly.

She calms down. It's easier when she can't see the horrible face. He's just been sick, think about it. You haven't cuddled for weeks. Much less fucked. It's just Daniel, after all. The same Daniel as always. If a little skinnier. Her Daniel who's employed by, and now the boss of, Kalim Enterprises. She caresses his stomach. Under his shirt. A little sexier. Presses against him. He strokes her lower back. Her neck.

Time passes. Eons. Nadine notices that she has a cock only a few centimeters from her nose. It's just there. Imagine. In the darkness, under the sheets. Early morning in the crypt. Kalim's bedroom. The room that smells of cinnamon and has snakes on the ceiling. It can only go one way. She does what's expected of her, almost too eagerly. He's rock hard. And she takes him into her mouth like she's been training her whole life for it. Like a Swedish girl. Like the boys in Hallunda can only dream of.

She sucks gently. Like he's made of glass and glacé and could shatter any second. He lies still. Stroking her neck. She forgets the heat and the menthol stench and just sucks. Three hot tips when you find a boner in the crypt. One: Make eye contact. Peek up through the tunnel of blankets and feverish chest and towards the gazing skull. Smile. And he smiles back. Two: When the telephone rings, don't stop. Because the skull is smiling and nodding. And you smile back as flirtatiously as possible with a mouth full of meat. Three: Don't panic when he starts speaking Arabic. Because he's smiling and smiling, hoping you're in on the joke.

She manages to pretend like nothing's wrong for half a minute. Without his noticing. Almost a minute. She doesn't bite down. Then she throws off the duvet. Mimes 'gotta pee' and stumbles out of bed. Naked, with her ass to the wind. Death's Head Daniel grins and waves. Naked from the waist down. A skeleton with a hard-on. Who can speak Arabic.

In the bathroom everything is menthol and nausea. She rinses her mouth. Brushes her teeth. And rinses her mouth again. She's never done that before. Not once. Not with the two before Daniel. She's never felt so disgusted. When did he learn Arabic? What the hell is going on? What the hell is with him? Dementia makes you forget. Not learn new things. 'Brain damage only goes one way.' That's what Katarina at the retirement home said. Don't bother trying to teach them anything.

She collects herself. Quickly. She must not show her fear. Or surprise. Or anything at all. Listen: nothing happened. Nothing at all. Just a little misunderstanding. There, there. She splashes water on her face. Suddenly aware of how naked she is. She grabs a pair of panties and a T-shirt from the laundry basket. Puts them on. Tries to understand. But she doesn't understand. She's just scared.

Death's Head Daniel is lying in bed, reading in the candle-light. A book. One of the weird books from the little dining room. A Kalim-book. That alone is fucked up. He looks up and waves. Nadine smiles and waves back. She goes to the kitchen and makes a couple of sandwiches and pours some juice. Everything tastes like menthol.

It's afternoon now. She thinks. She does the dishes. Does another load of laundry. Waves to Daniel. She paces back and forth and back and forth. Eats some toast. Changes clothes three times. She brings bundles of clothes out into the dining room so he won't see her naked. She only wants him to see her in nice clothes. It seems so important. To be loved. By Daniel. By the thing that looks like Daniel. She calls Shopper James and asks him to buy a set of ladies pajamas or two. Luxurious ones. 'I'll find something that makes you look even more fantastic.' And sheets. 'Black?' Good idea, darling. She kisses Daniel on the forehead fairly often.

Late at night she wakes up. Or dreams she does. He's rubbing her chest with that damned ointment. He's gotten her top off somehow. He plays with her nipples. Pinches them teasingly. Everything looks like a movie to her. His yellow nails against her Greek skin. White skin vs. nougat. She whimpers a little. She screams when he bends over her. His face has fallen off. All that's left is a black hole whispering in Arabic.

He's sitting in bed speaking French on the phone. The new black sheets make him look even paler. She sits beside him watching Ricki Lake. Red hot in off-white silk lingerie. Crazy fat-asses are arguing on TV. Daniel thinks it's funny. Just like old Daniel did. Although new Daniel has never heard of Halo. Nadine brings in the new Xbox. The 360, with a supersized hard drive. She hooks it up to the TV in the bedroom.

'Play a little?'

'Play what?'

'Halo? We're only halfway through.'

Daniel looks indifferent at first. Then the skull straightens up and says: 'I'm a little hazy again.'

'Again?'

'I'm sorry.'

'Sorry?'

'That I don't remember.'

'You don't remember Halo? The MasterChief?'

'No.' Daniel looks sad. Nadine shrugs. Downplays it.

'Oh well.' Nadine looks kindly at him. Speaks in her retirement home voice. 'Let's do something else then.'

She laughs inside her head. Because she's realized something. That Daniel's never told anyone how much he loves Xbox. Playing Halo with a glass of wine. Everyone at his job, his old job, tried to get him to play golf. But Daniel wanted to play video games. And he was afraid they'd think he was immature. Nadine is suddenly sure. Daniel has some kind of amnesia. He's not himself. And what are you if you're not yourself? Someone else. Except not like the demented old hags at the old folks' home. They turned into nobody at all. Whoever was home in their old heads moved out and left nothing behind. This was different. She's got to read up on personality changes.

Another day goes by. Daniel speaks more Arabic on the phone. And another day. The vigil ticks on and on. Erections and toast and a bunch of weird kinds of tea Daniel suddenly has a taste for. They have ten different tins of them in the kitchen. Nadine has stopped keeping track of what day it is. They sit in bed like usual. Half naked and half asleep. Nadine staring at the TV and Daniel 2.0 with a book. Then, suddenly, the doorbell rings. They both jump.

'Who is it?' Daniel sounds almost scared. Nadine turns off the TV.

'No idea.'

'Could it be the negro with the food?'

'He doesn't come unless you call him.' Nadine swallows at the word 'negro'. A word Daniel never would have used.

The doorbell rings again. What time is it? Afternoon?

'Check who it is. Through the peephole.' He grabs her arm. 'Shh. We're not home.' He sounds completely insane. 'Don't open it for anyone. Understand?'

Nadine nods and runs out into the hall. Who is he afraid of? Has he tried to rip off Kalim's family? Are they here to demand their share of the inheritance? Are they going to kick the door down? She creeps up to the door. Checks the peephole.

Eva-Lena Engman is in the stairwell. We weren't prepared for that. The mother-in-law strikes back, darling. With shawl and beret and in all likelihood orthopedic shoes. Nadine can't see them. There's a bag of groceries in the way. Eva-Lena tinkers with her phone. Looks concerned.

Nadine runs into the bedroom. Daniel is up. With a book and a bottle in his hand. Kalim-junk. He had been to the little dining room to grab it. Inconceivable. His boxers are bulging like usual. He looks ridiculous.

'It's your mother,' she whispers.

'You didn't open it, did you?'

'No.'

'Good.' Daniel looks relieved. 'Is she alone?'

'She's alone. She has a bag of groceries with her.'

'I don't want to see her. Not like this.' Daniel calms down. Puts the book and bottle on the bedside table. 'We'll just wait for her to leave.'

'I can handle it. I'll say you're sleeping.'

'No, she'll want to come in. Does she have a key?'

Daniel's phone starts to ring. It rings twice before Daniel presses busy.

'I want to be left alone. It's enough having you see me like this.'

'It's not so bad.'

'Yeah, it is. I look like a zombie.'

Nadine nods. Tries to take control. She called Eva-Lena on like, the first day. Told her Daniel was sick. Not much to do but wait. No, he wasn't going to die. Otherwise we're good, thanks. Take care. They didn't speak very often. And she hadn't talked to Evert Engman. They were divorced and Evert lived in Tranås. A boring old man. Of course she hadn't talked to her own family. What did they have to do with it?

She turns on the TV again. Daniel gets up to shave. Comes back and takes out his book. Kalim's book. He reads something handwritten. Like it was nothing new. Nadine lies staring at the snakes on the ceiling. If you squint, they almost look like they're moving. She's so tired. So tired.

'Shall we order some real food?' Daniel sounds totally normal. Just a little hoarse.

'In a bit.'

'When then?'

'When I've slept.'

'OK. Sweet dreams.'

She sleeps. And sleeps. Daniel smears her with ointment again, or so she dreams. He talks on the phone. English and that language that has to be Arabic. The snakes crawl down from the ceiling and all over her. They creep under her new pajamas. Fondle her. She dreams that she wakes up when she comes. And Daniel is still asleep next to her. He smiles in his sleep.

The next day she gets breakfast in bed. Sushi. Daniel has called Shopper James and ordered some real food. He's in a good mood. He feeds her fish and jokes about his memory loss. It feels like he's teasing her. He talked to one of Kalim's relatives. They've buried Kalim. There was some issue with the fact that Muslims are supposed to be buried within twenty-four hours, but they worked it out.

'Was Kalim Muslim?' She puts her sushi tray on the floor.

'About as much as you're Greek Orthodox.'

'And what about the company?'

'As far as they know there is no company.'

Nadine tries to keep up with the legal jargon. Or pretends to at least. 'So they had no idea that Kalim had a company that sold books?'

' "Antiques" is what it says on the document.' He makes a gesture that Nadine doesn't understand.

'Antiques.'

'It's got to say something.'

'Anyway.' Nadine feels how impatient she's getting. 'What *do* they know? What happens with the money?'

'Nothing.'

'What?'

'They don't know anything about the company.' Daniel grins. Looks down at her. Strokes her cheek with his index finger.

'Huh? What does that mean?'

'That they get nothing. They can't inherit something they don't know exists.'

Nadine is almost holding her breath. Tries to understand. 'Are we ripping them off?'

'Kalim is.'

'But he's dead.'

'Yeah. But a corporation doesn't die just because the owner does.'

'So who owns the corporation then?'

'Now, or in a few weeks?'

'In a few weeks.'

Daniel smiles his death's head smile. Draws tiny circles on her cheek. Outlines her mouth with a sharp fingernail. Fiddles with her lip. It's both sexy and annoying. 'A guy who you're soon going to throw yourself at and kiss.'

Nadine blushes. And exhales for an eternity. 'Is it true?'

Daniel nods. His finger gently pries open her mouth. Like a hook in her lower jaw. Like she was a fish. He pulls her towards him. Up to a sitting position. The finger tastes dry. She follows along with his movements. Pulling herself up until she's on her knees in the bed, wearing only panties and a pajama shirt, and sucking his finger. She holds him around the waist and wonders who he is. He is *so* not Daniel. Daniel is the teddy bear type. Despite being skinny. A nice, skinny teddy bear, she thinks while she sucks his finger. Never porn-star moves like this. Her pajamas just fall right off. He works another finger into her mouth. Nadine sucks hard. One part of her rubs her breast against his stubborn erection. Another part doesn't know whether to laugh or scream. A third part wants to ask an important question.

He lets her off the hook. Runs his fingers through her hair.

She kisses his stomach. Presses herself against him. Searches for something to rub against. A knee, anything.

'How much?' she asks, breathing heavily. 'How much?'

'You're so nosy. How much what?'

'How much money?' You can almost have an orgasm just by saying 'money', darling. It all depends whose money you're talking about.

'Maybe three million kronor in cash and bonds.'

Nadine can only moan.

'Plus fixed assets.'

'What's that?'

'Apartments. Books.'

'How much in total?'

'Forty million kronor maybe.'

Nadine falls out of bed. Her legs just, like, disappear. And the bed too. And there she is, lying there. In her panties. On the floor. Pretty ugly panties, too. With pain in her back and neck. Daniel looks down at her. He looks surprised. Then he smiles. Tries not to laugh. Holds his hand over his mouth.

'You okay?'

'Uh huh.'

'Don't get too euphoric.'

Nadine has never heard that word before. But she can guess. Some gay lingo for horny, maybe. She smiles. Mumbles something. Covers herself. She's got to shave her legs. She's really let herself go.

'Be careful, babe.' Death's Head Daniel watches her pick herself up. Scrutinizes her. Doesn't lift a finger to help her. 'I've got to get myself together before you suck me dry,' he says. 'You'll have to contain yourself for a few more days.'

He keeps staring at her until she goes out to the dining room to get dressed. Rich and constantly stared at. Strange. Everything's so fucking strange all the time now. Daniel's on the phone in the bedroom. Speaking what could be Italian.

He sounds more and more like Kalim. She's got to shave her legs.

Later. He's asleep and she's watching a movie. She peeks over at her very own millionaire every now and then. He actually looks quite all right in daylight. Healthier. The sushi did him some good. Ridiculous, but true. He's a little healthier. An enormous weight lifts off her chest. However nuts Daniel's become, he's going to survive. Now they can focus on Kalim's money instead of gnawing on kiwi.

She watches as the dust swirls around in the light from the living room window. It's not raining. She thinks about calling Cecilia. Or Eva-Lena. She needs advice. She realizes now that Death's Head Daniel is worth a ton of money. And with all the changes, personality-wise, he could very well decide that he needs some personnel changes to match. Daniel and Nadine could become just Daniel at the drop of a hat. That's a tough one. So, how does one become a part of Kalim Inc.? One gets pregnant, or marries the death's head. Or else one tries to become a shareholder.

The simplest thing was to get pregnant. Death's Head Daniel is a horny dude, so it shouldn't take much. Then she'd be stuck with a kid for the next twenty years. One year per million. Thanks, darling. Nadine isn't really into children. So that would mean making him share the load. But Nadine is pretty sure the new Daniel wouldn't go for it. It's just not his style. He wants to go around with his office in his back pocket, Kalim-style. So for her that means getting a spot in the pocket.

The sushi has perked Daniel up. Or the thought of being eaten. Either way, he's gotten healthier and healthier. But he still looks pale. And the strange bruises are still there. Along with the yellow nails and the relentless erection. He reads a lot of Kalim's books. Stares at her a lot. Sits in his office writing emails. He starts getting weird cravings. He wants steak. And then fruit. And then lots of beans. Like he's pregnant or something. He orders things he's never eaten before. Chick-peas. Halloumi. Even more tea and wild honey. Weird pastes smeared on bread. James had a lot of running around to do. Nadine starts ordering wine too. Chugging wine is nice. It takes the edge off it all. Every time he smiles and says something friendly, she answers. Just as friendly. Thanks! A little olive oil on bread really is good, darling. It's just that Daniel liked butter and salami on his sandwiches. He didn't call her 'baby' all the time. But he did spend a lot of time in his office. As much then as now. Among the stacks and stacks of paper. Yellow and white and gray and old. She stands in the doorway and sees him sitting in Daniel's chair. With his back to her. With a teacup and an old book in front of him. The one who used to be Daniel reads slowly. The text looks handwritten. Sprawling and smudged. Medieval doodles. Daniel never drank tea. The only thing medieval he ever did was watch *Ivanhoe* on New Year's Day. Daniel watched football and sit-coms. *Friends*. Or *Weeds*. Fake reality, he called it.

Nadine looks into prenups online. Without any written agreement, she has rights to all of her clothes and jewelry if they get divorced. And a reasonable share of all household items. Every second frying pan sort of thing. Half the coffee mugs. Death's Head Daniel gets Kalim Inc., Nadine gets the monster microwave. She looks up personality changes too. Could be symptoms of something called Huntington's disease. Or dementia. It doesn't say anything about learning new languages from dementia. To suddenly know a new language used to be considered a sure sign of demonic possession. See 'exorcism'. And take a big swig of wine.

Two days later, Daniel's healthy. All of a sudden, darling. After one last feverish night. When Nadine wakes up he's in the shower. Without having woken her up. She wasn't expecting that. She hears him come out of the shower. Hears him making bathroom noises. It makes her feel safe.

She pretends to be sleeping when he comes back in. Watches him through her eyelashes. He's naked. Walking all on his own. Jesus Christ, he's skinny. A walking skeleton, darling. With bruises from his groin to his armpits. And a boner, as per usual. We need a long vacation. A few weeks at least. Lots of food and sun. Until we're as brown as ginger snaps. And see if we can't tire out that cock a little.

'Are you sleeping?' he wheezes.

And we'll drink tequila until his voice returns to normal. And tea with honey.

'No. But I'm dreaming.'

'I feel good.'

'Good.'

'Really good.'

'You have no idea how happy that makes me.'

'Tonight we celebrate. What do you want to eat?'

'Sushi?'

'You have no imagination. I'll call the negro and order a little Greek food.'

Nadine really hates it when he calls James 'the negro' but she smiles with her whole face. 'Awesome.'

They smile like idiots, both of them.

'I've got to get dolled up.'

'Me too.'

Daniel tidies up. Cleans a little. Moves some furniture around. Takes out things they've put away, and puts away others. Nadine locks herself in the bathroom with her Ladyshave and boxed wine. Lies in the bathtub for over an hour. Shaving and plucking and drinking wine. It feels so decadent to smoke in the tub.

When she's finally done in the bathroom, the apartment looks different. It still stinks of that damn cinnamon. Do the candles never end? It takes a while before she sees what else he's done. Daniel's moved stuff around. Taken out things they had put away. And vice versa. The apartment looks more and more like the first time they saw it. The way Kalim had it. A bunch of Kalim's stuff is on display. Candlesticks and weird bowls. And there are books everywhere. It's like the mess in the little dining room crawled out into the apartment again.

Nadine tries to wrap her head around it. The doorbell rings. Daniel yells from his office. 'The negro's bringing food. Open if it's him.' She loses her train of thought. Forgets what she was thinking about and runs to the door. In 800 kronor panties and a silk kimono. So Östermalm.

James is a ray of sunshine. He sets the food down. Eyes her up and down shamelessly.

'Sweetie,' he says, sounding gayer than gay. 'You look wonderful.'

Nadine smiles. 'All women look good like this.'

'Don't be so modest.'

He sniffs. Takes in the smell of the apartment. 'So,' he says. 'Incense. Kalim's back. Where has he been?'

Nadine answers without thinking. 'Abroad.'

'Could have guessed. He must be filthy rich.'

Nadine nods. And realizes she can't run away in only kimono and panties.

'Good catch,' winks James. 'I'm impressed. They say he mostly likes guys.' More winking. 'You must be something special.'

Nadine backpedals from the conversation. She hurries back into the apartment. Closes the door and stands shaking for a second. Everything falls into place. He thinks he's Kalim. Maybe it was the shock of Kalim dying. Did he panic? Did he decide that he would save Kalim's money by turning into Kalim?

Or even worse. If Kalim was gay? Were they lovers? Did they have a relationship? Incredibly fucking disgusting. Her boyfriend getting pounded by a bald old man. She should kill them both. Raging Macedonian morals.

She collects herself. Dries her tears. The scent of cinnamon is nauseating. She yells. 'Food's here!'

'I'll set the table!' shouts the person she shares an apartment with. Whoever it is. 'You go get dressed.'

Nadine puts the bags of food in the dining room and goes to put her makeup on. It's hard to put on eyeliner when your hands are shaking. She hears Daniel Kalim Engman doing something in the office. Hears him walk by outside. She's afraid. Afraid of him. And angry. And so not sure what to wear. Whether she should seduce him or kill him. Or eat a little tzatziki and pretend it's raining.

A dress? Too much, darling. Something more casual? Pajamas? What clothes signal what? She wants to be stunning. But for whom? And what kind of stunning? And why? What does she want from Daniel Kalim Skullsson really? A share of the money? To avoid having to move out? If he's really lost his mind, then he needs help. Should she play along? Try to talk some sense into him? Or run for her life?

Five tips for a successful date night with a mentally ill boyfriend you don't want to piss off. One: Stay calm. Two: Stay calm. Three: Stay calm. Four: Stay calm. Five: Don't wear too many clothes. He calls and Nadine comes. She glides through incense and cinnamon. In only kimono and lingerie and heels. She feels like a fucking porn star wearing heels indoors. Daniel thinks so too. He's staring. With Kalim's eyes. He's lit the candles in the dining room. Both their new ones and a couple of old. There must be thirty candles burning in the room. And the table is set with a mess of antiques and disposable cutlery. Same as always when Daniel and Kalim set the table. Östermalm-trashy, darling. No music, just the noise from the street.

He gestures to where she should sit. Half a table away from where he's sitting. In Kalim's seat from inbred-joke night. In a white shirt. Egyptian cotton. Just as white as he is. Daniel's seat is empty. There's something on his chair. Mr Adell's package.

'Souvlaki? Bifteki?' Daniel gestures towards the contain-ers on the table. 'It kind of turned into a buffet.'

He pulls out a dusty old bottle of wine. 'Our present from Mr Adell. Very exclusive stuff. Greek, appropriately enough. The wine of rapture. Awakens the inner passions, and so on. Perfect for a night like this.'

Nadine smiles. Daniel pours the wine. Nadine tries to remember Daniel's mannerisms. Does he really pour wine like that? Has Daniel ever used the word 'rapture'? Does Daniel really stare so much at her tits? Did he ever do that? He did once. Inbred joke night. The night she sat exactly like this, between them. And after Kalim had left, she understood that they were fighting over her. Competing for her attention. Kalim won one round, but Daniel's the one who got to stay in the apartment with her. And fuck her. Stake his claim. On the dining room table. As soon as Kalim was gone. It was great.

Daniel *had* to remember that. It was one of those moments. It was powerful, and hot, and wonderful. They were newly rich and newly in love and newly moved in. They bought her the fur the next day. Like a thank you, or a sign of things to come.

They talk about the future. Never about money. Daniel wants to go on vacation. Some Greek island. Rest, tan, and swim. Eat tzatziki and lamb and sheep's cheese. Except it's so cold there this time of year. Better try somewhere further south.

'Jordan?'

'And meet the relatives? I can probably swing a trip from the company.'

'The Canary Islands?'

'Thailand.'

'Isn't it super expensive?'

'Is that a problem for us?' The skull smiles.

Nadine smiles too. 'Us' sounds good. She takes a big gulp of wine. Mr Adell's white wine. It's yellow. Thick, sweet, and lukewarm. And fantastic with kebab. Who needs to go to Greece? We have the Östermalm food hall. She tries to concentrate on the food. Not furs and sex and split personality boyfriends on trips to Thailand. She wonders if Kalim is more the marrying type than Daniel. Wonders if that thing over there would get married. Despite the fact that she's a woman. She smiles her brightest smile. Clinks glasses with him. The wine goes down easy. And straight up to her head, darling.

'I could live like this for the rest of my life.'

Daniel Kalimsson smiles and raises his glass. 'The rest of your life? Without ever going out?'

'Once in a while, maybe.'

'The rest of your life with me?'

'Yeah. You can teach me – ' Nadine doesn't say 'Arabic'. She settles for 'accounting or something. So that you can hire me.' The wine rushes through her. Now she knows it's no ordinary wine. And takes another sip.

'The books are in pretty good shape right now. But thanks anyway.' Daniel smiles his skeletal grin. Perv-skull grin. Mean, arrogant, and contemptuous. Nadine realizes that the money is the only thing keeping her in the room, in the apartment, in his presence, in all of this.

'Don't you have any other skills?'

'I can cook and clean.'

'You can't cook.'

'That depends who you compare me to.' Daniel is a decent cook. Kalim buys pre-made stuff that he can arrange and make it look like he did it himself. Cold cuts. Haloumi. Bifteki. Daniel hasn't made anything more complicated than toast since he got back. It doesn't prove anything.

'And you really want to be my maid?'

'Who do you think does all the cleaning around here?'

Daniel ponders for a second. Nadine tries to grab another kebab. It's really difficult. The skewers keep, like, moving around. 'You?'

Nadine nods. Smiles, like there's nothing wrong with the fact that Daniel has yearlong gaps in his memory. And the fact that she's already drunk as a skunk.

'You can be my little servant girl. You'll scrub my floors on your knees?'

Nadine nods. Again. She doesn't even blush.

'Excellent.' He grins that same greedy grin. With bifteki in his mouth and a glass of wine in his hand. 'You said you could live this way for the rest of your life.'

'I could live this way for the rest of my life.'

'Scrubbing my floors?'

'Scrubbing your floors.'

She tries to get up. To walk away, from everything. But she can't. She can hardly keep herself on her chair. The wine rushes through her. Her ears are ringing. Wailing like sirens. And all she can see is Death's Head Daniel sitting and chewing. And observing her drunkenness. Like some kind of experiment. And smiling that new, crooked smile. He looks like he's had a stroke. She wonders if he can explain it. If he's aware of how he's changed. Aware that he's someone else now.

She takes a sip of wine and dips some bread in olive oil. She prepares herself for the attack. The one she's been planning for days.

'What TV shows do you watch?'

'*Weeds*,' Daniel answers without hesitating. And without looking up from his food. 'I love *Weeds*.' She knows he's enjoying the shocked look on her face. That he's dying to see it.

'Favorite food?'

'Whatever you cook.'

'But I can't cook.'

'I know, babe.'

'What do you call my mother?'

'Sofia? Mrs Kirovski?'

'What else?'

'The hydra from Heraklion.'

'Heraklion is in Crete.'

'The monster of Macedonia?' He looks up. Studies her expression. 'No, I just call her Sofia. Same as you, actually. You never call her "mother". And we rarely see her. And we were in Heraklion two years ago, so I know that it's in Crete.'

'What was the name of the hotel?'

'No idea. Do you remember?'

Nadine thinks about it. She doesn't remember either. Something with Blue or Wing or Sun. They all have names like that. And it was the second vacation they took together. And so far, she can still back out of the interrogation. Pretend she's just worried about his memory loss.

'Do you?' He smiles. 'I only remember the cats.'

'Oh yeah.' Sun-something hotel was swarming with cats. 'Do you remember our cat?'

'At the hotel?'

'No, here at home.'

'We've never had a cat. There were so many at the hotel, I can't remember if we named one.'

'Me neither.' Nadine nods. She agrees with that part, at least. Takes a big swig of wine. 'But we did have a cat.'

'Did we?'

'Yeah. On Gullmarsplan.'

'You're lying,' says the thing pretending to be Daniel, matter-of-factly.

'Nope.'

'We have never had a cat.'

'Yup. Her name was Maya.'

'Maya?' He looks down at her. Without getting up. He suddenly seems gigantic. Black-eyed. Threatening.

'Yeah. Maya. She was black.'

'You're lying.'

'No.'

'Why are you lying?'

'Why don't you remember?'

'Why does it matter what I remember?' He stands up. Walks around the table. Nadine has to clench her hands to stop them from shaking. She doesn't dare look up. She can feel him breathing. His eternal boner against her shoulder. He pats her on the cheek. Tenderly and carefully. The hand moves towards the back of her neck. Nadine thinks about sex and about dying and her bottom lip trembles. 'Are you afraid that I'm going senile?'

Nadine nods. 'I want you to be healthy.'

'Because you want to live like this for the rest of your life.'

'I want to live like this for the rest of my life.'

'I am healthy. But I don't remember any cat.'

'We had a cat. Her name was Maya.'

'Why don't I remember that?'

He has his fingers around her neck. In her hair. Stroking her cheek with the other hand. She feels his breath. Everything smells like cinnamon. He can see right into her cleavage. Her ridiculously expensive bra.

'Maybe there's a gap in your memory?'

'You mean that it's gone? That I forgot Maya?'

'Yeah, you must have forgotten.'

'What did she look like?'

'Black. Kind of small.'

'And we had her when we lived on Gullmarsplan?'

'Yeah, she died last year.'

She looks at him out of the corner of her eye. Death's Head Daniel looks concerned. Shakes his head. 'I can't remember.'

Nadine reaches up towards him. Rubs his head. His hair that's turned almost white. Daniel smiles and walks back to his seat. Toasts with her. They have a moment of silence for Maya. A long moment.

'There's just one thing,' says Death's Head Daniel after a while. 'You're allergic to both dogs and cats.'

Nadine almost falls out of her chair. She blushes. She knows that he knows.

'Daniel asked you specifically about sable. Don't you remember?'

Nadine nods. And starts to cry.

'Sable too. It makes your eyes water. But you can take it. Because you've got a fur coat that's worth a hundred thousand kronor. You can take a little suffering for that.'

Nadine doesn't answer. She fights against the shakes. Fights the seasickness from the waves under her chair. Daniel gnaws at a kebab and looks at her.

'Mr Adell makes a strong wine. It does things to one's judgment. You've tried it before actually. You got a little sample that night we watched TV. And fucked like rabbits.'

Nadine blinks. And blinks. She wants to kill him. Drive her fork through his bony eye socket. Claw his face off. Stomp it to mush with her high heels.

'You've drunk much more of it this time. Soon you'll be gladly doing what I ask. Because you want to live like this for the rest of your life.'

'I want to live like this for the rest of my life.' Nadine raises her glass to her lips. Even though a part of her screams 'stop', she takes another sip. Streams of mascara run down her cheeks.

'Listen,' says Daniel's voice. She doesn't really see him so much as hear him. It's like a voice in a dark tunnel. 'Either you go, now. You get dressed, take your handbag, and walk out of here. You never hear from me, and I never hear from you again.'

Nadine can't even comprehend it. It takes her a small eternity just to say, 'But why?'

She sees his yellow nails. They play around the rim of his glass. They spin around and around and around. Nadine can feel them deep in her stomach. Under her stomach.

'Because you helped me. And I'm grateful for that.'

Nadine doesn't reply. She just gestures for him to continue.

'Or else you can stay here. And scrub my floors.' He doesn't even smile. He just gets up and walks out into the kitchen. 'Don't slam the door when you leave.'

Nadine looks out the window. It's already dark. All the light from the dining room is reflected in it. It's nice and cozy. She can see herself between all the yellow dots. She can be out and down the street in five minutes. Cecilia will let her in. She might need a roommate. It might be nice to live in Hallunda again. She's got to remember to take her jewelry with her. It might be worth a bit, at least. She can fill her pockets. And her passport. And a few clothes. What can she get together in five minutes? She sees herself walking down Styrmansgatan. With a bag full of panties and pockets full of gold. Leaving Östermalm, darling.

She has control over her body. She can get up. She can run. Jump out the window. Crawl down the stairs. It's nice to feel like you have free will.

She looks at the table. At the big candelabra. A little bubble in the olive oil. Waits. Until the Death's Head is reflected in the window. Behind her.

'Are you in the peerage book, my dear?'

He doesn't even kiss her. He just lifts her up and tips her forward. Down into the tzatziki. Olive oil between the ass cheeks. Greek foreplay. Fast and rough. Don't tense up or it'll fucking hurt.

'There's something I have to tell you.' The voice above and behind her is a little out of breath. It belongs to someone totally foreign to her. Not Daniel. Not Kalim. 'Before I took Daniel's body, I also took him like this. He too had a weakness for Mr Adell's wine. The last thing he got in life was pounded, poor thing. Ass-fucked to the very end.'

Nadine finally sees how deep the abyss really is. How wrong she had it all. She realizes she may have promised too much. But she doesn't struggle, doesn't try to get away. She thinks about the sable fur that cost a hundred thousand kronor. About apartments in Paris and Istanbul. About the only advice Sofia Kirovski ever gave her about men. 'Play along and pretend you like it. It tires them out quicker.'

She lasts one minute until she starts to scream for real.

# FRAGMENT IV

Fredman called the bloated woman's emissary on Tuesday night. It rang five times before she answered. She read her phone number aloud. One digit at a time. Like an old-time radio operator.

'It's me. Fredman.'

No greeting, just 'Where are you?'

'Kalmar. Like we said. Do you remember?'

It's silent for a few seconds. The bitch has had a stroke, he thinks. She's walking around with shit running down her legs and drool trickling from the corners of her mouth.

'Yes.' She speaks clearly. Articulates. Still like a radio announcer. 'Konrad Landin.'

'That's right.'

'Have you found him?'

'Yes. In a scatter garden. Him and a couple hundred other hillbillies.'

'That goddamn . . .' The Bloated Woman's Emissary swears in a language Fredman doesn't understand. And probably doesn't want to understand. There's a crashing sound on the other end. He's glad he isn't there.

'Well?' she says after a while.

'No idea. Back to square one. I still believe in Bengtson. Or Wildmark. Or one of the really old ones.'

'Like Strindberg.'

'I don't think that's the right path at all. You know that.'

'You're just afraid to have to dig him up.' It's not just a joke. And easy to say if you never have to take any risks yourself.

'When are you coming to Stockholm?'

'In a few days. I was thinking of doing a bit of sightseeing. Check out the emigration museum. Visit an old acquaintance in Borås.'

'One of the furies?'

'An old fury. Municipal bigwig.'

'Ah, I see.'

'You've got to have a bit of fun. Even at my age.'

'You are a miserable old lech.' She says it with warmth.

'And as long as I stay that way, I'm happy.'

'He who knows eternity, need not hurry.'

'True.'

They say their farewells. Ring off, as people used to say.

Fredman stretches out on the bed. Takes in all the banal details in the little hotel room. He could have been anywhere on Earth, lying there with half a bottle of cognac, a paperback, and the remote control on the nightstand. He takes a hearty swig of cognac. Washes away the irritation and the taste of subpar steak. Clicks around on the TV. Game shows. Soaps. Sports. More sports. CNN from Iraq. Bloody bundles on a street. Crying women and stunned American soldiers. Some kind of boxing on Eurosport. Two tattooed hulks kicking at each other's knees and groins. Rock music on distorted speakers to make it look dangerous. Like the real thing. Silly. He yawns. Takes another swig of cognac. It's not that late. 9:30. He should call now. He's put it off for several days already. Soon it will be too late.

She answers on the second ring.

'Frida Nilsson.'

He hesitates. Notes that she's using her ornery mother's surname. He should have drowned her father. That self-absorbed, cowardly, ungrateful shit. Of Fredman's three children, Martin is the worst. The others are just weak and stupid. But Martin, he goes out of his way.

'Hi. It's me. Grandpa.' He almost says Ingmar Fredman, too. In case she's forgotten him.

'Wow, so nice to hear from you, Grandpa. It really is.'

Fredman exhales. Hears street noises behind her. 'I hope I'm not calling too late.'

'No, no. I've just been out with some friends.'

He can hear a car honking. Someone is speaking close to her. A man. She's out with a man. I'll be damned! What is she? Twenty-one? Is that old enough to date?

'Is that so?' He puts on his grandpa voice. A little nicer. A little dumber. One who would never discuss the merits of trying to dig up Strindberg. *The* Strindberg. August Strindberg. The cranky old devil. 'How nice.'

'How are things with you?' She sounds interested. Not like his other backward relatives. Fredman can smell genuine interest from miles away. He has to think about it. How is he, really?

'Fine. Considering the circumstances. No heart attacks or anything.'

The only response he gets is engine noise. 'And you? How is the writing going? On the internet.'

'With the blog you mean? How did you know that I have a blog?'

'I keep up with some things.' And Berit Nilsson keeps him informed. Frida's ornery mother's equally ornery mother. A praline-eating, inflated suburban monster. As deep as a puddle. Fredman calls her up now and then to hear her complain about her grandchildren.

'It's going really well.' An honest tone. 'I'm not going to get rich off it, but it's getting lots of attention. I'm getting invited to exhibitions and vernissages and stuff like that. It's pretty cool.' It sounds like she's had a bit to drink. Fredman reminds himself that he hasn't seen her in five years. She was sixteen then. Not yet old enough to drink. Or to go messing around with boys in town. Or do they do that nowadays? Fredman can barely remember what it was like to be sixteen.

'That's nice.' He takes a deep breath. In family conversations, it's all about getting past all the talk about the family itself. He couldn't give a shit how they're doing. What they're up to these days. If some wretched little bastard has learned to walk or not. And he can't stand to pretend otherwise. 'That's sort of why I called. About the vernissage.'

'Oh, really? Wait a sec.' There's talking. She says she'll be in in a minute. In where, Fredman wonders. One of those rock bars on Södermalm? Some kind of artist bar? Fredman likes the rock bars better, even if he can't stand modern metal. Artist bars make him feel old. All that pretentious prattle. He has no time for it. Never has.

'Which vernissage?' she says, finally. Just to him.

'My Witt's. I read that you were going.'

'Yeah?' He can hear her hesitate. What does her grandpa know about these things? Does she really want to talk about My Witt with Grandpa?

Fredman smartens up. 'I know this sounds crazy, but don't go. To the vernissage.'

'What?'

'Please, don't go.' Fredman hears how strange his own voice sounds. 'I know it sounds nuts.'

'Yes, it does.' She laughs. Nervously. Like you do when a senile old relative is about to do something stupid.

'But . . .' He takes a swig of cognac. 'It's important.'

'How come? I don't understand.'

'There's going to be trouble.'

'Of course there is. You know what kind of exhibition it is, right?'

'I do. And that's not what I'm worried about.'

Frida laughs.

'But I know something bad is going to happen and I don't want you getting involved, and don't ask me how I know that, because I can't tell you. But this is important.'

'It sounds kind of weird.'

Fredman breathes deeply. Don't get angry. On Thursday

you'll be meeting Mrs Fury. 'It doesn't sound weird, my sweet child. It sounds insane. And you must think I've completely lost my mind.'

'No, I don't. I just don't understand.'

'Just don't go. I'm begging you. I'll never ask you for anything else. Just trust me on this.'

Then he practically screams at her.

Once he's hung up, it only takes him a few minutes to finish the bottle.

# MISS WITT'S GREAT WORK

MY WITT WAS SATISFIED. Unbelievably so. The gallery had been packed for six days straight. Seriously, like sardines. For a photo exhibition. She'd never heard of anything like it before. Many of the visitors were just curious. Many of them were press. Many of them were the cultural elite. And she sold well. *Porn Star* was hot right now. Controversial. The flavor of the week. The month, even. Maybe the year. There was all sorts of chatter in the culture pages and on feminist blogs. People were pissed and had been for weeks. Since way before the vernissage. So much smoke before anyone even saw the fire. Endless gossip at the gallery. So much *what do you think about this* and poorly hidden irritation. So much controversy. People stormed out. And My Witt loved it.

There was a protest outside the first two days. Damn good advertising. Twenty feminist antifa punks and their boyfriends. Black hoodies and a sign saying 'crush sexism'. Five police officers standing by. Svarvargatan looked completely crazy. A protest, a police van, and the vehicles from the brewery across the street. Thankfully no stones were thrown. Despite the fact that three different TV channels were there. My's assistant Linda Sivhonen invited them all in for coffee. And that night a few of them even came to the party. They drank free wine and gazed wide-eyed at a world they would never understand. Two plainclothes cops showed up too. One of them, Stefan, was nice. Even a little yummy. Cops were underrated. There was a sullen seriousness to them that My liked. And she loved their crazy stories. A mixture of disgust at all the insanity in the world and empathy towards the victims of that insanity. She should do something on police. Something kitchen-sink realistic and on their side. Ordinary guys and gals vs. the scum. Like *The Wire* or *NYPD Blue*. With cool guy Stefan as Andy Sipowicz.

In any case, they were closed today. Six days of success, now it was time for a little paperwork. If she felt like it. She got to the gallery at four. Sent a few invoices. Paid a few others. Surfed the internet for a while. Googled her own name. Checked what the evening newspapers were saying about her. Refused to turn on her phone. Or answer the gallery line. Thought about getting something to eat. Went and bought a yogurt at the corner store. Took out the garbage. Not much of a workday.

Now My Witt was sitting alone in the office with a glass of wine, looking at Polaroids from the vernissage. She and Linda had taken almost five hundred photos. Pricey. But she had a plan. Yet another idea. She could make an exhibition out of it. *The Porn Star Party*. An exhibition of photos of a party, debuted at a new party. And take photos of that one too. Celebrities gathering to look at photos of celebrities. There was something there. Some kind of statement about that world. A Warhol-esque meta-joke. All it needed was the right caption. The right preamble. A bit of text that pointed in the right direction. Maybe they could use the internet somehow. Cultural commentary in real time. She'd have to talk to web guru Christopher about it. See if they could stream it all on www.mywitt.com. The cultural mafia's funhouse mirror. Or something about Russian nesting dolls. With the right phrasing you can sell pretty much anything.

The pictures from the *Porn Star* party turned out great. Brazen. A little bit intrusive. Everybody who's anybody in the Stockholm art scene was there. Brash, wasted, and dressed to the nines. Culture journalists with champagne. Professional freeloaders with champagne. Wannabe artists with champagne. Bloggers of the week with champagne. Cops with champagne. Antifa bimbos with champagne. The little gallery was jam-packed. People waited outside. Danced on the sidewalk. The whole street was blocked by taxi cabs. It was glorious.

And then the afterparty. When the majority of people had left and Linda had closed the curtains. Champagne and a little nose candy, then a little Porn Star for real. Linda Sivhonen, art historian and submissive as they come, went down on all of them one after another. And loved it. Once everyone except My had gone, she lay on the little sofa in the kitchenette, positively beaming. Half naked and sticky. 'That was the best night of my life,' she said. Over and over again. And laughed. Out of her mind. But the photos turned out great. No matter what they used them for. Besides teasing Linda. My loved the picture of the two of them. My at the desk. Exactly where she was sitting now. Only leaning back a bit more with a champagne glass in her hand. She looks drunk. Hot. Flushed and freckled. Her makeup smeared. Her long, rusty red hair everywhere. She's grinning and talking to someone outside the picture. Gesturing with long fingers. Filippa K jacket unbuttoned. A glimpse of a bra underneath. Linda's ass and feet are sticking out from under the desk. On her knees for the boss. She's lost a shoe and her dress has drifted up. The flash lights up a pair of white thighs above stay-ups, red panties and champagne glasses. 'Do what you do best, sweetie.'

Linda was a catch. A fantastic assistant. And now they were in some kind of relationship. Both interesting and unexpected. They met when My was living inside one of the NK department store's Christmas displays for a week. *My Witt doesn't do Christmas. See the serenity your Christmas is missing.* Linda was working as a PR assistant at NK then. They kept in touch after that. And by August she'd started working for My. While My made ads for LLW. They wound up in bed together after a couple of months. It didn't take long at all for them to find their roles. When they were alone, My liked to slap her around. Or finger fuck her while she was on the phone. My loved it. Loved the situation more than she loved Linda. It was lovely being boss. It was lovely selling art. It was lovely being in the newspaper. It was lovely fucking her secretary.

Life was good. It's good to be My. My thought about calling Linda and inviting herself over but decided against it. She needed to sleep. Alone. She took one last mouthful of wine. She was about to get up when there was a knock on the door. At 9:30. Who the hell could that be? She went out into the gallery.

She drew back the curtain on the door window. For a split second she imagined that antifa had waited until she was alone to throw a bomb at her. She'd be burned to death by a molotov cocktail.

There was a woman outside the gallery. An older woman. Maybe sixty-five. Well-groomed. Dress, fur coat, and gloves. Dark colors. A thick layer of powder on her face. Gray hair pulled back tightly. She should have been wearing a hat too, My thought. She had no idea who it was. The woman smiled. A single gold tooth caught the light. She was holding a portfolio.

My cracked the door open.

'Mrs Witt?' An idiotic question. If she knew that My Witt still wasn't divorced from Peter Engelman yet, then she knew damn well what she looked like. She was in the tabloids all the time. She was 'Royal Theater actor's artist wife', whenever Peter disgraced himself. 'Engelman's little Witt' in lighter times.

'It'll be Miss again soon enough,' said My. Smiled her starlet smile. 'How can I help you?'

The woman smiled, flashing more gold.

'My name is Anette Glasser. I'd like to commission an artwork.'

My hesitated. She'd had quite a bit to drink tonight, once again. Fucking boxed wine. You can never tell how much you've had.

'What kind of artwork? For whom?'

She opened the door and Anette Glasser stepped inside. My took a step backward. Glasser was standing a little too close. My took another step back. Glasser smelled like spicy food and cigars. She cleared her throat. 'I represent a group of private collectors of modern art. We'd like to start by purchasing your entire current exhibition.'

'There are some numbered lambda prints left.' My tried to take inventory in her head. Did they still have copies of all the photos? Were they out of *Porn Star #14*? Maybe? Probably. She needed to call Linda. 'Can you drop by tomorrow when my assistant is here?'

'I wanted to meet you first. My assistant can speak with your assistant later.'

'Right, of course.'

Anette Glasser smiled. She had a lot of makeup on. Almost like warpaint. Lots of white and red. And she wasn't one to be put off. Or made to wait. 'The truth is, we've already purchased the series. One copy of each. On the day after the vernissage.'

'Oh, that's right.' My tried to think. They must have been the ones who paid 72,000 kronor in cash. How had she missed that? The day after the vernissage meant the day after the afterparty, that's how. Linda had slept over and had gone down to open. My had stayed in bed until 1:30. An hour and a half later. As hungover as a Royal Theater actor. Linda had looked like a Finnish ghost. The work had sold like hotcakes. But who were Glasser's collectors? She'd have to check the receipts.

'Right, of course,' My said again. The collectors obviously had money. Best to play along.

Glasser looked around. Saw the little green upholstered

couch, in Karl Johan-style. 'The butcher's block', someone at the *Daily News* had called it. 'Look, there it is. The mirror and the table too.'

'Yup. The whole set, actually. The only thing different is the flowers in the vase.'

'And over there we have your outfit.' She peeked into the back room. 'In a floating glass frame. Lovely.'

My nodded. 'Yeah. I like how they're presented.'

The maid's uniform and black lingerie were wrinkled and stained. They were tastefully mounted on a white backdrop.

'It reminds me of Gustav Adolf's regalia at the Royal Armory.'

'I've heard that a few times. But the inspiration was a framed wedding dress I once saw.'

'And this is your wedding dress?'

'You could say that.' My smiled. Back amongst the clichés. Glasser smiled back and leaned closer.

'Do people dare sit on the sofa once they've seen the photographs?'

'Actually they do.'

My took a step back. Glasser followed. 'Anyway, we would very much like to commission something from you. We see such great potential in you. Even if, to tell the truth . . .' Anette Glasser weighed her words, '. . . we weren't so impressed this time around.'

'What a shame,' said My Witt, without sounding either angry or surprised. She could be a marvel of self-control. At least there was something to be gained being married to an alcoholic primadonna.

'But they're nice pictures.'

'Nice?' *Porn Star* was hardcore porn. Well-made hardcore porn, though.

'They are truly beautiful.'

'Thanks,' mumbled My. Thank God for that. *Porn Star* was hot as hell. *Matrix*-cool meets Fassbinder's monstrous mundanity. My and her photographers, Jens and Rico, spent ages on the lighting. But still, it was hardcore porn. That was the whole point.

'But, like I said: not terribly original.'

My didn't know what to say. What did this old bitch Glasser know about hardcore porn? What the hell went on in nursing homes these days?

'And what a stylish gentleman.' Glasser grinned and winked at My. Her makeup almost cracked.

'Yes,' said My. 'The gentleman' was porn actor Danny Hard. A swarthy mountain of muscle from Kalmar. A nice enough farm boy with an odd accent. And an erection that doesn't quit. The *Porn Star* session took over six hours and Danny had a hard-on from start to finish. Unbelievable. His damned thermos of a cock was in each and every photo. Penetrating My to varying degrees.

'I especially liked numbers eighteen and nineteen. You were at your peak in those.'

My smiled. And nodded. The mere thought of those two photos made her nauseous.

Glasser caught a glimpse of eighteen and nineteen in the back room. 'There they are!' She took My by the arm and pulled her along to photo nineteen. My didn't even want to look at it. Much less discuss it. Not now, anyway. People usually hurried past those two photos. Rarely ever commenting on them. Danny was gripping her neck with both hands and pressing hard. It had felt like she was choking on a two-by-four. And they had held that position while the photographers tried out different angles. Not exactly what you would call pretty. Unless you were Anette Glasser. 'You look absolutely spellbound.' She smiled, studying nineteen closely. My's elegant chignon was unraveling and her little white bonnet was crooked, along with her lace collar. She looked sweaty and sticky. The tears were real. They had to touch up her makeup several times. The fear in her eyes was also real. Getting dressed up and having sex in front of four other people was nothing. Almost suffocating was worse.

'We give our all for art,' said My Witt. Tastefully ironic. 'I do my own stunts.' 'Witt sells her cunt, but at least she does her own stunts' was how a certain blogger had put it. She took a step back from the photos. But Glasser stayed put.

'It must be difficult to stay still while almost being choked to death? It makes you want to thrash about. Scream and fight back. But you had to remain still. That takes true self-mastery. And yet you can see a hint of panic in your eyes. I think it was rather skillful of you to eroticize your panic, to make it a part of the artwork.'

My wanted to ask Glasser to leave. Or to elaborate. She felt sick. Glasser leaned even closer to the image. Turned towards My, then back to the photograph. And one more time. As if comparing the replica with the original.

'This one is the best,' she said at last. 'This one shows what's inside of you. The group I represent all agreed about that. We can see your potential in it.'

'For another piece, you mean?'

'Precisely.' Glasser traced her finger across the photo, almost touching it.

'I don't know how I feel about commissions. I'm not some ad agency that has to take any offer that comes my way.'

'I know. But we pay well. Ridiculously well, for the right work. We have no problem paying a lot for something that is going to be extremely valuable.'

'We'll have to talk it over before I commit to anything.'

'How did it work when you did those images of the girls cutting themselves?'

'Someone I knew at the ad agency mentioned that they were doing something for BRIS, the children's rights organization. The concept wrote itself.'

'That's when you first caught our eye.'

'You're not the only ones.' Thank god for that. Helena

Illyria, who carved 'HELP ME' into her thigh. And who looked like she hadn't slept in a week. They put up posters in the Stockholm subway last year. Helena had gone from pin-up to women's rights hero overnight. And My won several prizes. And a page in *Time* magazine. Not too shabby.

'Is it true that the wounds were real?'

'Yeah. But I did most of the cutting.' My skipped the part about Helena being too drunk to do it. 'And she was under local anesthetic.'

Anette Glasser stood silently for a moment. Then she said: 'Coward.'

'Sorry?'

'It's a cowardly thing to do, to weasel out of the experience you're trying to depict. How can people trust in something that is not authentic? What tricks did you use in these photos, hmm?'

My had been asked that before. 'No tricks. Besides a little lube.' She pointed at eleven, twelve, thirteen. The anal trilogy. 'It wouldn't have been possible without it. I'd have ended up in the hospital.'

Anette Glasser nodded. 'I believe that's all I needed to know.' She reached out her hand, glove on.

'Okay then.' They shook hands. Obviously the bitch had claws of steel. My squeezed back. 'Tell me more about this piece you want from me.'

'We'll get back to you about it. If you come up with any ideas, let us know. Something that will make all this seem – ' she grimaced, ' – innocent.'

The visit was over. Anette Glasser walked towards the door. My followed her. Out on the street, Glasser stopped.

'Did he wash it off?' she asked.

'I'm sorry?'

'After number thirteen. Before you put it in your mouth again.'

My Witt blushed. 'Yes.'

'Cheater.' Anette Glasser laughed. An evil clown laugh.

And walked away, towards Igeldammsgatan. 'Good night, Mrs Witt.'

My Witt stood there in the doorway. Only when Glasser had disappeared among the cars up by the corner store did she finally exhale. Her hands were shaking. She suddenly noticed she was furious. She needed a cigarette. Or a drink. Or someone to scream at.

She locked the door. Closed the curtains. Shivered. Poured another glass of wine. She was this close to calling Linda just to have someone to scream at. Glasser, that bitch, had mocked her in her own gallery. Called her out. And the worst part? She was right. And then she had challenged her. 'Something less innocent.' That cunt was going to get something less innocent, all right. My Witt would show her. She'd decorate a Christmas tree with the bitch's entrails if she had to.

She sat in her office for a long time. Rest of a box of wine-long. She surfed aimlessly. Art sites. Ad agencies. Online portfolios of illustrators, photographers, and ten types of models. Ordinary fashion models. Goth models. Extreme models. Body modification. Tattoo artists. Weird porn. Hentai. Cosplay galleries. Up-and-coming artists' galleries. Amateur artists' galleries. Millions of pathetic fucking wannabe artists' galleries. Plagiarisms of plagiarisms of plagiarisms. It was all so fucking cute. She Googled Anette Glasser and found an address in Täby. And that an Anette Glasser was on the board of a foundation My Witt had never heard of. Nothing else.

She went home. And went to bed without washing up. She just stepped out of her clothes and collapsed. Slept. A heavy, lifeless sleep. She woke up sweaty, cotton-mouthed. Hungover as a culture journalist. Showering helped. After fifteen minutes in scalding water, she felt human again. Her hangover demanded food and cigarettes. Hungover My always wanted cigarettes. That's why she never kept cigarettes at home. Not since moving out of Peter's place. Peter who smoked everywhere, all the time.

Not until she was putting on her makeup did she remember. Anette Glasser. 'Innocent.' That fucking witch. If she pulled her hair into a hard bun at the back of her neck, she even looked a bit like Glasser, all she needed was the white makeup. My Witt was porcelain-white already. She just needed to powder over her freckles and paint her eyebrows on a little thicker. The gray, knee-length dress made her look stern.

It was drizzling as she hurried down Kronobergsgatan. A truck driver honked his horn at her. My Witt gave him the finger. She bought coffee at the Västermalm mall. Turned on her phone. She had twenty-seven text messages and nine missed calls. It took her a block just to open them all. Most of them were from her idiot husband. Engelman was drunk. Engelman was sentimental. Engelman mumbled cheap insights. 'I know I drink too much.' Is that right, genius? Everybody in Sweden knows that. Any time you've been out partying, some reporter calls me the next morning asking for a comment. 'I want to be your husband again.' Fat chance, buddy. She wondered where he was living these days. She had changed the locks on the apartment after he threw a flowerpot at her. Now he's forced some extra or drama school grad to let him stay with her, no doubt. Some young bimbo who's somehow starstruck by the old burnout. And who would put up with any amount of humiliation.

Linda had left a message about interviews. There was already somebody waiting in the gallery. Three magazines, two women's rights groups, and a gallerist had gotten in touch so far. And Benny. Bearded Benny. Her lawyer slash accountant. Benny congratulated her. She was, for the moment, 'quite rich'. My Witt smiled the whole way to the gallery. It was good to be My.

Linda greeted her with a kiss on the cheek. And a compliment on her hairdo.

'Don't we look serious today.'

'Just you wait.'

Linda smiled. Her look for the day was a white dress and knee-high boots. A biker shepherdess. The world was their oyster, but there were people waiting for them at the gallery. Linda had already sold two prints. She pointed at the woman waiting. She looked pissed off. And twenty-five, tops. She had clearly never heard of any color besides washed-out black.

My Witt smiled her best smile. Introduced herself. The girl in black was named Ida. The interview was for a gay site. And for a gender studies paper. It took My two minutes to realize Ida was no journalist. She was socially awkward and dull as all hell. She had no questions prepared. Only theories about porn she seemed to want confirmed. My Witt couldn't help with that and didn't understand Ida's way of speaking. She was an artist, not a gender studies expert. The whole conversation was running on empty. After half an hour, Ida asked about My's orientation. My didn't understand the question at first.

'Orientation?'

'Your sexual orientation.' Ida blushed.

'Why?'

'My readers want to know.'

Do you even have any readers? thought My.

'I was married to a man until just recently.' She sounded unnecessarily annoyed. 'That's enough of an answer.'

'You can sell pictures of yourself having sex, but you don't want to talk about your private life?'

'I can make a lot of money off those pictures. Are you going to pay me to tell you who I'm sleeping with? Are your readers going to pay me?'

Ida didn't answer. My Witt looked around for a lifeline. A customer. Linda. Anything. They sat quietly for a while. Listening to the music. Today Linda was playing something classical. Satie? Ida shuffled through her papers.

'You see.' My stretched out her arm, switched on her

artist persona. Pointed at the nearest photograph and raised her voice. 'This is a blank slate. It's up to you to decide what these images mean. Art is not what I show you. It is what you see in what I show you. It's your own private experience that defines it.'

Ida looked attentive. My was an artist all of a sudden. She raised her voice even more. Pretentious and inflated and self-confident. Linda smiled. The other people in the gallery stopped talking and stepped closer. The artist was speaking. Explaining the magic. She lied herself blue in the face with self-absorption and hyperbole. She turned towards Ida-in-black. 'What do you see in this picture?' She pointed at number five. Oral foreplay. Mrs Witt is on Mr Hard like an ice cream cone. Witt's staring into the camera. With her bonnet on crooked. Blouse undone. Her hairdo has begun to loosen. Hard's trousers are around his knees. His cock is like a flagpole.

'Well?'

'I think it's an extremely vulnerable image.' A middle-aged woman pierces the silence. Librarian-type. Cat eye glasses. Gudrun Sjödén from head to toe. My nods at her.

'If my boyfriend were that big, I'd have TMJ.' People laugh. My nods and turns back to Ida.

'Well?'

Ida searches for her words. Blushes. Nine pairs of eyes stare at her. My sneers with her back to them.

'I just think it's distasteful.'

Someone laughs. The blond boy maybe?

'How insightful. Is there a different photo you like better?'

'No.'

'Any you dislike more?'

'No. They're all equally distasteful. It's just porn.' She spits out the P-word.

My Witt gives her a look that says 'idiot'. 'Who says? And what do you mean by "porn"?'

'Speaking of porn.' The blond gay boy butts in. Without noticing the tension in the room. 'Has this Danny Hard done any gay porn? I'd love to see him play on my home turf.' Laughter. My cuts Ida loose. She's been humiliated enough. She's already going to write something long and angry about My. And she'll make sure it gets wide distribution.

She turns towards the blond gay. Smiles her friendliest smile. 'He said he's done some softer stuff with other guys, but couldn't really get into it.'

The blond gay pouts dramatically. 'What a shame. He would have been wonderful. He's got a real Tom of Finland figure.'

My nods.

'Can I ask you something?' The librarian. Her date, a man in a corduroy jacket, looks terrified.

'Yes?'

The woman clears her throat. As if she was about to recite poetry. 'Did you practice sword-swallowing or did you take some sort of muscle relaxant before taking these pictures?' She points at the dreaded number nineteen. 'I've read that it can help.'

The collective gaze darts from the librarian to My. Linda stands behind the crowd, smiling. Ida is already on her way to the door.

'I'm a terrible sword-swallower, as you can see from the other pictures. I did have a rather large glass of wine before-hand, but I'm not sure if it helped.'

The conversation flows on. Total strangers in an art gallery discuss the finer points of cocksucking. Casually, as if talking about soccer. Or how to get rid of aphids. Mrs Librarian and Young Master Twink exchange sex tips. Without an iota of embarrassment. As the conversation picks up, My sneaks away. She pinches Linda's ass. No panties. Slut. You'll get yours. It's going to be a whole lot less innocent.

Back in the office she remembers. Anette Glasser. The

bitch who bought the whole series. For her friends. She rummages through the receipts. Linda has arranged them chronologically. Neat and tidy. Good help is so important. There it is. Seventy-two thousand kronor. Cash. Signed Linda Sivhonen. Buyer: 'The Carcosa Foundation'. Never heard of it. Where was the money, by the way? I suppose Linda deposited it. Where's the bank receipt?

Outside, the door chimes. Linda's saying goodbye to someone.

'Linda!' Mistress voice. 'Come!' Linda practically sprints up to her. Her blue-gray eyes glitter like ice crystals.

'Yes?'

'Have you deposited all the money?'

'Not yet.'

'Why not?'

Linda throws up her hands. 'I've been a little busy.'

My slaps her. Not too hard. More loud than painful. Linda doesn't defend herself. Her bottom lip quivers. She stands completely still.

'Where is the money, you slut?'

'In the vent in the pantry.' Good thinking. One more slap, though. 'I'm so sorry.'

'Well then.' My steps closer. Presses Linda against her. She's shaking. Fabulous. 'You'll pay for that tonight. Go to the bank. Now.' Linda nods.

My grabs Linda by the back of her blond pageboy haircut. Gives it a tug, bending her backwards. 'Okay?'

'Yes,' Linda gasps. Her mouth is begging to be kissed. From the gallery someone shouts 'Mrs Witt?' Footsteps approach the office. My releases Linda with one last hair-pull. Straightens her skirt. Linda smiles and gives her a look that says 'busted'.

The librarian is at the door. She looks at Linda. Swallows a question. 'Right,' she says.

'Well?' says My Witt.

'Just a quick question. Then I'll leave you two alone.'

'No problem.' My smiles her most genuine smile.

'You have another interview in twenty minutes.' Linda seems compelled to say it.

'Right, well. I heard from Anette Glasser that you're going to be doing a big commission for her.'

My nods. Linda looks questioningly at her. My wants an extra large glass of wine.

'That is so exciting.' The librarian's eyes twinkle. 'Can you say what you're planning to do?'

'I don't know yet, actually.'

'It's going to be so exciting. Really. Good luck!' She turns around and leaves. My thinks about going after her. But changes her mind. The phone rings.

Linda answers. 'Witt's Gallery.' My can hear her soon-to-be ex-husband's voice. 'No, she's not here right now.' Linda sounds as neutral as an answering machine. Peter yells something at her. And hangs up.

'He called me a "Finnish rug-muncher".' Linda sounds surprised. 'Do I still have time to go to the bank?'

'Make us some coffee instead.'

Linda blows a kiss and leaves. My peers out from the office. There are three middle-aged men in the gallery. She goes out to mingle and manages to sell three prints before Linda gets back. They ask her to sign their programs. Thank her. Say: 'Nice to meet you.' And leave, each with their very own autographed, insanely expensive piece of porn.

The next interview is right on schedule. My has time for half a cup of coffee before then. The journalist is a coat rack of a man with big eyes. He writes about arts and culture for chick magazines.

'Like *Frida*?'

'Like *Frida*. And *Seventeen*.'

'Are there even any words in *Frida*?'

'More than you might think.'

'And you've seen my photos?'

'They're fantastic. Great lighting.'

And just like that, they're friends. The hour passes painlessly. A photographer shows up to take pictures. Linda powders My up a little extra. A couple of construction workers stand outside, watching. My blows them kisses. She says almost nothing sensible the entire time. But she does say art is not a profession. And that aesthetic education is a waste of time. That you're better off taking accounting than drama.

'And one more thing: Art is never cute.' Some major wisdom there. The big-eyed coat rack jots it down.

The afternoon flies by. One more interview. A German culture writer. He speaks Schwarzenegger English and is ultra-liberal. He buys five prints. For a collector. The phone rings. GQ. Three different talk shows. All wanting Witt on their couch. Witt smiles and says things like: 'Visual art as we know it is dead and gone. You might as well weave tapestries. Go outside and ask the first person you see to name one modern artist and it's Picasso, guaranteed. And he hasn't been modern for sixty years. Besides, he's been dead for thirty.'

A journalist calls. She asks My to comment on a spokeswoman from the Feminist Initiative calling her a 'speculative misogynist'. My says that she's a feminist too. And waffles on for a few minutes about interpretive precedents and a leftist feminist hegemony. Peter Engelman calls two more times. First tipsy, then so drunk that Linda can't understand a single word he says. A couple of high school boys come in. Starry-eyed and snickering. They stare at the pictures. Whisper. Sneak glimpses at My. An old woman sticks her head in, screams 'Filthy cunt!', and runs away. The high schoolers boo her. Another older woman buys a print of number eleven. Doggy-style against the couch. A third woman asks bizarre questions about numbing creams and anal sex. She could have been Glasser's sister. Fucking Carcosa Foundation. If only My had fifteen minutes at a computer. Some friends from art school in Gothenburg drop by. On their way to a party. They promise to call. My has her first glass of wine at three. Eats sushi standing up around four. Smacks Linda around in the kitchenette at five.

At six, My bums a cigarette from a visitor and steps out into the drizzle. She smokes slowly with her back to the gallery. Svarvargatan looks like a back alley, all it needs is evil little hags running around screaming 'cunt' and 'commission please'. When she comes back into the gallery again, a courier has dropped off a fruit basket and two bottles of champagne. Good labels. The basket is the size of a baby carriage. There's a card between the bottles. A white postcard. 'The Carcosa Foundation looks forward to our joint enterprise. Regards, A. Glasser.' Enough with the Carcosa Foundation. I'll show you innocent, you cunts.

My Witt tells people to help themselves. 'Hurry up before we close.' She takes a few grapes and walks back to the office. There's a marking on the card. A symbol. It looks like three question marks intertwined at the bottom. To form a three-pointed star. The kind of thing someone would doodle on their message pad, or else cleverly designed to look that way.

She calls Bearded Benny.

'The Carcosa Foundation,' she says without a hello. 'What is that?'

'A foundation?'

'Well aren't you as clever as always?'

'I'm at home.' The sound of children in the background. 'I'm not working right now, if you'll excuse me.' My Witt realizes that there are people who haven't spent the last week inside a gallery. People who haven't had three glasses of wine by 6:30.

'Linda! What day is it?'

'Tuesday!' At least five people answer.

'Are you even talking to me anymore?' Benny sounds annoyed.

'Yes. Sorry.' My wonders if she's drunk. If he can hear it in her voice.

'Anyway, the Carcosa Foundation, what do they want from you?'

'Do you know who they are?'

'Not really. They seem to be an old foundation with too much money and too little to do. There's a lot of them like that out there. Can I go make my kids dinner now?'

My hangs up. Turns on her phone. Six missed calls. Not horrible. Eleven texts. One call and three texts left after she's deleted all of Peter's. The girl from the Sunday morning show on Channel 4 called. Can't wait for Sunday. Yeah, duh. They're going to talk about pictures they can't show on TV. How dumb is that? My pours more wine. Reads texts from two people she doesn't know. 'Porn profiteer. Prepare to die.' 'Gender traitor.' My wonders how they keep getting her number. She usually changes it once a month. One text from Linda. 'May I massage mistress's back tonight?'

Out in the gallery they're eating fruit and trying to decide where to go next. Some distant acquaintances and their friends. Linda used to work with the freckled one. The one outside smoking has something to do with culture at one of the newspapers. They want to go party. My just wants to go home. Plan her big commission. Or get a massage.

She picks another grape. She'll never know if they're poisoned or not. If they're what triggered it all. 'Shall we open the champagne?'

'We should probably eat first. Anywhere good around here?'

Linda gives them restaurant tips. Sushi? They eat more fruit while they're talking. High-class Italian? La Famiglia? There's a Greek place on Fleminggatan. My thinks about what makes great art. About that dumbass Peter. Wonders if the grapes were drugged. Wonders how someone she's never met could want to kill her. Everyone's up for Greek. My says:

'But I've actually already eaten. You guys go and I'll catch up with you. I've got some stuff to take care of.' They all laugh understandingly. They already sound tipsy. See you in a bit and darn it, Linda just remembered she's got to help the boss.

They leave the champagne where it is. Turn out the lights. Go into the office. Shuffle paper around aimlessly for a few minutes. My thinks of asking about the Carcosa Foundation. But the thought breaks. Everything breaks. The levee breaks. A moment later and My has Linda down on the sofa. *The* sofa. The porn sofa. She rides her face. Restrains her arms. Pulls her hair. Linda kicks and twists and her eyes sparkle. It's violent and cruel and totally amazing. Over her shoulder, My Witt can see out into the street. There's just a thin, transparent screen covering the window. Someone standing out there could see it all. Someone with a camera. That would be a treat for the blogosphere. Witt the Slit rides again. She comes, hard and convulsive. Linda almost suffocates between her legs.

Afterwards, Linda stumbles to the bathroom. My Witt stays on the sofa. Bent over, with her skirt around her waist. She really is wonderful, Miss Sivhonen. It's funny how things work out. She wants to just lie there and bask in it. Preferably for hours. But it's time to go.

At the Greek restaurant, they're already loudly drinking dessert by the time My and Linda get there. My is instantly annoyed. They're midnight drunk at eight o'clock. All five of them. How the hell did that happen? When she sits down, My realizes that she doesn't know any of their names. And that she doesn't have a clue why she and Linda are there. She'll have to ask Linda. But Linda's at the bar ordering wine. They talk about arts grants and blah blah blah. Linda comes back with the wine. One of the five drunken strangers offers them vodka. My rants that any art that needs government support is dead by definition. At that point it's just a museum piece. Or propaganda. They laugh. Buy her more wine and My drinks it up.

Someone calls. Some blog goblin. What are My's views on sexual politics? How the fuck is sex political? And blah blah blah. My hangs up. Returns to the conversation, nobody bats an eye.

'What do your parents think about all this?' It's the culture journalist talking.

'Nothing.'

'Nothing?'

'They're dead. Car accident when I was nineteen.'

'Oh, Jesus. Were you with them?'

'No, I was at school. My little brother was, though. He escaped without a scratch.'

'Is he your closest relative?'

'Yeah, but we hardly see each other. He lives in Nyköping.'

'Would you be doing stuff like this if your parents were alive?'

'Maybe,' My lies. 'I hadn't thought about it, to be honest.'

Anette Glasser comes to mind again. Fucking Glasser. The foundation sitting at a table passing number nineteen around. Old women in clown-white makeup cackling. Carcosa-cackling and passing judgments. Heckling. They want to see real blood.

'Innocent, but promising.'

'She could have puked.'

'That would have been the least she could do.'

'It's borderline cute.'

'Give me an example of "great art"?' My asks the table. Interrupting some drivel about musical theater.

'The pyramids.'

'Classical art, you mean?'

'Nine-Eleven.'

'Anything Van Gogh did.'

'Something that you measure all other art against.'

'It's in the eye of the beholder, obviously.'

'Everything's in the eye of the fucking beholder,' My hisses.

'Art is temporary,' Linda interjects. 'Only reputation is eternal.'

'But how can I make art that everyone will compare all future art to, when people don't know shit about art?'

'Aren't you selling "people" short?' The one bickering is the girl My dislikes the most. The cultural journalist's girl-friend. She makes quotation marks with her fingers when she says 'people'.

'People?' My copies the gesture. 'No. It's not derogatory to say people don't know about something. Especially something that isn't remotely useful or rewarding to know about. People know a lot about Henke Larsson, Buffy the Vampire Slayer, and who's fucking who on Big Brother that week. But people don't know shit about art. That's why art is dead. It died, and nobody even noticed!'

They all look at her. Everyone else in the restaurant is staring at her too. She's talking very loudly. 'Sorry.' She My Witt-smiles around the room. Lets her hair down. Poses. She theater-whispers: 'If art is dead, how can I make great art?'

'By making art that redefines what art is.' The freckled one is awake, apparently.

'And what does that mean?'

'Redraw the entire map.'

'And how the hell do you do that?'

'Good question.'

'What art has ever really "redrawn the map"?' Air quotes.

'This century?'

'Last century.'

'Sergeant Pepper. *The Wizard of Oz. The Matrix.*'

'I'd like to add early Elvis, the Berlin Olympics, and *Dumbo.*'

'*Dumbo?*'

'The flying elephant. Unbelievable visuals for its time.'

'What am I missing here?'

'You're noticing that we haven't named any visual artists?'

'How can you say the Berlin Olympics?' The woman is just as freckled as My.

'What do you mean?'

'It was the Nazi Olympics.'

My smiles and doesn't care to respond. Linda attempts to explain. It's modern iconography. Series, traffic signs, and brand names. Look at Nazism as a very well-established brand. Commercial art. Goebbels created such good art, they made it illegal. Linda is good at explaining My's theories. My is God. Linda her prophet.

The night continues in the same fashion. They argue. Shut each other down. And don't have much fun doing it. Every woman walking past on the street outside is Anette Glasser. My starts giving monologues and Linda grows increasingly quiet. My teases the air-quotes lady. Linda gropes her under the table. They drink way too much. Their conversation makes less and less sense.

They take a taxi home to My's place. Four whole blocks. Drunk and tired. Linda holds My's hand. The taxi driver stares at them in the rearview mirror. His face is strangely pale. As if he's wearing makeup.

They sleep in Peter Engelman's gigantic bed. Half dressed and without saying goodnight. They've just been bickering over something stupid.

My wakes up, nauseous and sweaty. Linda is snoring and hugging a pillow. It feels like she's miles away. My dreamed about angry old ladies. Carcosa hags in clown makeup watching hardcore porn. Sick, violent shit, straight from the floor of some slaughterhouse. And My is in it. She's crawling around on a tile floor. Through shit and vomit. She's drunk. And half naked. And the Carcosa women are laughing at her. 'Art is never cute!' they scream.

The phone rings as she's drinking her third glass of water. She usually turns it off. Fuck. She answers without checking the time.

The officer apologizes for calling so early. It's early Wednesday morning. Peter Engelman is in jail and wants to talk to his wife. What did that idiot do now? And My is not his wife. Not for long anyway. There was a fight at KB. In the bar. And outside. Assaulting an officer. A great work of art if ever there was one. My Witt asks if she has to talk to Peter. No.

She wishes the officer a pleasant day and hangs up. Drinks one more glass of water and calls Felicia. Felicia blogs about celebrities. She's half asleep, but quickly gets the picture. My lays it all out. Feed the vultures. Feed the press. *Hänt*, *Aftonbladet*, and the rest. Peter E. in the drunk tank again. His wife 'the porn artist' – use that phrase – is crushed. 'We were almost back together,' she lies. And make sure you call me Witt. Not Engelman. Only drunk theater actors go by that name. Keep whatever they pay you for it. Just don't stop writing about this, please. Hang Engelman out to dry. That's right, 'porn artist', thanks. She hangs up and goes to the bathroom to puke.

When she comes out of the bathroom, the phones start ringing. First her cell, then the landline in the kitchen. However the hell anybody found that number. Then Linda's phone. All three ring and ring. The vultures are awake. Linda's awake too. My tells her to ignore the fucking phones.

She stares off into space for a while. When she's had enough of the phone on the kitchen wall, she smashes it with a frying pan. She almost cries. Fucking Engelman. I'll show you great fucking art. A statement to make the world stop turning. She's going to declare war on someone. Fly into a skyscraper. Kill someone on live TV. Or be killed on live TV. I'll show you innocence, Glasser.

She sits on the laundry basket, brainstorming, while Linda's in the shower. 'There might be something there,' she tells the shower curtain. Like a live installation. Killed in the name of art. How hard could it be? Just tease the nearest Muslim till he explodes. We can sneak into a mosque and record a porno. Or just be the wrong gender. All we have to do is document it. Piece of cake. Earn yourself a fatwa and then livestream yourself. Constantly. Here I am! Suckers! And a website that keeps time. 'My Witt has survived for three days, two hours, and thirteen minutes.'

When Linda comes out of the shower, My is already at the computer. Rambling about headlines and fatwas. She's talking loudly. Too loudly. Later on, Linda would say that's when she first felt afraid. When My Witt started arguing with her laptop. Or with someone sitting beside her.

She gives Linda a ten-minute head start. Through the window, she can see three probable photographers loitering along Kronobergsgatan. As discreet as house flies. She swears about them while doing her makeup. Tight bun. A lot of powder. Bright red lipstick. Like a silent movie star. Her lips clash with her red hair, but it'll have to do. By the time she leaves there are five photographers. The cameras click like machine guns. Her phone won't stop ringing. She calls Bearded Benny in the deafening noise of Fleminggatan. Benny sounds half-awake. How do people find time to sleep? She barks orders. To both Linda and Benny. Make an ad for the Channel 4 couch on Sunday. She's going to speak out. Spill the beans. And debut a new artwork. Something innocent, don't worry. No porn this time. Linda will send the stuff.

People take photos of her with their phones. Four times on St Eriksgatan. Three on Alströmergatan. She wants to scream at them. There are other celebrities besides me in Kungsholmen. Stenmark! Frank Andersson! Mauro Scocco! She does scream the last one. 'Fucking Mauro Scocco!' There are three photographers outside the gallery. My smiles at them and hurries inside.

The day is one long phone call. The phone rings and rings and rings. My gives comment after comment. Linda answers the phone and sells pictures. My wants to fuck her. Hard. But there are always people in the gallery. Instead, she eats fruit and stares at the protesters outside. God knows when they showed up again. But there are some girls outside passing out flyers. They stare back at her. Peter's out of jail at two. The phone rings and rings with new intensity. My gives more comments. Peter calls and screams at Linda. For five minutes. My ignores him and Googles herself. She's hot today. Porn queen and a drunken pig's poor, poor wife.

My preaches to anyone who will listen. About tattoos. The limits of the human body. Today's *Porn Star* will be a test of endurance. The limits of Miss Witt's body. My wonders how she can exploit her pale white skin. Could they get her to look like an anemic saint? She rambles for a while about crucifixion. Soon she'll be the same age as Jesus. There's an art to suffering. A beauty to it. To suffer with dignity. Like some kind of fakir.

'You mean like David Blaine?' asks a guy in pinstripes. In ten years he'll be dead sexy in pinstripes.

'Who?'

'The British guy. He holds the world record for a human being going without oxygen. And he once starved himself for over a month.'

'That's the guy who . . .' My waves an apple and searches for the words. 'Sat in a cage for a long-ass time right?'

'That's him.'

'I sat in a window display for a week once. Just before Christmas. Five days. It was mostly just boring. But I gained a new appreciation for the plight of the goldfish.' Standard joke. Standard laughter.

'Aren't there any feats of endurance that really test our moral limits?' A man. About fifty. Professor-type.

'Fakirs?' suggests Pinstripes. 'Don't people with piercings and body modifications test our limits?'

'What does sticking a needle through your tongue have to do with morality?'

'Can you really have moral endurance?'

'Priests?'

'Someone incorruptible?'

'Porn stars,' My proclaims, dead sure of herself. 'One of those chicks who bangs hundreds of guys on camera. Talk about testing your limits.'

No one answers. My calculates. Conceptualizes. Visualizes. Strategizes. Her ideas begin to take form.

'I'm going to build a mechanical fuck machine and let it loose on me, and see how many hours I can take it.' She raises her voice. 'Linda! We're going to build a fuck machine!'

'Right now?'

'We've got to start planning.'

The planning goes so-so. At three o'clock she sends Linda out shopping. For food and wine and both evening newspapers. They eat sushi standing up and take turns reading aloud. My got five pages in *Expressen*. Four in *Aftonbladet*. The reading gets more and more theatrical. The gallery is packed. And there are fifteen people outside staring. My rushes out onto the street and wails, 'My Witt devastated after Engelman brawl.' Inside the gallery, Linda gets the guests to chant the headlines. There's at least one blogger on-site writing live from the scene. About My Witt. They film her with their phones. My Witt reads aloud from a blog that's one hour old. Soon the best parts are on YouTube. A vicious circle. A cat chasing its tail. My hopes they include her imitation of Peter. 'I'm not drunk,' she slurs. 'I'm just tired. Being a thespian really frays your emotional fibers.' She turns the word 'thespian' into a dry heave.

A woman My has never seen before is trying to explain what's going on. She's speaking loud and clear in an oratory voice. This is breaking news tattle-journalism. Livestream scandal. There's so much data coursing through the air you can practically see it. My sits on the sex couch eating jumbo shrimp and absorbing the babble. Someone next to her uses the term 'sensationalist feedback loop'. Does she only know pretentious dorks? Is she just a magnet for phrasemakers?

She swallows the last shrimp as Linda comes by with a glass of wine. The size of a volleyball.

'Where did you get this glass?'

Linda shrugs. 'It was in the pantry.'

My nods. Takes a sip. And another. They're talking about art beside her. Again. It seems like that's all people do. And she follows suit. Shouts into the air. 'Art is in the moment.' She notices people are listening. 'The first experience. When you see a work a second time you're not revisiting the work itself, but your feelings about it.

'Maybe we're making history here. Fifty years ago, jazz music turned in on itself. By artists, for artists, all that crap. Soon it was so distanced from its audience that it didn't even notice it had been completely bulldozed by rock and roll.' It might just be My, saying all this. 'Visual art has gone the same direction. It's been bulldozed by film and photography and advertising and God knows what else.'

She returns to the fuck machine. Rants about it. Throws ideas at Linda. She's probably never seen one in real life. Neither has Linda. But it's an interesting idea. A kind of mechanical action that just goes and goes. Automatic. Repetitive. Like a piece of outrageous gym equipment. An ejaculation feedback loop. Something for the culture writers to chew on for weeks.

'Just imagine what an uptight feminist with two semesters of gender studies could make of such an image. And imagine how different the reception would be if it was a man or a woman strapped into it.' My Witt takes a giant swig. Tells Linda to hold down the fort, pulls on her black overcoat and walks outside. It's dark out. She turns off her phone and bums a cigarette from an anti-Witt protester. The protester doesn't recognize her.

It's drizzling. My walks down to the canal. With the giant

glass in hand. Looks in people's windows. Ordinary apartments containing ordinary lives. There's a little terrace on the stairs down by Kungsholmsstrand. She sits on a bench and watches the canal. There's one solitary boat at the quay. The water looks cold.

Anette Glasser comes and sits next to her. It feels totally expected. She stinks of perfume.

'Quite the performance back there.'

'Thank you. Just doing what I do best.'

'And what's that, exactly?'

'Raising hell.'

'Too bad you can't put "raising hell" in a museum.'

'Art,' spits My, 'exists only in the moment.'

Anette Glasser laughs. An unpleasant sound. 'So true.'

My nods.

Time goes by. A lot of it. My considers asking about the fruit, but resists. After a while, Anette Glasser starts talking again. 'My foundation consists of a number of connoisseurs. We collect only work we commission ourselves. Exclusive pieces that suit our tastes.' Glasser tries to find the words. 'Pieces of an . . . extreme nature.'

'Should I be flattered?'

'All the ambition in the world is no replacement for raw talent. Although ambition *can* produce impressive forgeries.'

'Andy Warhol?'

'Stephen King. You yourself are a charlatan. And you know it.'

'And if I am . . .' My fills her mouth with wine. An entire vintage. 'What are you doing here with your exclusive tastes?'

'You have potential. That's how we work. We find an artist with potential and make sure he or she can fully develop that potential.'

My Witt doesn't answer. A car drives by behind them. Someone laughs, far away. A train pulls into the station on the other side of the canal.

'I'm so tired.'

Anette Glasser nods. She looks like a kabuki mask.

'My ex is driving me crazy.'

'And you exploit it so well. Let that anger motivate you.'

'It's tiring being angry all the time.'

'How would your work look if you were content and in love?'

My Witt grimaces. Steals a glimpse at Glasser's makeup. Fascinating really. Monochrome and thick as stucco.

'I think I am in love though,' her mouth says. My Witt's mouth. To My Witt's surprise. 'Peter was drunk and violent and I feared for my life. I needed to sleep somewhere. One thing led to another.'

'Oh dear. Who's the lucky somebody?'

'My assistant.'

'The Finnish girl? How risqué.' Glasser smiles.

'Risqué?' My laughs. 'Love triangles in '30s movies are risqué. My life is a lot more than that.'

'You're not the first person to fall for their secretary.'

My Witt laughs and laughs and laughs. It echoes down Svarvargatan. 'I love her.' The words burst out of her. She laughs even more. It's totally crazy. And Anette Glasser smiles even more. A sympathetic kabuki grin.

'Best of luck to you,' says the mask. 'See you tomorrow.'

My Witt nods with a mouthful of red wine and giggles. Anette Glasser nods. And leaves.

My stays seated on the terrace for a long time. Empties her glass, trying not to think about anything in particular. She waits for serenity, the reward for a hard day's work. Waits for peace.

But she finds none. Only an unpleasant vertigo. She's drunk. And needs to check her phone. She can't just sit here and zone out forever. She's a part of something. A flow. She needs it. She was born from a torrent of gossip and slander. Outside of it, she's alone.

She walks back to the gallery. Past a couple of women on their way home from work. A boy on his way home from school. All three stare at her wine glass. She has no idea what time it is. She'll have to ask Linda. And tell her what she told Glasser. It's important. Crucial even, suddenly.

As it turns out, it's five-thirty. And the excitement at the gallery has transformed into some kind of pre-party. Linda has plugged her phone into the computer and is playing Peter Engelman's best and worst drunken outbursts. You can hear his drunken nonsense from the street. Ingenious. The front window is full of headlines from the last few days. Tons and tons of porn and debauchery and Peter and My. Linda has dimmed the lights and pointed spotlights to illuminate the headlines from behind.

'Just beautiful,' My says to one of the protesters. Twenty-one. Female. Archetypal porn-hater. Man-hater. My-Hater. She stands there reading the headlines. Unsure of what she should think or even what she does think. She can hear Peter's voice inside, crying: 'You miserable Finnish cunt.' Fantastic in-the-moment art.

A man My has never seen before steps outside. He tries to invite the protesters in for wine. He invites My too. Seemingly without knowing who she is. My goes inside. The protester doesn't. Just another party night at Gallery Witt. Linda has put out a couple of wine boxes. They never run out, apparently. My wonders who pays for them all. Probably her. And the foundation provides the fruit. Just taste it.

She nods at people. Walks over to the sex couch. No one seems to want to sit on it. So it's just for My. And Linda. She sits down. Linda glides past and whispers, 'Tired?' My nods and gets a kiss on the cheek. Her enormous wine glass gets a refill. She leans back. Listens to all the talk, the theories, the hot air. The spinning wheel goes round and round. Tides of babble wash over her. It belongs to her, this sea of whispers and rumors. Her swells and squalls. Her world.

A middle-aged woman is standing by the sofa talking to two other people My has never seen before. The woman shoehorns the words 'drama school' into almost every sentence. 'When I was in drama school . . .', 'My time in drama school'. Why is it that everyone who studies drama has to say 'drama' with an extra long, extra pretentious A? 'Draaama.' Peter Engelman is the same way. She should strap both Peter and the drama school woman to her new fuck machine. That'll show Anette Glasser. Can you say 'thespian' with a giant rubber cock in your mouth, darling? Or does it fray your emotional fibers? Just call it Bergman-esque and everything will be okay.

Linda comes by again. They talk about the sex machine idea some more. Amidst all the partying and Engelman-shaming, Linda's somehow managed to call around. Custom mechanical workshops, prosthetics manufacturers, and companies that sell gym equipment. She's made a bunch of tidy little lists. It's all about working with professionals. They can start building the machine tomorrow. They draw on a sketchpad. Like two stuntmen. How should the victim sit? Lie down? Victim, is that the right term? This machine is meant to make you feel bliss, after all. Passenger? Client? We'll come back to it.

Linda hurries off to explain something about in-the-moment art. My Witt blinks and suddenly knows what she has to do over the next few days. In one crystal-clear, sober second she knows what it's going to take. To finish her big commission. It's all so clear. What she needs to do. Where she needs to go. What she's going to show. A work in three parts. An unforgettable work. The brilliant idea is taken care of. Now she just has to execute it as profitably as possible.

My Witt sits quietly for a long time. Alone on the green upholstered Karl Johan couch. She smiles to herself. Experts on My Witt's later period all agree that it was then, that Wednesday night, that it began to happen. My transcends to a new level. Mostly mentally, but maybe even physically.

They let the party continue until eight. Then they close the gallery. Send the guests off to various bars around Fridhemsplan and promise to meet them there. They do the dishes. Get things in order. Pick up all the paper. My cleans the toilet. Linda sweeps the floor. They close the curtains.

They walk home like a totally normal couple. They turn off their phones on Alströmergatan. Walk practically hand in hand. They slink into the mall. Discreetly. My is wearing her giant sunglasses. Linda does the talking. They buy a little food from the deli. Indian chicken. Shrimp. Nobody photographs them. Some stare. Some whisper. But that's all.

They go back to My's place. Shower. First My, then Linda. Everything is quiet. Purposeful. Home after a long day. Neither peeks as the other gets out of the shower. They change into sweats. Warm up the food. Sit at the little kitchen table. Open a bottle of wine. Talk about how badly they want a cigarette. About how they haven't watched ordinary TV in over a week. News. Morning shows. That kind of thing. They talk about locking themselves in for a few days. Eat candy and watch TV. After the commission, says My. Is everything ready for Sunday? For the livestream? Linda nods. Everything's good to go. You'll have to be there bright fucking early. Wonderful, I'm going to be a zombie. But at least it'll be over with.

Linda is curious. She begins to nag. What are you going to show? What's the plan? My often waits until the last second to explain. It's exciting, but frustrating. Do we need to buy anything? My makes a list. Fine-tip markers, half-inch cotton rope. A stand for the webcam, some kind of cross. Linda writes it all down.

'What kind of cross?'

'The kind you crucify people on.'

'And where do you think we'll find one of those with ten hours' notice?'

My thinks. Takes a gulp of wine. 'I want to be able to hang

someone up in the front room. Suspend him or her from the ceiling. Can I do that without a cross?'

'I'll figure something out. When do you need it by?'

'After lunch. Early afternoon.'

'Done.'

They clink their glasses. Semi-ironically. Loose and flirty. My starts thinking about Lindarnas Allé, lined on both sides by basswood trees. She'd like to go there with Linda. Maybe they can go after all is said and done. She notices that she's daydreaming. All while Linda's making small talk about sex machines and Indian food. A funny combo. My is dreaming in new directions. Linda's thinking about sex machines. My is traveling to new dimensions. Linda is talking about bank withdrawals. They somehow manage to hold a conversation despite My being in another room. Another part of the world. Weird. She's in two places at once. Linda clears the table. My sits there smiling. Linda pours more wine. My is in the Hyades.

They surf a little porn. An asexual reconnaissance mission. Getting rammed with robot cocks mostly looks pretty goofy. A lot of it is amateurish and badly lit. They sketch their own idea. Brainstorm on the couch. Plan it out. Like an old married couple building a sex machine. It's their last evening together. Before all hell breaks loose. Before My puts them over the edge. And they probably both know it. They hug. Make out a little. Like old friends. Like small children hiding from the world. Before it all comes crashing down. They sleep together. Hand in hand.

By Thursday afternoon everything is ready. My is ready. Linda is ready. Everyone has been warned. Linda has opened the gallery. Made all the phone calls. Set everything up. Everyone who needs to know is prepared. The buzz on the internet has already ramped up by lunchtime. Did you see what she did yesterday? What's she going to do today? My goes for a long walk while the excitement builds. Along the streets of Kungsholmen. She daydreams about Carcosa. Wonders. A city-within-a-city. How is it possible that she's never seen it before? Which street is that goddamned dome on anyway?

Linda has put up two large hooks in the ceiling of the outer room. Hung up chains. Rigged up two cameras. Summoned Johan and Rico to film it. She's gotten the website ready. Bought thirty markers. Written a press release. About the press's right to defile. Freedom of speech as a threat to freedom. The free word versus the free woman. Sounds plausible. Well done. People start trickling in by 1:30. The usual professional vultures. The newspaper crowd. The culture muppets. There's a metal rod on the floor. A 'spreader'. Linda had to explain it to My. It's a piece of metal with a cuff on each end. Four feet long. Holds your legs apart.

My undresses in the office. Linda has brought her a bathrobe. It feels safe not to be naked. She puts her hair up. In a tight Glasser bun. Puts on a g-string. The size of a postage stamp. Black. My decided that morning. She would wear panties. She had limits, plain and simple.

Linda walks in. She's holding a number thirteen in her hand. 'Look what I found!' She lays a piece of cardstock on the table. The size of a playing card, made of some kind of brown paper. 'It was behind the photo.'

'Where?'

Linda points. 'Here, on the back. Behind the frame. I was just straightening it.'

My turns the card over. Glasser's symbol. Carcosa. The intertwined question marks.

'What is it?'

'No idea,' My lies. She's found scraps of paper like that all over the gallery. In the fruit bowl. In drawers in the office. On the toilet. She knows what they are but can't explain.

She walks out into the gallery. The air is thick with anticipation. A whir of cameras. Whispers. The usual. What will she do now? My Witt, the maniac. My Witt, the porn artist. My Witt, the innocent. She wants to punch someone in the jaw. Scream something hysterically.

Linda makes sure the cameras are rolling. My wonders if digital cameras actually roll. In some way or another. Her thoughts wander. When did someone put all those notes there? Linda takes her robe. Makes a face at her panties. My makes a face back at her. A private moment amidst the chaos. Portishead plays on the stereo. Linda straps My's ankles into the spreader. Her arms to the chains hanging from the ceiling. Looks at her beloved, spread-eagle to the world. My on the cross. She kisses her. The mob whispers. Excited. Takes in My's stomach, her breasts, her ass. My is skin and bones and white as a ghost. She's covered in freckles. She's a natural redhead, as you can tell from the pictures in the room. My sees the people outside the gallery. Sees her own reflection in the window. Sees a lot of faces she recognizes. She knows the name of every third person in the room. That guy over there was at the sleazefest after the vernissage. She sees Anette Glasser and the whole foundation standing over by the little table. She doesn't see any friends. Linda puts the ball gag in her mouth. She can only shut up and stare.

'That'll shut her up,' someone says. The crowd laughs and stares as My looks out at nothing. She concentrates on what she saw that morning. A colossal dome. Beyond Arbetargatan somewhere. Linda passes out markers. Points to piles of newspaper clippings on the little table. Everything they wrote about My and her divorce. Go ahead. Over there lies a bundle of printouts from blogs. Internet forums where the nameless ooze hatred towards those with names. Go ahead. My continues to stare blankly while the crowd reads and contemplates. They hesitate. Nobody wants to be the first. Everyone wants to watch, but nobody wants to participate.

'My God you're shy!' Linda exaggerates her Finnish

accent. 'Here, watch!' She walks up and writes 'Gender traitor' crookedly across My's abdomen. Black marker on white skin. Someone gasps. Someone snickers. Linda gives her marker to a culture reporter. My strains not to look him in the eye. Slimy fuck. He hesitates. Someone starts writing on My's shoulder. Another on her back. The culture reporter leans over. His eyes glow with malice. He writes something on her cheek. Slowly. All while trying to catch her eyes. He would spit on her if he could. It makes a perfect image. My hopes the guys are filming.

Then they pounce on her. They write on her shoulders. On her stomach. One woman writes an entire headline on her forehead. Someone writes along the edge of her panties. They hesitate to write on her face. They avoid her breasts. For a while. She closes her eyes. Someone's started scribbling on her lip. It stinks of marker. There are hands everywhere. Tiny, sharp, marker tips. A cacophony of cameras. Flashes. She should have set up a mirror. She wants to see what it looks like. What she looks like. Now some asshole is writing on the inside of her thigh. Someone else has taken her feet. They mumble about censorship, the body as art, and tattoos. Someone makes a big display of writing on her nipples. My dreams of Carcosa. The dome just a few blocks away. She wonders if it's a church. There are monsters outside, watching. With three and six and eight eyes. Carcossians. Hidden behind clown-white masks. They wave at her. Smile. They are so proud.

Things calm down after half an hour. My is hidden under a layer of marker. Her eyes have started watering, and saliva is dripping from the corners of her mouth. It's hard to swallow with a ball gag in your mouth. She has to pee. Her arms hurt. And her legs. She wants out. But she's got to wait. Don't panic. Linda will release her when they're finished. Her shoulders hurt. She's freezing. She's dreaming. She's sleeping. Standing. Meditating. Floating. High on endorphins and ink.

She can't hear the cameras anymore. Or the voices. She's lev-
itating. She thinks about Linda. Sticky and beaming. 'That
was the best night of my life.' Would she ever say that again?

My spends a week in Carcosa before they pull her down
from the cross. Linda makes sure everything is documented.
The way they wipe the spit from her chin and throat and tits.
The way her arms cramp and twitch. They free her legs first.
Then her left arm. My falls backwards into Linda's arms. The
crowd oohs and aahs. Linda gently eases My to the floor.
Caresses her hair and removes the ball gag. Gets her some
water. My lies shaking in a pile, covered in marker and des-
perately needing to pee, while people applaud. She looks up
at them. Feels her arms cramp up. Sees the monsters outside
the window. Glasser's gang nods encouragingly. She smiles at
them all.

Even before Linda brings the mirror out, she knows. The
symbol is all over her. The three question marks forming a
three-pointed star. It says 'Finally, My can be happy' on her
forehead. She laughs. And laughs. And laughs. Linda helps
her up. Leads her into the back room. They've rigged up a
makeshift photo studio with lights and a white sheet for a
backdrop. Rico takes pictures of her. Portraits. Long-shots.
Details. She's completely covered. Except for her scalp and
the inside of her left calf. My poses, though she still has to
pee. She realizes that she no longer feels naked. Hidden under
all the marker.

She finally gets to pee. And put on a dress. A short white
one. More like a long tank-top. It must be Linda's. It makes
her look even stranger. Like the amazing tattooed lady in a
nightgown.

She grabs Linda by the arm. 'Do you remember, at the
party?'

'What?'

'The vernissage. After it.'

Linda nods. Blushes.

'You said it was the best night of your life. If we did the exact same thing again, would it be just as good?'

'It would just be a repetition.'

She hugs Linda hard. The camera sounds are deafening. They smile coyly, both of them. My sips a coffee. Chitchats with the crowd for half an hour. Greets them and thanks them. States the obvious over and over again. How will she ever wash it off? Hmmm. Your skin cells recycle themselves after a few weeks. Laughter. She listens to ten different explanations of what she's just done. Raped by headlines. A naked, mocked messiah. A desperate protest. My knows that she's succeeded.

She's had enough. She lets Linda watch the gallery, pulls on her coat and steps out into the street. Barefoot. It's dark out. She bums a cigarette off an anti-Witt protester. The protester is scared senseless. She and her companions look like they've seen a ghost.

'Always different in real life, huh?' My grins. Then she sees it. They've strung up a doll on the wall across from the gallery. A mannequin with a bunch of knives sticking out. The doll is wearing a maid's uniform and a red wig. Images from the *Porn Star* exhibition run up and down the mannequin. There's a sign around its neck. 'Gender traitor', it says. Its face is an ordinary mannequin stare. My is grateful for that.

She walks down the street. Towards the canal, by Kungsholmsstrand. The cameras flash and flash. Following her. A few weeks later, a video will pop up on the internet of My Witt walking down Svarvargatan, her hair in a messy bun, and legs so scribbled-on that it looks like she's wearing leggings. She walks out into the street between two cars. And disappears. Into nothing.

The party rages on. But My Witt won't come home tonight. Linda closes the gallery. Shoos away the last of the vultures. My Witt is out on a long walk. Linda sits alone in the main room. On the floor under My's chains. Where the floor is stained with marker and saliva. My Witt took a trip to the Hyades. Linda looks at the hanging mannequin across the street. It's perfect. My has become a legend, larger than life.

My Witt listens to the artists on Gianitogatan. They're talking about sacrifice. About giving it all in exchange for immortality. She watches them dance. Around and around and around. Like cats chasing their tails, catching their tails, swallowing them. They brag to one another. I left my family for my calling. So I could live completely for myself. I killed my children because they took up too much of my time. I left the love of my life because she interfered with my work. I murdered a whole congregation. Just to satisfy my curiosity. To see how it feels, if only for an instant. The fall.

'Can the artist ever really experience their own art?' My asks. 'If my work only lasts for a moment in the viewer's mind, can I ever know how other people feel about my work?'

'You can see it in their eyes,' a man answers. 'The true reflection of your creation. For a moment you can see them fall. That's as close as you're ever going to get.'

What happened to My Witt on Thursday night, no one knows. She disappeared from Svarvargatan at five in the afternoon and came home to Kronobergsgatan at six-thirty on Friday morning. Twelve hours of My's mythos is missing. She's spotted here and there around Stockholm. Mostly in Kungsholmen, but even in Stora Essingen and Södermalm. And in Duvbo, on the street where she grew up. By the house where her parents lived. She's easy to recognize. Black knee-length coat, barefoot, marker all over her. Her hair is one big mess. She seems to be in a hurry. Every time they see her. She bums a cigarette on St Paulsgatan. Rushes along Fleminggatan. She walks through Rålambshov Park, asking everyone she meets if they know where she can find the building with the dome. She waits for someone by Kungsholmen Church.

'Not a bad start,' says Anette Glasser. The whole street

stinks of roses and pansies. Few things in the dream are human.

'Thanks.'

'We appreciated the Christ imagery.'

'By "we", do you actually mean you, or are there more of you?' My uses air quotes.

'We are many.' Anette Glasser smiles. A horrific sight. 'We are Legion.'

My Witt snickers. Anette Glasser giggles. It's an unpleasant, sawlike noise. Flakes of makeup fall from the corners of her mouth. She's starting to fall apart.

'You can take your mask off now,' My snickers. Anette Glasser widens her eyes. Bubbling with laughter.

'I'm not wearing a mask.' They shout the reply in unison. And laugh and laugh and laugh. Until their faces melt. Until the huge black birds fly from the roof of the dome and fill the sky with a cloud of black wings.

She asks a few different people where she is. Stora Essingen or Hjorthagen? And My is seen in stranger places than that. At the Skönvik mental hospital. An insane, powder-faced woman in a black coat is seen late at night outside the old Grand Hotel in Falköping. She's shaking from the cold. She asks for directions to the building with the dome in Lindarnas Allé. None of the three girls she's talking to can help her. Furious, she walks back into the hotel. The hotel that's been closed for over thirty years.

My Witt comes home early Friday morning. Reeking of sweat and permanent marker and zoo. Trembling hands and bloodshot eyes. With cuts on her feet and claw marks across her throat and legs and buttocks. She throws off her coat and goes straight to the kitchen. Linda finds her sitting at the kitchen table. Wearing only panties. She's eating leftovers. Cold. She put everything she could find in the refrigerator on one plate. Indian, sushi, and a big slice of pizza. She's shoveling it down.

'Sorry,' she mumbles with her mouth full of food. 'I was so hungry.' Her eyes are gleaming white in a black mask of marker.

Linda opens her mouth, closes it again. Opens it again. 'It's okay.'

My ignores her and keeps eating.

'Where is your dress?'

My looks around. Looks down at herself surprised. As if she hadn't noticed she was almost naked.

'I have no idea.'

'You were wearing it when you left.'

'And now I'm not, apparently. At least I'm wearing underwear.' My laughs hoarsely.

Linda fidgets with the belt of her robe. Fidgets and fidgets and fidgets. My chews and chews and chews. A police siren passes down the street. 'Where have you been?'

'Me?'

'Who the fuck else would I be talking about?' Linda screams.

'Leave me alone!' My screams back at her. 'You wouldn't get it anyway! Go back to bed and let me be!'

Linda runs out of the kitchen. She's still crying when My walks into the bedroom. My lies down without a word. Rolls herself up in the blanket and falls asleep. Linda lies there awake until the morning light creeps into the room. My Witt is dreaming and snoring. Her phone rings in the living room. Then Linda's.

Their phones are lying side-by-side. People calling about this and that. Linda answers My's first. Old habits die hard. Jens Fredriksson. Asking about the photos My's supposed to take tonight. Linda hasn't heard anything about it. Who's shooting? Jens has no idea. My called yesterday. To shoot at her place. Kronobergsgatan. At seven. Are they going straight online, or what's the deal? Linda has no idea. My will call later. Meanwhile, on her own phone, it's Peter calling. Drunk and in a rage on a Friday morning. My had left a message, he claims. Linda tells him to go to hell. In Finnish.

She jots down a note. 'Call Jens about photo. What's going on?' She doesn't want to go in and ask. She doesn't want to talk to My. Not alone. She's afraid. Afraid of her mood. Of how distant she's become. Afraid of how she's suddenly stopped touching her. Stopped flirting. Stopped reprimanding her. Stopped pulling her hair in that wonderful way. Afraid because she only talks about art and Peter. She's afraid she doesn't understand her anymore.

But Linda takes care of the gallery like a good little girl. All traces of the marker performance are gone by the time they open. She welcomes everyone. Holds court and explains. There are so many questions. What happened yesterday? What happens next? Today? Linda answers their questions with questions. 'What did you think it meant? What should happen?' Classic My rhetoric. My's little servant girl sells prints. But she has nothing to sell from yesterday. Although Rico has already sent her all the photos and film clips and an enormous bill. The work is done and ready to publish.

They've gotten almost a hundred emails about the Illustrated Woman. Or the Tattooed Lady. The Painted Pariah. The Graffiti Woman. The Headline Whore. They should have come up with a snappy title. Half the world is requesting a comment. Photos, anything. What happens next? There's a long letter written in what Linda thinks is Polish. Another in Spanish. She recognizes the name of the gallery that sent it. It's legendary. If they want to show My's work then she has made it. The evil bitch has done it. And if Linda decides to stay, then the sky's the limit for her. Secretaries get rich too. Richer than lovers. All she has to do is play along.

The gallery swarms and swarms with people. Linda has to answer for My. Because Linda is the closest thing. My is God. Linda, her prophet. But she can't answer for what My plans to do next. Yes, there will be more. The next performance is tonight. Full-grown adults go totally gaga when she says it. They ooh and aah and don't know what to say. They demand to know more. Beg for it. Make childish gestures and faces. Ask about websites and links and times. There are Witt-watches. Telephone chains, email lists, text if you hear anything. We'll call you if anything happens. Can you say where, at least?

'It doesn't get any more real-time than this,' says a radio voice. 'All we know is that My Witt will do another installation tonight. Be prepared.' Linda puts the quote on repeat over the stereo. The well-known voice whispers over and over again: 'Be prepared.'

The mistress phones and the servant answers. Peppy as can be. Linda is always on alert. No matter what My throws at her. Grumpy girls get the boot. Or My may suddenly decide to switch teams again. Opportunistic bisexuality equals job insecurity. But My mostly sounds tired. Neither-nor-sexual. Just tired. She asks how it's going. Tells Linda to forward the more important emails. Is everything ready for Sunday? Linda is on the ball.

'We talked about this already.'

'Did we?'

'Several times.'

My sighs in resignation. Linda promises to send the details again. She doesn't tell her about the galleries. My will get to discover that for herself. Maybe it'll cheer her up. 'Be prepared,' the radio voice whispers.

'When are you coming down?'

'I've got to get ready for the shoot. Buy some flowers.'

'Are we shooting in the apartment?' Linda notices how diplomatic she sounds. *We* are shooting, but *My* calls the shots. We play house in My's apartment. Not our apartment.

'I said that, right?'

'No?'

'We talked about it already. I do nothing but talk.'

'I don't think so.'

Linda can almost hear My thinking. Searching her memory. 'Beats the shit out of me. Anyway. Jens is dropping by at four. Rico will come get you. When you close.'

'All right. What's the plan? Do I need to pick anything up?'

'It's all here. I've done nothing but shop all day.' She suddenly sounds like the same old My. Full of energy and ideas. 'You really can buy anything online. Even locally. You're going to love the machine.'

Linda swallows. Feels the butterflies in her stomach. My and a fuck machine, you just can't lose. I wonder what she's planning? Linda wants to ask and ask. If she should bring something to eat. Clothes? But My hangs up.

'Be prepared.'

All of Sweden is calling the gallery. So is London. Barcelona and Atlanta. The man from Atlanta asks if Linda is 'that Ms Siv-honen, the new girlfriend.' He is 'so thrilled' to speak with her. Linda doesn't really know what to say to that. She's just glad to be there. Proud of her girlfriend again. Happy to be part of the action.

Linda takes care of the gallery like a good little girl. Closes it on time. Wishes everyone a pleasant evening and thanks for coming. No, she can't give any details. No, Rico doesn't know anything either. He's just been told to stand by. With Linda and his camera gear.

'Be prepared.'

They flee the apartment at midnight. Stumbling down the stairs. Rico and Linda. In a panic. Rico without his cameras. Linda without a coat. They run down to Fleminggatan. It takes a while to hail a cab. Linda is so bloody that no one wants her in the car. People look away. Pretend not to see them. No one asks if they need help. Eventually, Rico drags Linda with him into the street. Cars swerve around them.

There's honking and screaming. Finally, a taxi stops. The driver asks if Linda is drunk. If she has AIDS. Rico screams at him. Linda screams. All the way to the emergency room at St Göran's hospital.

They give her priority. Two doctors. Clean clothes. Sixty stitches. She's missing three teeth. An officer asks her about Rico. Did he hit her? No. Who did then? Someone on the street. They just attacked her out of the blue. They? Was there more than one of them? No, she didn't know. Another officer questions Rico. Where were they? At a friend's house. Is that where she was beaten? By you? She says it happened on the street. Rico and Linda lie clumsily. Both the doctors and the police are convinced that whatever happened to Rico and Linda, they don't want to talk about it. And that it wasn't Rico who hit Linda in the face at least thirty times.

They leave the hospital on Saturday morning. Escape, some say. Are discharged, say others. Then they lie low until the catastrophe is public knowledge. They're too scared to warn anyone or interfere. Some people blame Linda Sivhonen for that. Usually without realizing how badly injured she was. She's bedridden for a week after that Friday night. Locked in her room in Aspudden. Cut off from the outside world. What could she have done, anyway?

In the panic that ensues, no one asks about Jens. No one asks what happened to Jens Gunnar Fredriksson for almost a week. And when they finally do ask, there are no answers. No one knows where he went. Rico and Linda assume that he left My's apartment and is just keeping a low profile. He might have left the country. He has family in Sandviken. A girlfriend in Gothenburg. But they never hear from him. And he never comes home. Never calls anyone. They find his jacket in My's apartment. But never his clothes, his shoes, or his wallet. His phone can't be traced. His insanely expensive Hasselblad camera is gone. The pictures that Linda Sivhonen and Rico Lundström know are on it never show up in some dark corner of the internet. They're gone, just like the camera. And with it My Witt's other great artwork. *My Love, My Sacrifice*.

Linda never talks about the piece. Or what happened that night. No matter how big of an authority on My Witt she is. The one they call 'the bride of the monster', the main character in articles like 'Lesbian Love Leads Artist to Death Pact'. And she is both the love and the sacrifice. They manage to get that much out of Rico before he stops talking to the media and then stops talking altogether. Nor does he have any photographs. They find his camera at My's place. Surrounded by hundreds of flowers. In a pool of blood and machine parts. There's no memory card inside. Nor does My ever say where it might have ended up. She never shows any pictures of what happened that night. They're out there somewhere, people say. Maybe wherever Fredriksson is buried. If he's buried, that is. My Witt couldn't have had time to bury him, according to the timeline, people say. Theories, theories. There are always theories when there are no facts. First of all, how did My Witt gather up a thousand pounds of gym equipment and machinery in two days? Not to mention all the flowers. Were there more than four people at My Witt's apartment that night? Were there more than two the following night? The police report is inconclusive. What do all the signs and symbols that My Witt painted on her walls mean? We may never know. The equipment is locked up in evidence. The apartment has been repainted.

My slept in. She was sweaty and sore all over. Her knuckles were bleeding. The apartment stank of flower water. Her sheets were stained with blood and ink. She sweated ink. When she showered, the water around her feet turned gray. It would take days to wash off.

Linda wasn't home. Neither was her stuff. She must have come back sometime that morning and gotten it. Clothes, underwear, laptop, makeup. My wondered if she'd been sleeping when Linda came back. Or if she'd been somewhere else. And if Linda had found her sleeping. Why hadn't she killed her? Had Glasser been there? Or Jens? She didn't know. In any case, the gallery would have to be closed on Saturday. The staff had abandoned ship. It's so hard to find good help these days.

Luckily she didn't have much left to do. The artwork was as good as finished. Glasser would be overjoyed. When the moment arrived. Then My would take some time off. A good long time.

Peter answered her text message three times. He would love to drop by and have a glass of wine in his old apartment. And talk about where they went wrong. It was about time. Peter was probably hoping for a quickie too. For old time's sake. He managed to sound drunk and horny in his texts. Peter was a good lover. When he was sober. My had leaked that information to the evening news six months ago. When the actor no longer impressed her. When she realized that some mistakes can't be forgiven. They stick to you. Like tattoos. Or hooks in your skin. Love was for morons. Marriage for masochists. My walks around among the flowers and machine parts, talking to herself. In sickness and in health. I'll show you sickness. I'll show you how sick love really is. Maybe that'll be the name for the fuck machine. 'In sickness and in health'? A victim of marriage. Something like that. She test-drives the machine again. Test-rides it. On low speed. It works painfully well. Orgasmically well. She remembers Linda at the vernissage party. My honestly felt like she was falling for a second there. When she saw her on that couch. Sticky and exhausted and endlessly beautiful.

She decorates the machine. The Sacrificial Scissors. A good name. Risqué. She goes out to buy more flowers and a dress. Tons and tons of flowers for the machine. To make it look inviting. And a dress, to make her look inviting. She's not so sure she wants to fuck Peter. But that's what he'll want. He's always up for it. No matter how drunk he is. The Sacrificial Scissors are for him.

At Melange they stare at her, but still sell her a dress. Tight and red. With a pattern that matches her face. The girl in the flower shop stares too, and pulls out her phone to film her. So My leaves. She takes a long aimless lap around and buys flowers from the kiosks and little stands on Lindarnas Allé. So many flowers. Roses and pansies. She buys as many as she can carry. Three massive bouquets. Along Fleminggatan. In broad daylight and biting wind. She goes home and decorates the apartment. Dances the dance of the spheres. She's completely out of her mind. And she loves it. She's a great artist now and her great new work is almost finished. My is going in a whole new direction. A new dimension. My has no concept of time. A week goes by in Carcosa. Hours in Kungsholmen. It's all so confusing. Only a few days ago, everything was so much simpler. Monochromatic. She does a bit more work around the house. Tidies up. Decorates her bed. And takes long walks in Carcosa. It's only one step away now. From her apartment to the city and back again. Totally bizarre. Once you know what to do, the rest takes care of itself. St Eriksgatan, Lindarnas Allé, Artists' Square, the Alleys of Eibon, Alströmergatan. My walks through a new dimension. My walks through a My dimension. The light changes and there she is. Maybe the light is the secret. Something about wavelengths. Some things can only be seen in the right light. Another light shows her another city.

The Hyades shine through the clouds and color the sky a weird reddish-purple. She walks along Alströmergatan. Past the nursing home. There are birds on every roof. Huge, fat, black birds. Or are they really birds? Bats, maybe. They sit in rows along the balconies too. By-ak-he, they're called. You learn something new all the time. My moves in a new direction. My moves in a My direction. She sees a lot of things that she's not sure she should believe. The old man with the orange helmet. The fat woman down in the Jewish cemetery. The shrieking ice cream truck. The dogs fighting over something between two cars. The sounds of screaming from an apartment. The cute little boutiques. The sound of car alarms and fire alarms. Sirens. Everything smells of garbage. The cemetery smells of death. They haven't had time to bury everyone who died at the party tonight. Soon the mourners will come with roses and pansies. For a silver coin they'll cry all day long. For a gold one they'll gouge out their eyes.

There are cars parked everywhere. And all the alarms are going off. Or maybe it's from the fire truck. The one down there by the corner store. At the very top of Svarvargatan. My Witt crosses through colors and dimensions. Lands beside the fire truck. Amidst the smoke and screams and confusion. The street is packed with people. Everyone is in each other's way. Police push people aside. Someone yells that they have to let the firefighters through. And My knows exactly what it is that's burning. And who started the fire.

The left display window is smashed. The right has been spray-painted: 'This is a blank canvas.' There isn't much fire. But there sure is a lot of smoke. The whole front room is full of smoke. There are people cheering. On the other side of the police.

'That's my gallery,' My says to a fireman beside the fire truck.

The fireman looks at her. Is startled. Stares. A policeman who's trying to walk between them stops too. Mid-step.

'Right, you mean this?' My says, pointing at the squiggles on her face. 'I'm an artist. This isn't a mask. I can't take it off.'

The firefighter looks at her for a long time. He nods. My nods. The policeman nods. All three of them smile. 'Someone smashed the window and threw a fire bomb inside,' says the policeman. 'Just a small one, I'd say. It didn't work very well.'

'When did it happen?'

'We got the call about, hmm, let's say twenty-five minutes ago.'

'Gender traitor! Die! Die! Die!' chants a chorus of female voices. My realizes that she has no idea what time it is in Stockholm. She left her phone at home. The sun is going down. Four? Five? In the afternoon? She watches as two other firefighters spray water through the window. They are calm and methodical. Behind them stands a woman with a stroller talking to a police officer. She owns a little hair salon two doors down. A third firefighter comes out through the window. He's wearing an oxygen mask and carrying an axe. He looks like Grassman's third icon. Human perseverance. He gestures at My's fireman.

'Was anyone hurt?'

'No.'

'Good.'

'Those guys got it all on film.' He points at a car covered in TV station decals. There are two men standing beside it smoking. Talking to the police. They see My at the same time she sees them. They bend down to pick up their cameras.

My pulls a strand of hair out of her face. Tightens her bun. Becomes the Painted Pariah. The Tattooed Lady.

'What were they doing here?'

'The photographers?'

'Yeah.'

'How should I know?'

'I don't know, maybe you asked them?'

'Burn, burn, burn!' chant the female voices. They sound younger and younger. Before long, they're children's voices. Irate five-year-olds howling about gender politics. A rock lands beside the salon woman. A beer bottle hits the fire truck. My's policeman looks around nervously. The TV guys don't know what to film. There's a camera in every window on the street. Everything that's happening here is being documented. Livestreamed. Arson as a live performance piece. Exquisite.

My steps closer to the fire. Shoves the police aside. The children shriek on and on. She feels the warmth. Smells the gasoline. We just cleaned the place. She can feel the TV camera burn a hole in her back. They've got her in their crosshairs. In the spotlight. Through the smoke she can see Glasser's fruit basket. On the floor. Broken. The floor is one giant pool of water. There are program brochures everywhere. And mashed fruit. And Linda's cardigan. Soaking wet. Fucking vandals.

'I've got to get my dress,' My says to no one in particular. She takes the fireman's big flashlight. And steps in through the window. Glass crunches under her shoes. Good thing she wore her boots today. Stupid that she's naked under her coat. The firemen shout after her. She holds her breath. Feels the smoke in her eyes. But there isn't much fire. Hardly any at all, in fact. The little table and program brochures are smoking. So is the radiator cover. The wallpaper. The entire Carcosa Foundation is sitting along the walls. They look at her. Surprised and confused. Is she about to die already? 'Careful!' they shout. Don't get arrested. Not yet, anyway. Who would finish your artwork then? You're not invincible, Miss Witt. Look! The sex couch is smouldering.

She hears them bickering as she walks into the kitchenette. She reaches up to the vent. Pulls off the grate and feels for the cash bag. It's gone. Linda has taken her severance pay. Not totally unexpected. My crouches to the floor. Takes a careful breath. Not healthy. There's a ton of shit in the air that ends with -ide. She's got to get out, quick. She hears someone shouting in the front room. She must be able to save something. Her reputation? Anything.

She grabs a box of wine and a glass from the sink. Takes as a deep breath as she dares to and gets out. She asks the fireman to see if they can save the frame with the clothes in it. It's the only thing that feels important. He says something incomprehensible behind his mask. Nods. My climbs back outside.

The pictures turn out amazing. My Witt sitting on an electrical box across from the gallery. With a glass of wine in her hand. She watches the firefighters. The police and the protesters. The bystanders. Fire hoses, crushed glass, and photographers. The box of wine is on the ground next to her. Beside her, the framed maid's uniform and the black underwear tastefully mounted on white fabric. Her hair is flowing out over her coat, which has fallen open. You can almost see her tits. The firefighters walking past stare blatantly. Is her whole body covered in scribbles? Or are those tattoos? The ones on her face are smudged. So it must be marker. She looks like a deranged badger. With red hair. Artists. Idiots.

My sits there for an hour watching the fire. She talks a little with the firemen. A little with the police. Does she suspect anyone? Not particularly. She has no enemies. But she did ruffle a lot of feathers. Suddenly she remembers she's got to go. She has company waiting. She takes her box of wine, her framed uniform and leaves. The cameras follow her until she disappears into the Alleys of Eibon.

They say that she took a taxi. To the Channel 4 building on Tegeluddsvägen. At six-fifteen in the morning, long before the sun came up. They said she was wearing a coat, overalls, and a stained undershirt. She looked like she'd been awake for several days straight. Her hair was all over the place and there were still traces of marker on her face. She was dragging a large duffel bag. A security guard said that it left a trail of blood behind, but he was probably exaggerating. One of many My Witt stories that would soon spread like wildfire across the internet.

Afterwards, both the receptionist and the show's host said that My seemed tired but focused. She looked like a runner, someone said. A long-distance runner who's closing in on the finish line and already knows that she's won. Tired, but happy. No one knew. No one had a clue. My Witt, the madwoman. She's already at home in hell. She greeted them all. Charming and light-hearted. She commented on the fire in the gallery. So sad. So scary. It was on the news. Story number two. Her assistant had been beaten: story number three. So scary. So sad.

She said that no one was allowed to open her bag and left it in the middle of the studio. I'll open it later. Once we're live, she said. It'll be more exciting that way. Art in the moment. The first reaction to a work is just as important as the work itself. The host agreed. Immediate. Spontaneous. Truly *live*. Everyone agreed. Good idea. Fresh. Cheeky. People walked right past it and had no idea.

They said that My Witt showered for a long time. That she scrubbed all the remaining marker from her pale white skin. Or at least from her face and neck. They said that she changed into the clean clothes she brought with her. But no underwear. Someone picked up on that. She brushed out her long copper-colored hair. They did her makeup. Hide the marker, she said. Give me a lot of powder. The white goes with my red hair. Thanks. The makeup girl said that she fell asleep in the chair. That's how calm she was. It was like putting makeup on a corpse.

They said that she sat in the green room in her Filippa K dress, eating grapes. Cool and collected. My Witt, the madwoman, sat there making small talk. Weather and wind and how did anyone get up this early? She talked to the band that would play. The economist who was going to speak. The chef for the cooking segment. Everyone said she seemed calm and content. Happy. The artist who was about to present a great work of art. She was worried that they had made her look too pale. That she looked haggard. They reassured her. Your skin looks lovely. Your hair is shining. You look gorgeous.

She went on after the ten o'clock news. Thin, starving,

pale, and endlessly beautiful. They talked a little about the fire. So tragic. So sad. My Witt said that she didn't feel any hatred, any anger. Whoever burned down her gallery just had a very strong reaction to her art. Violent maybe, but a reaction. She was understanding. Angelic. Perfect. She didn't mention her assistant.

Then came the time for her to show her new work. So exciting, said the woman beside My. Truly, added the host. My Witt lifted the bag onto the table. And pulled out Peter Engelman's head. Just his head. No body. The studio went quiet. His face was covered with small black symbols and he had an enormous rubber dildo shoved down his throat. The inch-long nails driven into his forehead made a pattern. They noticed it afterwards. Once they had arrested My Witt. The nails depicted three question marks, merged together at the bottom. To form a three-pointed star.

*Stockholm & Linköping,* 2008

# ACKNOWLEDGMENTS

Thanks to Lars Johansson, Elin Whilde, Mia Klintewall, Tobias Eliasson, Göran Björkman, Jan Kristian Fjærestad, Bengt Johansson, Kjell Lindgren, Tommas Arfert, Stefan Olsson and Randal Rudstam for all kinds of help.

A thirteen years later thanks to Hilda Lidén for helping me iron out nuisances in the translation.

Anders Fager was born in 1964 in Stockholm. After a career as an army officer, punk rocker, and game designer he rather accidentally turned to writing full time in 2009, when he released his first volume of Lovecraftian short stories, *Svenska kulter* [*Swedish Cults*]. The book was a critical success and a hit with readers and led to an expanded version, *Samlade Svenska kulter* [*Collected Swedish Cults*] in 2011. His work has so far been published in Finland, Italy, and France, where he became the only Swedish writer ever to have been nominated for the Grand Prix de l'Imaginaire. He has written six novels, the acclaimed graphic novel *The Crows* (with artist Peter Bergting) as well as material for role-playing games such as *Kult* and *Tales from the Loop*. He lives in Stockholm with a tank full of fish and is very happily married.

CPSIA information can be obtained
at www.ICGtesting.com
Printed in the USA
BVHW071003300822
645842BV00006B/490

9 781954 321571